THE GHOSTS OF RATHALLA

THE GHOSTS OF RATHALLA

By Matthew K. Perkins

RESOURCE *Publications* · Eugene, Oregon

THE GHOSTS OF RATHALLA

Resource Publications
An Imprint of Wipf and Stock Publishers
199 W. 8th Ave., Suite 3
Eugene, OR 97401

www.wipfandstock.com

PAPERBACK ISBN: 979-8-3852-0809-8
HARDCOVER ISBN: 979-8-3852-0810-4
EBOOK ISBN: 979-8-3852-0811-1

02/15/24

To my mother, Mary Lynn Perkins—the woman in the arena. A transcendent fighter. A warrior among warriors. Rest in peace, courageous angel.

Map Illustration: BMR Williams

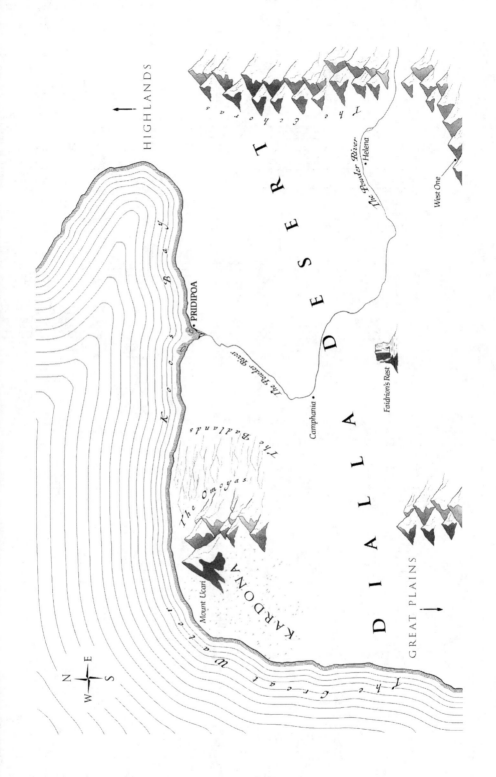

Contents

PART I

The Dialla Desert

S creams echoed out of every corner of the night-shrouded camp, and they were of an unsettling variety.

The loudest were the ones of pain, and these ricocheted off the large cedar trees that towered around the camp's enclosure with an unmistakable pitch that originated, time and again, with gravely wounded warriors. Some wailed at a bloody stump where a limb used to be, some gripped futilely at the shaft of an arrow that had found its way to a vital organ, and some lay, awash in their own blood, with wounds unseen. Many of them called for their mothers. When a new volley of arrows whistled into the camp from the dark tree line, more screams chorused into the night sky, while some were silenced forever.

The most disturbing were the screams of bloodlust. These began deeper in pitch, but quickly sharpened until they ended in a wild shriek summoned from each warrior's own primal history. These cries accompanied every axe and sword-wielding man that charged into the tree line, and every one of the same that charged out. A heavy and warm rain fell. The smell of smoke and blood. The clash of iron on iron. The thump of an axe against a wooden buckler. The crunch of where a heavy mallet met bone. An understanding among these screamers that the only way to stop violence was to conquer it with a superior violence.

The many fires that burned around the camp also carried on their aimless embers the screams of fear. The foundation of every scream, these were also the quietest—at times not heard at all but only seen in one's eyes. A dignity to hold it in, but also a concern to what it would be if unleashed. Would it come out as one of those wild shrieks and the warrior be lost to bloodlust? Would it come out as a whimper and the warrior be forever a coward? Such doubts only begot more fear and this fear hid behind the very eyes that scanned the scene at the camp and had the courage to ask, *Is this what we are?*

Through the middle of the camp's carnage, illuminated only by the abandoned campfires whose orange flames twisted against the falling rain, two women scurried. The one in front was older—streaks of white hair and visible wrinkles—and behind her, being pulled along by the forearm, was a woman much younger, and very pregnant. The young woman's gait was awkward and ghoulish, with knees bent and hips set wide, shuffling along at the older woman's pace as best she could. The baby inside of her was well on its way into this world. They were terrified but quiet. Screams of fear hidden in the singularity of the eye's pupils. Another volley of arrows hissed into the camp with one of them burrowing into the wet soil just paces away.

"Courage now, darling. Almost there."

Ahead of them in the camp were more than a dozen large yurts crafted from animal hide. Men in green cloaks scrambled around each structure's exterior, arming themselves from weapon racks before charging into the darkness against the unseen attackers. The women hustled past dozens more warriors and several more yurts before the older woman said, "Here."

She pulled aside a mule deer hide that acted as the door of the tent and pushed the pregnant woman inside before stepping in and letting the hide drop back into place behind them. The thick, leather walls muted much of the outside chaos and a large fire burned with the smoke leaking out of a single hole fashioned into the center of the structure's roof. Around the edge of the circular yurt were cots filled with wounded men and women.

When the physician saw the two newcomers she hustled over to the older woman and said, "What are you doing here?"

"Isn't this the hospital?"

"They're all hospitals now."

"We need a physician. The baby is almost here."

The pregnant woman gasped for breath but managed to lift her wool tunic enough to show the physician between her legs.

"Goodness, the baby *is* here."

They guided the pregnant woman to one of the few empty cots and helped her to a lying position. The physician said, "What is your name?"

"Ayune."

"Ayune, is this your first child?"

"Yes."

"How is your pain so far?"

Ayune's forehead was beaded with sweat and her breath came in short gasps, but she managed to say, "Bad."

"Okay. That's normal. I'm going to give you some herb, okay? It should help with the pain. I want you to tuck this into your cheek and I want you to concentrate on your breathing. I want short breaths, like you have now, but I want you in control of them. Like this." The physician demonstrated a few, huffed exhalations as she reached her blood-covered fingers into a pouch at her side and pulled out a dark brown pinch of mossy substance and handed it to Ayune.

A sharp cry came from the far side of the room where a wounded man began thrashing in his cot. The physician snapped her fingers at the older woman who had escorted Ayune and said, "You. Go to the next hut over. North side. Tell them I need help in here. Now."

The older woman nodded and slipped outside again just as an arrow thudded softly into the tent's flank right above Ayune's cot. The physician saw the panic in Ayune's eyes and said, "Ayune. It's too late to go anywhere else. We have to trust that the camp will hold. Your baby is here, and I need you here with me. Do you understand?"

Ayune nodded and slipped the herb into her cheek.

"Okay then. It's time to push."

A second physician entered with the older woman, and he began tending to the wounded while the two women hovered over Ayune with whispers of instruction and encouragement. Outside the sounds of battle continued and so did the patter of rain on the yurt's roof. The corners of Ayune's eyes stung from the smoke and from the pain.

She pushed for less than a quarter-hour before the pressure between her legs was relieved and she knew that her baby was born fully . . .except that it was *quiet*. "What's happening? Is it okay? What's happening? Please."

The two tending women stood, hunched over the form of the child cradled in the physician's arms—blood up to her elbows on both sides. *Grab me a linen from there. We need to dry him.* The physician turned the little figure in her hands, first face down and then up, while she spoke to it with a soft, but urgent tone. *Come on little one. Come on. It's time for the world. It's time. Come on.* The older woman returned with the linen and they worked together to wipe the baby clean of the milky biofilm that covered its body but still it was quiet. *Come on now. I see you moving those arms. I see you. Come on. It's time to meet your mother.*

"What's happening? Please."

Come on little man. Come on. The physician positioned the baby's head in the bend of her left elbow and began to tap lightly at the child's chest with her right hand. *Time to wake up. Come on.* She wiped his face again with the linen, and this time, as she tapped his chest, the child's lungs filled with air, and he screamed.

The wounded men around the tent went quiet. Outside the sounds of battle vanished. The rain fell and the child screamed again. And again. And again. Every living breath now a scream to end all screams.

"Okay," the physician said. "Well look at you now, with those lungs."

Ayune's face was a picture of exhaustion and relief. She said, "He's scared."

The older woman said, "No darling, he's not scared. He just needs his momma."

"You hold him and we'll get you fixed up," the physician said.

She handed the baby to Ayune and immediately the screaming stopped, as if the child knew that it had found its source of food, warmth, nurturing, love. There was no lust for blood in the child. No pain. Not yet.

The night deepened, and the green-cloaked warriors streamed back into the camp from out of the dark forest, signaling an end to the ambush.

The older woman sat at the bedside of Ayune and the baby, now fast asleep, before stepping out of the yurt for a taste of fresh air and to see the returning warriors. The physician was already outside, covered from the neck down in dried blood and blood still drying and she dipped her red hands into the pouch at her side and tucked a bit of the herb into her own cheek. The older woman approached her and together they stood in the dim light of the fires and watched the camp get resettled.

"I've never heard of an attack like that at night," said the older woman.

The physician spat and said, "It's a first for me."

"Why tonight?"

"I got a pretty good guess about it."

"What?"

"It's the third night since they killed Udura Atun in battle up north of here. I'd bet that every Samsaran camp out there was attacked tonight. Looking for newborns—looking for someone like your girl in there."

The older woman gasped and put a hand to her mouth. "So it's true?"

"Everything I've heard says it is."

The older woman shook her head in despair. "Gracious me. All this madness. This war. When will it stop?"

The physician spat again and said, "The birth of that child in there is assurance that all of this madness has just begun."

He moved through the crowded street like someone unfamiliar with the feeling of fear. From underneath the hood of a wool cloak he stole nervous glances over his shoulder, causing numerous collisions with other pedestrians and leaving in his path a wake of angry cursing. He was in the market district of the city of Helena, where the smell of cardamom and ginger wafted from wooden booths that lined the streets and supplied the market with its signature aroma. Ahead in the street he caught a glimpse of two spearpoints towering over the crowded people—Olerian soldiers—and he cursed out loud before redirecting himself to one of the street's thin alleyways. While leaning against the stucco exterior of the alleyside corner, he pulled a small brown substance from his cheek and, after discarding it in the dirt, pulled a linen pouch off his belt and tucked a fresh pinch of the stuff back into his mouth. He closed his eyes and steadied his breathing.

It was late in the afternoon and the angle of the sun left the alley deep in shadow compared to the street. Beggars and the sleeping bodies of beggars lined each side with faces and hands so dirty in the darkness that their skin color was imperceptible. Helena was the second largest city in the region— set along the Powder River and comprised of one- and two-story adobe structures that snaked along the riverbank for miles. At the city's perimeter stood a wall that just eclipsed a dozen feet in height with a stone base and mortar filling that had long since been bleached white by the desert sun.

His cloak was the color of dry clay and he pulled it tighter around his face just as he dared to peek off of the alley's corner and back into the street. Nothing. He exhaled a deep and deliberate breath of air.

"Getting myself all worked up," he muttered quietly.

He made his way down the alley on the balls of his feet, carefully skirting around the scraps of discarded wool blankets, waste, and humanity that was housed there. The alley went sixty paces deep before he hit a T-junction and had to decide left or right. Both were equally dismal and, as he reconsidered each, he looked back up the alley from where he had come to see two cloaked figures watching him from the street.

"Shit."

He hurried off down the left junction and took two more turns before reaching another street, where he hopped and pulled himself through more bartering crowds of merchants and buyers. Being careful not to anger everybody around him this time, he went with the flow of the crowd for a short distance before ducking into a small stable. He opened the iron latch of the first gate in the stable and slipped inside before closing it back behind him. Even before his eyes could adjust to the darker stable, he was able to see that he was sharing the stall with a chestnut-colored mare on the opposite side of the stall. Crouched now and sitting with his back to the gate, the man held a single finger up to his lips toward the mare, whose long face expressed nothing in return. They both stayed still in the silence and the man looked down with pity at his sandaled feet in the stable's muck and he adjusted their crisscrossed leather straps while listening to passing conversations on the nearby street. After many minutes passed with nothing to note, the man left the stable and nodded to the mare, *thanks, old girl.*

The number of people on the street thinned out as dusk approached and he put the market district behind him. He'd spit and then he'd look over his shoulder, and then he'd spit again, and he settled into this rhythm all the way to the eastern end of the city. He came across another thin and dark alleyway, but there were no beggars in this one. He paused at the entrance for a moment—long enough to hear the muffled voices coming out of the darkness—and he walked down it. When he came to the end of the alleyway he came to the end of the city. It opened up to a flat, open area of dirt with the bleached city walls on one side and a handful of the two-story adobe structures encasing it on the other. Men and women sat around on the dirt ground, but they were not beggars. Garments the color of wine and gold were piled with helmets and weapons upon packs that formed an unofficial ring around the area, and the owners of these items were the Olerian Empire's soldiers on their downtime. They drank water and wine, and the atmosphere was jovial, and casual, except for the two men in the modest dirt arena.

Equipped with small bucklers and shortswords made of wood, the two soldiers sparred intensely while the others around the area watched on for entertainment. The newcomer checked the alley behind him—nothing—and then scanned the faces of the watchers until he focused his attention on a woman across the way. She wore sandals like his and a cloak too, except her cloak was folded neatly on top of her pack that she put on the ground along with many of the others. She was built athletic, and lean. The linen pants she wore—also like his—were tapered off just below the knee so that the leather straps of her sandals twisted and overlapped to her calves.

One of the soldiers—bearded and obviously drunk—split from the crowd and approached him with purpose, but he held his nerve long enough to hear the soldier ask, "You want to make a wager?"

The cloaked man spat and then pointed with his chin toward the woman, "Is she fighting?"

"She's next."

"How much for her?"

"We stopped allowing bets on her."

"Why?"

"Because she never loses," the soldier said, and he spat too. "I'll tell you what I'll do though—every one silver piece you wager on one of her opponents and I'll pay you fifteen back if they beat her."

He shook his head and dismissed the soldier with a wave of his hand and continued to watch the woman until the ongoing fight was settled. As the prior combatants left the arena, she stepped in and picked up one of the sparring swords and twirled it deftly in her right hand, getting a feel for its balance. The crowd quieted noticeably just at the sight of her and those along the wall and the ground sat up a little straighter to get a better view. One voice called from the building side of the area and said, "Are you really one of them Copperfoots?"

She held both her arms out wide and said, "Why don't you come find out?"

The man gave a theatrical shake of his head and people laughed at him before a murmur came from the crowd, signaling a challenger. It was a young man with the same sparse facial hair sported by so many others in the crowd. His tunic gave him away as an Olerian soldier. The other onlookers whooped and hollered as he picked up one of the swords and he relished in the attention bestowed upon his thin shoulders. He met her eyes to check if she was ready and, with a slight nod of her head, he went storming forth. The young man displayed proficient fundamentals, but the added adrenaline made him sloppy. His leather riding boots sent a small cloud of dust up around their knees and the woman could hear the sharp, trained exhalations of breath every time he took another cut or stab with his sword. His initial assault was a four-move combination that she didn't even bother to parry—sidestepping each overzealous cut with liquid agility. When he spun on her and attempted a hard, overhead chop she sidestepped again and, for the first time, moved her sword, bringing it in a hard horizontal cut across the man's larynx.

An empathetic moan came from the crowd as he collapsed into a heap, clutching at his throat and desperately grasping for air. She crouched briefly at his side and put a hand on his shoulder and said *he'll be fine* as she stood again. She used her foot to kick the sparring sword away from the downed soldier, toward the rest of the watchers, and then gestured to the unmanned weapon. They were quiet for a moment but soon another young man came forward, drawing another round of cheers from the spectators. The new challenger was as young as the previous one, but he had learned from his predecessor's mistakes and took a more measured approach. He circled her slowly while she studied him with eyes that were the picture of focus. When it became clear that he wasn't going to be the aggressor she attacked him with the power and fluidity of a panther. Her level of quickness immediately put him off balance and their little wooden swords only made contact twice before she jabbed hers into his abdomen and then cracked it hard against his left knee. He collapsed not far from the first one and the crowd groaned again. She said *I'll take that* and she grabbed the wooden sword from the fallen man and tossed it again toward the rest of the viewers. They were all delighted by the entertainment, as they slapped each other's arms and laughed at their fallen comrades still writhing in pain on the ground.

The last man to step forth didn't have the young markers of the previous two. His hair was peppered with grey, and he was a seasoned soldier who had seen nearly two decades of combat. He was one of the best, most experienced swordsmen stationed in Helena. He made it almost a minute. As she helped him up from the dirt, broken nose and all, he smiled and gave her an admiring handshake.

DUSK SETTLED IN FULLY AND almost all of the soldiers had dispersed from their afternoon of entertainment. The woman stood over a small table made of ironwood and organized her pack before swinging her cloak over her shoulders and her belt around her waist. A cloaked man approached her and she watched him carefully out of her peripheral vision—her right hand inching toward the very real sword that was now on her belt. The man stopped a handful of paces from her and he asked, "Are you Bird?"

"I'm her."

The man spat and said, "You looking for work?"

She stopped packing and turned to the stranger to size him up properly. Her eyes lingered on his dirty feet and the hobnailed sandals he wore that were so similar to her own. She said, "There's no discounts for being Copperfoot."

"I'm not asking for any."

"Good," she said as she returned her attention to her pack. "What's the job?"

"I need to get up to West One, and I'll pay you ten silver to go with me."

She paused again to look at him. She asked skeptically, "Ten silver?"

"Yes."

She shook her head. "You're wasting your money. It's a tough hike, but West One is less than a day from here and the only people that travel that road are the soldiers coming from the fort."

"I know that."

"So why the overpay?"

"Because I heard you're the best."

"From who?"

"From everybody."

"Still feels like there's a catch to be had," she said.

"I'll have another job offer for you when we make it to West One. You're just as free to decline that job as you are this one."

"Why not just offer me that job now?"

He shrugged and said, "I don't know what it is yet. But it'll be big. It'll be lucrative."

She finished with her pack and slung its single, leather strap across her shoulder and faced the man. "What's your name?"

"Ernest."

"Ernest," she said, and the man nodded and she tapped a finger on her opposite forearm while she struck a thoughtful pose and it was quiet between them.

"When do you want to leave?"

"Meet me outside the southern gate when the sun breaks."

HE SLEPT POORLY AND MADE Helena's southern gate in the deep, dark purple of early morning, well before sunrise. She was already waiting for him and the two set off into the sleeping desert like shades into a dreamland. For the first half of the morning the travel was easy—the land was mostly flat, and they stayed on the well-worn horse trail between Helena and West One. She noticed how often he looked behind them on the trail but said nothing of it, and when midday came they each sidled up to the base of a tiny mesa that offered them a sliver of shade and ate.

He spat and renewed the herb-like substance in his cheek before devouring a corn tortilla dressed with black beans. When he finished, he noticed her studying him intently.

"What?" he asked.

"Hiring me comes with limits."

"What do you mean?"

"I mean if you stole something valuable back there—or you hurt a kid or something—your ten silver doesn't buy me standing between you and whatever mob is looking for you."

"Hurt a kid?"

"Your eyes have spent more time on the trail behind us than the one ahead. The last time I was in a situation like this, the guy was a gambler with big debts. They came for him and he thought I was going to put my life on the line over him being a degenerate. I'm not here to cast judgment—I'm just letting you know the rules."

Ernest shook his head. "I didn't steal anything. And I didn't hurt no kid. There's a lot of bad people in the world and a few of them might be out to hurt *me*. Might not be, too. Your employment is a precaution."

She nodded and finished eating and then said, "The second half of the day is a lot tougher than the first. Going to be a lot of uphill. Go easy on your water."

Tucked into the minor range that branched off of the vast Echora Mountains to the east, and placed because of a nearby watering hole, West One was the most southeastern fort in the Olerian Empire. Being so isolated, it had yet to play a major role in any war campaign, but in recent years of peace it became the foremost fort for training horseback riders and patrols.

It was well past midday, and the mountains rose to the east of them like the teeth of some long-jawed beast upon whose open maw they hiked. They talked sparingly between deep, heavy breaths. The sun burned behind them and the color of its flaming orb meshed with the soft ocher sand that covered the rocky and barren landscape of their ascent. The dust disturbed in their passing stuck to the sweat of their exposed faces and this they splashed away with water stored in goat bladders that hung off their shoulders by leather cords made of the same animal. They stopped in the mid-afternoon with their backs to the mountain and looked north into the expanse of flat desert below and beyond them. The Dialla Desert. What could be seen was brindle-colored earth with small aggregates of yellow and green vegetation. It ran on for as far as their eyes could see and disappeared into what their eyes could not.

"How much further do you think it is?" He asked.

"Not much."

They continued up the trail into the late afternoon when a duo of horseback riders came from the other direction, forcing the two companions off the trail to make room for their passing. They bowed their heads, but no words were spoken between the parties and when the horses were gone, the two continued to climb. It was hot and dry and, when they came upon a twisted tree by the trail, they sat in the shade cast by its mangled form. The sun was fast sinking in the sky, but the heat from it still rippled translucently over everything except for their thin branches of shade. She pulled the stopper on her water and splashed it over her dark brown hair that was pulled back into a tight ponytail. His hair was darker—flecks of grey betraying his older age—and he did the same before spitting out a thick brown mucus into the dirt. He said, "I don't have much water left."

"We're getting close," she said.

"I thought you've never been there before."

"I haven't."

They hiked on with her in the lead. He grew tired of coughing out the fine dirt that she kicked up, and slowly drifted back while the two continued to tread, lonely and upward, with their shadows baked into the mountainside. The shortsword at her side chimed quietly against the iron rings that bound it to her belt and her leather pack, like his, jostled against the outside of her wool cloak. As they gained in elevation, a hot wind gusted in from the monarch sun in the west and, as if wanting a better look, it pulled back her cloak to reveal another gleaming, claw-like weapon attached to her hip, opposite of the sword. It needed no such look at the man. At a glance, the two travelers, in their knee-length cloaks, linen pants, and hobnailed sandals, looked to be of the same mold, but he wore no vambraces, no armor, no sword, and, out in this desolation, looked no different than some city dweller lost on his way to market.

Just minutes before the sun began its plummet past the distant horizon, they spotted the fort—its small, earthen-colored walls and buildings were set over the trail within a slight bend of the mountain's spine. There were six small structures, and they were all made from a tan and reddish brick cemented together by a brown muddy plaster that caked the outsides of the bricks as well as in between them. Its worn nature gave it a look of abandonment, but atop each building and along the length of walls were the top halves of men's bodies and the spears they stood with. Even from the distance they could see the fading sun glint off the watchers' armor.

He said that it didn't look like much. She shrugged.

They entered the fort through a small, wooden side gate and, with the exception of a few nods, were met with indifference. They stood inside the large compound catching their breath and hiding in the structures' shade from the final moments of the sun. He coughed and spat and retrieved his small pouch. He pinched a glob of the mossy brown substance from it and pushed it under his tongue and then placed his hands on his hips and closed his eyes. She placed her small leather pack on the ground and brushed off its dirty exterior with her hands. She bounced anxiously on the balls of her feet while scanning the sleepy base and, without opening his eyes, the man said to her, "We're safe here."

She acknowledged the comment with a small nod before a young man dressed in garb of wine and gold approached them and, without introducing himself, said that the captain was ready to see them.

They walked toward the fort's largest structure and then descended downward into a series of damp, dark tunnels that were burrowed into the side of the mountain range. When they came to a room that appeared to be a dead end, the young soldier gestured for them to take a seat in front of an ironwood table and said that the captain would be along shortly. They each sat in silence in their thin wooden chairs as the rooms only light, a candle, flickered lightly and dully over their skin and clothes. He spat into a small copper spittoon that sat at the foot of the table while she rubbed her two middle fingers over each of her temples. The captain didn't enter from the same tunnel they had, but instead he materialized out the dark corner of the room that the candlelight failed to penetrate. He was dressed in the same wine and gold attire as the men outside. He took a seat behind the desk and looked dispassionately at the travelers before him. They offered him no formalities and he gave none.

"You are here quicker than I expected," the captain said. He spat too and leaned forward with his elbows on the desk and his hands folded into each other. He was nearly bald, with what little was left of his hair gathering around his ears and upper neck. His skin was dark and leathery from sun exposure and as he ran one hand over his cheek it made a scratching sound as it pulled at the skin and stubby hairs of his face. He said, "It might be that you could get on with your business right away, but your speed in getting here has confused my instructions."

Another man entered the room from the same entrance used by the two companions. He walked confidently over to the captain and leaned into his ear, whispering something that went unheard in the room's tiny darkness. The captain nodded to what the man said and then dismissed him with a wave of his hand. After he was gone, the captain turned his body and reached into a small leather purse that hung off the back of his chair, bringing forth a bulky envelope wrapped tightly with a linen cord.

"This is for a *Ernest*," he said as he looked between the two and he pushed the bundle across the table toward the man. "You'll recognize the seal."

In the darkness was the shuffle of feet and the muffled voices of men passing in the tunnels behind them. Ernest looked over his shoulder briefly and then leaned forward in his chair to grab the envelope. It was sealed with a bulky glob of yellow wax pressed with the image of a hare. He looked over his shoulder again before tucking the papers into his pack while the captain nodded his assurance. Bird's eyes glanced at the seal, but she said nothing.

The captain stood from his chair and adjusted his pant line. He said, "I'm not one to tamper with Lady Kira's plans with you two getting here early and all, and so you'll stay on the base for two days. You can leave the day after."

The captain looked at the woman and said, "What was your name again?"

"Bird."

"Right. I'll be staying in the officer's barracks tonight and tomorrow," he said as he gestured between the two travelers. "Ernest. Bird. You'll be in my quarters for as long as you're here. Pass the time how it suits you. The man outside the tunnel will show you where to go and take care of anything that you might need."

He pointed to Ernest's pack where the envelope hid. "Whatever is in there is clearly none of my business. You can inspect it to your own standards, but I'm sure that you'll find everything about it is authentic and untampered. I trust that you'll tell its sender as much. When the time comes to leave, I suggest you take the east pass for the same reasons that you took it here. I promise you that it's a much smoother commute going down."

THE EVENING SKY SET IN fully on the mountainside and the soft blue on the horizon was quickly being overwhelmed by a heavy purple color that brought with it innumerable stars and their distant silence. They were met outside the tunnel by the same young soldier who had shown them in. He was short in stature and had meager traces of facial hair swept across his face in no discernable pattern. He offered to carry their packs for them but they declined and so he gestured for them to follow.

"This your first time to West One?"

Ernest gave a noncommittal grunt and the young soldier led them across the north side of the courtyard. The fort looked completely different doused in darkness. Its color and imperfections were muted, and it appeared as lifeless as any structure would if not for the dozen small torches that lined the interior of the outer wall and several of the inner buildings. Bird's eyes adjusted quickly and she counted the men along the wall top, each of them as far from the nearest torch as possible so as to give their eyes the chance to adapt and spot something in that darkness—even if there was nothing to spot except for the darkness itself and each man was left alone with his thoughts and the stories of others gone mad atop the wall and of sirens and succubi who baited watchers into the wild darkness and fed upon their vitals before turning to their souls.

The young soldier continued to talk as they made their way through the courtyard. He told them that West One was originally a trading outpost for people in the southern Titian region. He pointed out the barracks, the mess hall, the training grounds—all of them soft and pale in color against the scanty torchlight. He said that there were never more than two dozen people stationed at the fort at any given time, and mounted patrols were

deployed on weeks long assignments to report on the more provincial por-
tions of the empire.

He said, "You probably saw a pair of our most recently deployed while
on your way here today."

Ernest grunted again and the soldier nodded and continued. "Those
two will be gone for up to three weeks. You familiar with the Weatridge
area? They'll be over there. It's important for even the most rural areas to
understand that they are protected and that we care for their safety. At pres-
ent, West One alone has sixty-eight men out to every corner of the empire.
If trends hold the same as they've been for the past three years, about thirty-
seven of those men should make it back here alive. Some die, some desert.
A lot of people sign up and go through all the basic training just hoping
they'll get assigned a horse and then they'll steal the horse and go back to
wherever it is they came. Used to have a big problem with that—stealing the
horses. I suppose we don't have to worry about that with you two, believing
how you do."

Neither Ernest nor Bird said anything more and they walked in silence
to the northwest corner of the fort where a small square building was tucked
against the outer wall. Atop the wall, one of the watchers shifted as the three
of them approached. Their escort rapped his knuckles on the ragged ebony
wood of the door and said, "This is you. If you follow that wall down to its
end you'll find the latrine. You share a wall over on that side with me and a
couple of others. That's where I'll be if you need anything. I've already got a
fire started inside for you as well as some food. It's nothing special—just the
stuff we send out on patrol—but you could do worse in these parts."

The soldier took his leave and Ernest muttered some complaint under
his breath. Bird opened the ill fit door, and the two companions dragged
their tired, dirty bodies into the small building.

It was a single room. Dark, even with the paltry fire that leaked smoke
out of the dwarfish chimney. In the near corner was a small table with a
single chair tucked neatly under it and on the opposite was a wood chest
the size of a person. She deferred the room's only cot to him. Next to the
fireplace was a small stack of wood and a large tin tub of water with a deep
blue that projected a deceptive depth. Ernest tossed his pack onto the cot
then sat cross legged in front of the water and sunk both of his hands into
the tub where the water grabbed at him like liquid mercury. With his newly
baptized hands he reached under his tongue, pulled out the dark pinch of
herb, and with a nimble move of his wrist he flicked it into the fire where it
hissed quietly among the flames.

She tossed her pack against the opposite wall and unsnapped the
bronze broach that kept her cloak on before tossing that next to the pack

too. What she kept covered underneath the cloak was an apparent armory. On her back was a matted, steel grey shield—slightly domed and perfectly circular—that fit snugly below the line of her cloak and two scapulae. Its circumference expanded beyond the width of her torso just slightly, as if the size of it was designed specifically for her. She retrieved it by reaching over her shoulder and pulling it off of two custom, U-shaped latches on the back of her armor that the shield's enarmes hung from, and then leaned it against the wall next to her pack. Sheathed on her right hip was the steel shortsword with an ornate handle composed of four small cubes of ivory that had been grooved and shaped to fit the clenched grip of its wielder, and on the opposite side of her belt was an exotic, three-pronged fist weapon that sparkled against the fire's light. She detached the belt and tossed it next to the shield and then unlatched and slipped her armor off over her head. The armor itself was as exquisite as everything else she wore—a segmented steel cuirass, similar in dullness to the shield, comprised of thirty-six individual steel slats held together by numerous leather straps and hinges that allowed her a full range of motion while wearing it. Underneath the armor was a beige colored, linen tunic, similar to his, and as she moved to detach the two vambraces around her wrists as she glanced at his pack sitting on the cot. She said, "So you're going to take a bad bath instead of reading that fancy letter?"

He ignored her and brought his cooled, wet hands to the back of his neck and to his face before running them through his dark hair that held a slight, natural curl.

She said, "Don't go mucking it up."

"I'm not."

"Don't go using it all either."

"There's plenty."

He finished his rinse and walked to the latrine while she took her turn with the water, dropping on both knees and plunging her entire head into the tub. He returned and dug a gray, wool shirt out of his pack. There was a brass candle holder on the small table, and he grabbed it and dipped the candle's wick into the fireplace and brought the new flame over to the room's chest. He sat on the floor against the chest and unwound the linen bind on the envelope. She added wood to the fire and commented on the coldness of mountain nights. He opened the papers meticulously and after several moments of scanning he held one of the papers in the air above his head and shook it. She walked over to him, snatched the paper out of his hand and returned to the fire where she leaned into the light and scanned the page. It was quiet in the room for many minutes, and they heard the muffled voices of two men changing shifts on the wall just outside their room. He grew

visibly agitated the longer he read, while she finished her short letter quickly
and read it again. She said his name, concern in her voice, but he waved her
off distractedly.

"What's in that letter, Ernest?"

"It's nothing good. I'll tell you that."

She pressed him to say more but he waved his hand and began reading the letter again. She folded the thin paper in her own hand and spun it
across to room where it landed near her pack. It was quiet for a while longer
and she lay flat on the floor staring blankly at the fire's light shift across the
ceiling. When he was finished reading, he gathered the letter, walked to the
fire, and squatted down to the level of the flames with his elbows on his
knees. He reached out deliberately with each page and torched them one
by one in succession until it was just him there empty-handed and with a
thought to the pain that he might be spared by throwing himself too into
the fire.

He pointed toward her pack and said, "Yours goes in too."

She sat up and said, "The shit it does. That's my contract."

"I know what it is, and you don't need it to get paid. Not by these
people."

She retrieved the letter and handed it to him to be tossed into the fire
like the others. When he was happy that there were no remnants of either
letter he added another log the fire.

He said, "Does this mean you're accepting the offer?"

"I might if you tell me what the hell it's for."

"It's for the same as you did so admirably today. Protect me, keep me
alive."

"The shit it is," she said.

"Honest."

"Then why is the rate tripled?"

"Because we've got to go somewhere that's far away."

"Where?"

He ignored the question and instead dug into his pack, retrieved his
pouch of herb, and pinched it into the side of his mouth. She said that when
people get paid that kind of silver it's because they're willing to do a job
nobody else wants to. He told her that sometimes people get paid that kind
of silver because they're *able* to do a job nobody else *can* do.

She said, "Don't flatter me, knave."

"I'm just saying it the way it is."

"You just need me looking after you because you can't look after
yourself."

"Damn right."

A night bird called quietly outside their room and again they heard the shuffling of feet atop the wall. The muttering of more voices. Ernest retrieved the food supplies left by the soldier from the corner table and tossed two hardtack biscuits at Bird and took two for himself and then lay down in the cot, nibbling and thinking. She added another log to the fire and the small hearth heaved its little warmth against the pressing darkness. Bird lay parallel to Ernest from across the room and propped her head on a bedroll from her pack. She stared at the ceiling and as it grew colder, she converted her bedroll to a blanket and used her pack as a pillow. They lay in silence for a long time, neither of them sleeping. Eventually the fire sickened and turned to coal and the wood's orange veins pulsed slowly and ominously as if its fiery heart was encumbered by the throes of death.

Her voice probed the darkness. She said, "Ernest?"

"Let's get some sleep."

"Ernest."

"What?"

"Where are we going?"

The room held the silence for several moments and she almost repeated the question, thinking that he hadn't heard her. But he had, and when his answer came back it was one word and when he said it a chill ran down her spine and she wasn't sure if it was from the temperature of the room or the dread in his voice.

He said, "Kardona."

***

By the Reutend calendar it was the year 151, marked from the date that the nation's founders declared independence from the Eodrans. Out east, by the count of the Eowari calendar, it was the year 392, coinciding with the Yuri dynasty's time in power. In Kardona the year depended on one's religion and if they followed the Cinios or Uqul calendar—years 258 and 272 respectively. For Oleria it was 1066, born from the date that Olerian ancestors crossed the Great Water and defeated the archaic Haudoans. The Haudoans were mighty and storied in their own right—their calendar was at 491 when no one remained to tally the next year. As far as the Olerians knew, their 1066-year-old calendar held in it more years than any in existence, and in a way had consumed the dates of innumerable tribes, clans, kingdoms, and nations that it had exterminated or absorbed into its own empire. Thirty-two years earlier, the year 1034, the Olerians nearly doubled the size of their already overwhelming empire by decimating the Eporisian armies, installing Olerian elders in all provinces, and giving the remaining survivors one timeless ultimatum—assimilate or be killed. The recipe was not a flawless one, and elders dealt with unrest and uprisings, but by and large those that were conquered had no recourse, and the protection and stability given to them as nominal Olerians was a perk that few else in the world experienced.

To the south of this newly conquered land, along the front range of the Echora Mountains and stretching across the Dialla Desert, was a people that kept no calendar. Their population was scattered, but not tribal. They were deeply religious, but they did not proselytize. They practiced agriculture, but they were not farmers. They forged invaluable weapons and armor, but they did not trade. They were fierce warriors, but not barbarians. They lived in proximity with the finest horses in the world, but they did not ride them.

In the year 1035, when a newly installed elder by the name of Cevrias sought to learn more about his neighbors to the south, there was little to be learned. He scoured historical Eporisian documents and interviewed the incumbent locals but found nothing notable. Over 400 years of nearness and seemingly the only thing he could confirm about the enigmatic people was their unwillingness to ride horses. As the empire expanded southward and contact with them became a daily occurrence, locals joked that you could always spot one of these mysterious outsiders by looking at their feet—perpetual walking made it so they always had a layer of the russet colored land caked onto them. By this way they came to be known as the Copperfoot, and though the name was initially used derogatorily, the people themselves came to embrace it and used it among themselves with pride.

The Olerians and Copperfoot rubbed shoulders uneventfully for decades before the relationship began to deteriorate, quickly. Though previously viewed as an ineffectual territory, and thus of little interest to Oleria, Cevrias discovered that not only did the Dialla Desert have the quickest access to the iron rich Echora mountains, which allowed the Copperfoot to mine and craft exceptional weapons and armor, but the wild horses that roamed the region were several hands larger than anything the Olerians had seen before and would be a vital addition to a military that relied so heavily on its cavalry. Cevrias sought to establish trade networks with the people and wanted to begin capturing and domesticating the wild horses, but he was routinely denied, no matter how lucrative the offers. Furthermore, Olerian vendors offered exorbitant amounts of silver for the weapons and armor crafted by the Copperfoot, but were perpetually frustrated by the inexplicable denials that came from the would-be trade partners. Later on, when independent military contractors and poachers entered Dialla with the purpose of abducting wild horses, another indisputable detail was discovered about the Copperfoot people—that they stood out as some of the most deft and brilliant warriors to walk the planet. Poachers that made it out of the desert alive returned to Oleria with stories of entire bands of men, sometimes numbering in the dozens, being obliterated by mere handfuls of the footed strangers.

For a few years their reputation as a dangerous and cunning people insulated the Copperfoot from any serious problems or threats. However, it was this very reputation that proved a double-edged sword—powerful empires do not prefer to be neighbored with dangerous and cunning people. During one of the longest stretches of peace the Olerians had ever known, they consolidated their vast territory and replenished military stores and ranks as needed. Then, as quietly as the world's largest known army could move, it did. For the next year soldiers from across the empire were reassigned and statiofned along Oleria's southern border, prepared for full-scale invasion. The Copperfoot knew nothing of these movements, and on the sixty-second day of the spring quarter, in the Olerian year 1053, the army crossed the border into the Dialla with the direct intention of destroying the mysterious desert people by any means necessary.

—Excerpt from Ilia's History of Common Regions, 1067

***

He woke late the next morning and, before he could draw a waking breath, he tucked a small wad of the herb under his tongue. She quietly performed a series of stretches and exercises in the middle of the room. A fire burned low in the room's small hearth and a plate of biscuits and bacon were on the table. "One of the soldiers brought that," she said. After eating he returned to the cot and sat rubbing his legs that ached from the hike the day before. He stopped and gazed into the fire with his elbows resting on his knees and she said, "What are you doing?"

"Thinking."

"If it's about finding a new job, I've been doing the same."

"It's not."

"Forget I said it then."

He laid down on the cot with his eyes open and his jaw shifting around the herb in his mouth. She said to him, "Since we're stuck here for an extra day, what do you want to do?"

"Lay here. Rest."

She grabbed a biscuit from the table and her eyes went to her armor, sword, and shield in the far corner of the room and she looked at Ernest—not a weapon on him—and said, "Do you know how to fight?"

"I'm a Copperfoot."

"That's not what I asked."

"It's been a long time."

"How long?"

"Forever."

She shook her head and said *shit* and he said, "Why's it matter?"

"Because Kardona is a warzone."

"That's why I hired you."

"I'm one person."

"But you're good.," he said.

"Even if I am . . ." she shook her head and the conversation died and she rocked her head back onto her neck and looked up with empty eyes into the dark ceiling.

It was his turn to ask her, "What are you thinking?"

"I'm thinking of making like a sane person and getting the hell out of here."

"You agreed to a contract."

"The same contract you threw in the fire?"

"Shit." He wrenched his neck sideways and launched a glob of spit into the fire.

"If you don't know how to fight, then what'd you do during the war?" She asked.

He just shook his head and she asked, "Deserter?"

His voice grew stern, and he said, "I'm no damned deserter."

She put up her hands in a gesture signaling that she meant no offense and she dropped the conversation. Outside of their room the base stirred awake with the sound of shuffling feet and hooves—the muffled calls of distant men and their answers. She went to the water bin and splashed handfuls of it onto her face and then blew the water off her lips in short bursts of moisture. He said, "I can try to get you paid more."

"It's not about the money. It's a bad idea to go there."

"I don't have a choice," he said.

"You better get yourself a weapon then."

"Will that make you feel better?"

She paused and then said, "It would actually."

"Then I'll get one."

She nodded and thought for a moment and said, "Okay. We have a full day here and we have a long journey out. We'll get you a weapon and use the time to get you some of the basics."

He shook his head again from his laying position and said, "I'm getting too old to be learning new tricks."

"Well, I'm not going to Kardona with some washed up deserter."

He shot her a glare, spat again, and then cursed under his breath before giving a resigned nod. They spent the rest of the morning in the training yard with two wooden sparring swords, but his effort for it was poor and so was his talent. By midmorning he gave up altogether and he sat in the shade of the outer wall, chewing and spitting his herb while he looked absently down at his dirty feet splayed in front of him. They ate again and in the hottest part of the day she disappeared beyond the fort's outer wall and returned a short while later with a bundle of dead acacia branches tucked under each arm. After a trip to the stable she was back in the yard with discarded hay and twine, and she worked on assembling the gathered products into a rough, humanoid figure. She found him sleeping in the shade of the wall, using his rolled-up cloak as a pillow, and she nudged him awake with her toe.

He looked the figure up and down and said, "You made yourself a friend?"

"I made you an enemy."

She walked him over to a spot several paces from her newly made sculpture and produced a small bow from under her cloak—hardly bigger than his torso—and handed it over to him. She used the toe of her sandal to scrape out a line in the sand and said, "Start shooting."

He handled the bow in his hands and eyed the dusty quiver that she tossed in the dirt at his feet. He held it to eye level and said, "This thing looks like it was made for a child."

"Suits you perfect then."

"The shit it does."

"It's small because it's made to be shot from horseback. Don't let it hurt your ego none."

"Where'd you get this thing?"

"From that little man that's always checking on us."

He shot all afternoon with limited success and she walked back and forth, retrieving the hits and the misses alike and setting the arrows at his feet while repeating the same instructions over and over—*elbow up, back straight, forward foot at an angle, anchor.* In the evening they stopped for dinner and took some roasted eggs and tortillas to the top of the north wall and ate quietly as they looked into the flat oblivion of the Dialla Desert. He continued to shoot into early dusk and as soldiers filtered into the fort from their patrols they took their dinners around the edge of the yard and watched him practice. Soon they were gambling on each shot and every release of an arrow was met with groans and cheers alike. She continued to retrieve arrows and when one of the soldiers told her that her friend can't shoot for shit she said, "I'm watching it the same as you are."

That night he sat on the floor of the room in front of the fire and soaked his right hand in the tin tub. Pink tendrils of blood seeped coolly from his pointer and middle finger and when she told him that they would continue to practice on the way to Kardona, he begged her to simply cut off his hand.

The following morning they ate breakfast in the yard and watched the patrols leave for the day. He complained about the pain in his hand constantly, so she disappeared to the barracks and returned shortly after with a leather archery glove.

"This should help protect those soft hands."

It did, and it immediately relieved the raw skin on his fingers. They shot for the rest of the morning and at lunch they again ate on the north wall and watched storm clouds skate across the distant countryside at eye level, dusting the earth with thin gray curls of rain as if the planet were a garden and this corner they inhabited was given water as some meager afterthought. When he was done eating he retrieved some of the dark, sticky substance from his pants and put a wad of it into his cheek before offering the pouch to her.

She declined and said, "I'll save you the time now and let you know that you never have to offer me any of that stuff."

"You're not even going to try it?"

"You think I've never had it?"

"Have you?"

"I've had it. It smells like goat shit and tastes worse."

"That's how you know it's the good stuff."

The day grew hotter as it progressed, and the afternoon found the two of them sitting in the eastern shade of the barracks as the sun dipped in the west when the patrols filtered in and took dinner in the mess hall.

At dusk, he returned to the room while she went to the mess hall. When she returned she found him sitting on the ground with his back to the wall opposite the fire. On one side of him was a bucket of cold water that his hand soaked in and on the other was a pot for spitting. They exchanged nods and she gave him a helping of beans and tortillas. Ernest continued to chew and spit into his cup as the fire sank slowly back into the wood in the same way the sun sinks into the earth and Bird began doing a series of balancing exercises in the dimming light. She rose onto both of her toes, held the pose for a minute, and then switched to her right leg only. Her left leg slowly eased up behind her until her left leg and torso were perpendicular to the ground, balanced neatly onto her right foot. Her shadow cast against the stone wall around them and replicated each move she made like some pallish anthropoid seeking to escape its plane of existence which was in itself nothing but two-dimensional specters making their way to this world by way of restless posturing. He seemed to look into this world through the weakened embers that glowed in his eyes just as well as if they were made of wood and it was the fire that was the reflection of some inner element hidden in him.

When she was done she motioned him from his position on the wall so she could lay down, as she had the previous nights, with her head on her pack. He removed his hand from the bucket and walked gingerly to the cot on his side of the room and settled onto the thin, feather mattress.

Bird spoke from across the room. "If your boss wants you to go to Kardona, then why come to West One first? It's a full day in the wrong direction."

Ernest held up his left hand with the middle and pointer fingers extended and said, "For two reasons—both involving caution. For one, the captain who you met is one of Lady Kira's most trusted associates and one of the few people in the world she would have trusted with that letter. Two, nobody could have followed us here. The land is too open and they'd have too many questions to answer if they wanted to approach the fort. When we leave here in the morning it will be with the certainty that we are alone."

"Who's following you?"

She heard the rustle of his head shaking on the wool cover of the mattress and he said, "I don't know. All down the line of her operation, the lady has had her people report that they're being followed, and then many go missing."

"You could've told me this back in Helena."

"Why do you think I needed a hired sword?"

"From the look of you? I was sure you were another degenerate gambler."

"Shit."

"Any idea what to look for with these people following you?"

"I think they're going to look like everyone else, just evil."

"Okay."

"From this point forward, it's best if nobody makes note of our passing."

"Okay."

"Discreteness is our friend."

"Okay."

"Like ghosts."

"You got it."

THE NEXT MORNING SHE WENT to the kitchen early with both packs and loaded each one with supplies. The fort's cook was a short, heavy man by the name of Serjio and he recognized Bird from his time stationed in Helena. He dipped into his specialty rations and handed her salted beef and goat jerky and offered fresh eggs from the fort's coop, and when she asked what she was going to do with fresh eggs out on the trail he shrugged and handed her four pieces of wrapped bread pudding. She went through the armory and took a leg quiver off one of the walls and when she gave it to Ernest he said, "What the hell is this for?" And she said, "Just put it on and look like you know what you're doing."

A short while later, Bird and Ernest walked out of the eastern gate with no pageantry and began working their way down the same trail by which they had come. They looked mostly the same as their ascent—the hobnailed sandals, the earthen cloaks—except for the small quiver and sword that now dangled off Ernest's belt, along with the small bow slung diagonal across his torso. It was overcast and cold in the morning, but by the time they stopped for lunch they each had the sleeves of their linen shirts rolled up to their elbows and they were routinely wiping sweat from off their brows before it found its way to their eyes.

The Dialla Desert extended north and west of them. The nearest stretch of it was the hottest and flattest of the region. Yearlong winds whipped around the intersection of the main Echora range and the branch that housed West One, and with no vegetation to ever hinder it, it battered down and swept up any half-measured attempt at life until the only thing left behind was rock and sand. At noon they found shade under a small outcrop and chewed loudly on a couple of biscuits while she looked out at the pastel clouds that blanketed the arid landscape and he stared emptily at the steep mountain peaks to the east that loomed over them like some invulnerable granite golem, and, in thirty-eight years of life lived under their shadow, there wasn't a day that passed where the majesty of the peaks was lost on him.

They reached the bottom of the mountain's trailhead in the early evening and agreed to stop for the night. They set a fire and shared the bread pudding with the Echoras looming over them like a fabled monster and their little fire acting as some diminutive spell cast against its inevitability. In the morning they packed up and when they were both ready to leave they instead stood side by side, each waiting for the other to lead the way. He gestured her forward with his hand and she nodded and then offered the same gesture back to him and he nodded too but they continued to stand there looking into the morning desert.

He said, "Are we getting to this thing or what?"

"Let's get to it," she said.

"I'd say it's your lead."

"And I'd say it's yours."

He nodded again but didn't move and then he said, "I don't know where to go."

"We're going to Kardona."

"I know where it is we're going but I don't know how to get there."

It was her turn to nod in understanding and when he asked her if she had been there before she said that she had and that she knew the way.

He spat and said, "Excellent. Let's get to it then."

"Sure, I'll lead it—for forty silver."

He spat, "I was witness to the agreement you made already with the price stated as it was."

"You were, but there was nothing in there that said I was to act as your navigator as well. I'd say forty silver pieces for a guided trip to Kardona and back is a fair ask."

He mumbled something about her not coming back at all and she said *what?* but he just mumbled even more incoherently while chewing over the herb in his mouth. He said, "Twenty silver."

"Forty."

"Thirty silver, then."

"Let's do the forty and call it good."

He muttered *god damn swindler*, but nodded in agreement and again gestured westerly for her to lead the way.

She said, "Is that the way you want go?"

"You just got a forty silver raise to be the guide and you're already asking me for some directional input?"

She kept a straight face and said, "There's more than one way to get there. We can go west as you've pointed out—stay south of the Badlands and the Omoya's and go in along the southern border. Or we can head north into Pridipoa and catch a ship across the bay and we'd make port on the western shore of Kardona."

"I'm not getting on no ship."

"It's faster."

"I'd rather crawl into a scorpion den ass naked than get on one of those oversized coffins."

"Okay, I hear ya." She gestured with her right hand in a chopping motion vaguely to the north and west of them and continued, "The Iron Road has trade wagons that come in and out of Camphania every day, most of them heading west. It's pretty easy to get on with them if you're willing to carry your own weight, or willing to pay a fee as a ride along. Either way it's safer than going the whole thing alone."

He nodded, and when he gestured again for her to lead the way, this time she did with him setting after her several paces behind. It was nearing the end of the summer quarter and the days would be brutally hot and dry before thunderstorms sailed through in the late afternoon, cooling the land briefly, before vanishing by nightfall like some fickle intentioned dreams. The two of them moved like ghosts across the countryside dyed of vermillion and sepia and in the hottest stretches of the day they napped nestled in the shade of mesas small and large and when rested they walked by way of old washed-out arroyos and arid lowlands. After two days they descended into the Dialla steppes and came in and out of small villages without a word as the people there stood in the doorways of their meager adobe houses with expressionless faces and their eyes made dark and dogs came out to bark at them half-heartedly but quickly returned to their places of shade, panting and dirty, while the children of the village followed them suspiciously for as long and as closely as their friends dared them to but they too quickly scattered back to their dwellings, sending the two outsiders on without acknowledgement and it was never spoken of and in time it was as if they had never come at all.

***

Just north of the Great Water, where a temperate climate enveloped an expansive area of luscious highlands, the Olerians built the foundation for their thousand-year empire. By virtue of what most in the world would call fate—and the other few, chance—the highlands were flooded with natural resources, such as copper and silver, and so rich was the soil and so forgiving the climate that nearly every pertinent crop in the known world could be grown there, and was. Hardships like drought and famine were strangers to the Olerian people, who never knew the way that a freezing winter could bite, or how a scorching summer could suffocate. Their army was fueled by beef and vegetables and their horses were made strong with grain and hay. Copper provided the basis for the bronze armor that every soldier was outfitted with and the silver coinage of the empire became the standard by which neighboring nations managed their own economies. The many rivers, lakes, and waterways that traversed the landscape made it difficult for invading armies to advance, and in times of peace provided an abundance of fresh water.

However, even given all of these advantages, Oleria failed to achieve any prominence outside of its small region until the rise of its first emperor, Gudrias the Great, circa 412. The son of a barley farmer, Gudrias came of age at a time when Oleria was a poorly run republic and relied on a conscription army to protect its borders. As a young soldier, he showed exceptional talent for the militaristic arts and, when his three years of required duty expired, he did something that few else did—he signed back up. He rose through the professional ranks and was honored as the youngest person to ever make the rank of general. Finally given the power to implement his own ideas, Gudrias quickly realized the opportunity that had been missed by his predecessors in harnessing the power of his homeland. The woodlands were his greatest weapon. When needing to move quickly, his armies cut and manufactured temporary bridges within hours, and the same was done when it became easier to build siege machines on site rather than haul them across the difficult countryside. Excess wood was sent to shore for ships and the size of the navy doubled during his tenure. When on campaign, his engineers could raise a fort in a matter of days, and they did so at any strategic location they could find. They were like carpenter ants in the way that they would advance, then build, then advance again, and to be on the receiving end of this aggression was to feel perpetually frustrated and hopeless. But Gudrias did more than protect Oleria's borders, he expanded them aggressively. Successful campaign after successful campaign ensued, and within eight years of becoming the youngest general ever, he became the first High Commander ever—the military's highest rank, created by Gudrias himself. With an army at his back that viewed him as an invincible conqueror, and a republic that continued to be viewed as weak, corrupt, and ineffective, Gudrias disbanded the nation's republic and declared himself the first emperor of Oleria. There were none who openly opposed him.

Aside from fundamentally altering Oleria's political structure, Gudrias's rise to power, which would be told, retold, historicized, romanticized, and immortalized in the following centuries, established a new norm for his nation—the path to power was through the military. No longer did Oleria need to conscript its forces— young men and women flocked to its ranks to be the next Gudrias. They taxed the people heavily and employed a full-time, standing, professional army, and with its civilians viewing the military as the ideal way to climb the social, political, and economic ladder, the Olerian ranks were flush with the best, brightest, and most ambitious people that the nation had to offer. Furthermore, because of Gudrias, the position of emperor would for a long time be viewed as a military position, and it would be over three-hundred years before an emperor would be named who was not previously a High Commander.

Their new identity as a militaristic empire, combined with their bountiful homeland, allowed Oleria to reach heights that it had never before imagined. Neighboring nations had their own virtues and advantages, sure, but none had the complete package to stand toe to toe with these new Olerians—full-time professional soldiers, bronze armor, horses, food and water in abundance, money and natural resources aplenty—and the more that they played at war, the better they became. Though no general, or any Olerian figure, would reach the stature of Gudrias the Great, each generation produced their own worthy tactical minds and leaders and the Olerian expansion continued steadily.

When they conquered Eporisia in the year 1035, it was the farthest south any Olerian army had ever been, and it was their first victory outside of the north highland region. Some of their higher generals had doubts about their armies' effectiveness outside of the highlands—worried that their tactics had grown too specific to the area that honed them—but the routine dismantling of Eporisia seemed to prove that such doubts were unfounded. Even though Eporisia was a coastal nation and much less arid than the desert to the south, the generals were confident that, in a war with the Copperfoot, similar results would be achieved.

They were wrong.

Their misplaced confidence would cost countless men their lives in the coming years, and one High Commander would be lost before they realized that the Dialla Desert was no place like they had fought before, and its brutal climate was a worthy enough opponent by itself, never mind the people that called it home.

—Excerpt from Ilia's A History of the Olerian Empire and its Origins, 1059

***

ON THE AFTERNOON OF THE fourth day, they intersected the Powder River where they spent the rest of the day bathing and cooling in one of its slow-moving meanders. They shadowed the river the next morning but relented to the heat at midday and sat under an embankment waiting for the worst of it to pass. She offered him a biscuit but he waved it off and she told him that there was plenty of food, but he waved it off again anyway. Occasionally a fish would jump out on the water and he lobbed large globs of black spit at the tiny minnows treading near the still surface water off the river's bank. She routinely would climb to the top of the embankment and check the surrounding landscape for people, but it looked desolate and lifeless as ever, and he said to her, "You can stop sticking your head up there every five minutes, there's nothing around here."

"Did you grow up in these parts?"

He gestured toward the mountains in the east and said, "A ways north and east of here. A little village by the name Ibria."

She perked up at the name and said, "I know that place. I didn't have you pegged as a mountain boy."

"You must've grown up in the southwest."

"How'd you know?"

"Because you guys call anything larger than an anthill a mountain."

"You wouldn't call that the mountains?"

"It's got some hills to it. Why would you be in Ibria?"

"Doing a job a lot like this one. The man was a cartographer—needed some looking after as he mapped out the Dialla."

"That's where those maps come from?"

She said, "Yeah. Just some old guy, like yourself, trying to make some silver by making a map."

"Did he?"

"Make some silver?"

"Yeah."

"I doubt it. It was an awful map."

"You saw it?"

"When he was finished he had me look over it to see what I thought, as someone who had lived and traveled the Dialla my whole life."

"Of course," Ernest said. "And what did he do when you told him it was awful?"

"I didn't. I told him it looked great."

"Why?"

She shrugged and said, "I'm no cartographer's consultant. Plus, the quicker they get some decent maps made the quicker there's going to be Olerians camped out in every corner of this place. Even here."

As she finished speaking, she gestured with her chin to the sandy desolace over her shoulder and he nodded his head and said, "They've already got them. I've seen them."

"Yeah?"

"Yeah. I think the war gave them a pretty good idea of the important stuff and they've figured out most of the rest since."

She nodded and said, "Something interesting he said to me once," as she pointed to compressed layers of sandstone at the foundation of the embankment. "You see the way that the rocks are layered there? He said those aren't any different than the rings inside of a tree trunk that tell you how old the tree is. Those layers there will tell you how old the world is."

"The earth doesn't have no age."

"Everything has an age."

"How old is it then?"

"I don't know. I don't know if anybody does. But it's old. Older than men."

"Of course its older than that. Otherwise there'd be no place for a man to be put."

The days along the river stayed hot and at night coyotes yelped restlessly into the emptiness and with no material world to reverberate the sound of their cries they perforated the darkness and were in turn devoured by it. They, or other living things, could be heard to come to the river's shore at night and drink from its water as the two travelers listened on like blind sentinels to the flowing before the eventual day's ebb, when vision was restored, and such living things returned to the dark and cool caverns of their existence, leaving only the sun-bleached landscape as the silent witness to their passing. The further west they traveled, the more ambitious the vegetation became and the river's shoreline occasionally sprouted large acacias and ironwoods that housed little thrashers that zipped to and from the highest branches and at night the two would settle under these for cover as if the stars above searched for them and they knew it was best to go unnoticed by such high things. It was late in the afternoon when Ernest and Bird were settling a spot among these trees when a large cloud of copper colored dust rose from the southwest. Bird issued a short, sharp whistle to get Ernest's attention and gestured with her head toward the cloud. He squinted toward it and said, "Riders out of West One?"

She shook her head, "I don't think so. It's too many of them."

"They're headed right for us."

She nodded and they exchanged concerned glances. She gestured toward his bow with her chin and said, "Just be ready."

He slid off the leather strap that held his sword's hilt into place, adjusted his quiver, and then moved over to one of the ironwood trees and leaned the small bow up against the trunk on the opposite side of the cloud's approach. By the time Bird adjusted her cloak, pulling it over each shoulder so that it covered the weapons on her hip, the cloud was close enough to make out the individual horses, numbering at least a dozen and moving at a quick gallop right toward their bundle of trees. Ernest's right hand gripped his sword handle tightly and perspiration began to show around his hands and on his brow. She looked at him and shook her head again and told him, "Hand off the sword. Look calm and be calm."

He nodded and wiped his sweaty palm on the inside of his cloak and tried to put on a casual stance. Finally, the horses got close enough to make out more details and as it became clear what they were, Bird cursed angrily under her breath and Ernest said, "Oh no."

There were eighteen horses all told, but only four of them with riders. Behind each rider was a handful of wild horses, all tethered together in a chain of leather blinders and girdles. The riders appeared to have seen the two of them but apparently cared little of their presence, slowing to a trot and each of them pulling their horse-led trains up to more trees just a couple dozen paces down the riverside.

Bird huffed and whipped aside her cloak, showing her weapons and walking toward the gang of riders. He fell in line behind her, quick stepping to keep up and pleading into her right ear.

"Please don't," he said.

"They're horse poachers, Ernest."

"There's no such thing anymore."

"There is to me."

He said *please* again as she approached the first rider who had just finished tying off his horse to the tree like a hitching post and as Bird walked toward him he waved a hand high in greeting.

He called out to her, "If the two of you don't mind, we'd like to share the area for the night." He gestured behind him where the other three riders were dismounting and hitching theirs and the wild horses. The first poacher continued waving and offered a smile but when he finally took note of the expression and gait of the advancing woman he took a step backward and was able to offer only a guttural sound of warning to the other riders who all looked toward him in time to watch his final moments. Her left hand shot down to her left hip, sliding it into the claw-like fist weapon and detaching it from her belt in one motion. The rider's one backward step bought him only one extra moment of life, because in the next one her armored left hand hammered into his trachea and in the same move her right hand unsheathed her sword and ripped it horizontally across the man's abdomen. His body buckled lifelessly at her feet and the other three men retrieved their own weapons from the backs of their mounts as she moved in their direction.

It's one of them, the nearest one shouted, and the other two could be seen to hesitate upon hearing this. Their hesitation cost the near companion any chance against the attacker, and by the time they decisively moved toward her she had disarmed the man and brought a vicious slash diagonally across his face, leaving him screaming and bleeding into the dirt.

Only the most galvanized of people could be a horse poacher in the Dialla Desert and not be dead inside of a week, and these two men had been at it for years. They had seen others die to snakebite, drowning, ruffians, horses, dehydration, starvation, any variety of illness—and they were seasoned survivors. But, despite their resilience, what neither one of them had experienced was to be the source of a Copperfoot's anger. As Bird quickly closed the distance between the two, she could see their eyes grow as wild and frightened as the captured horses. The two men were scared, but they had fought together before and they drew on past horrors to stand calm against their own surging fear. The one on her left sported a small longsword he gripped tightly with two hands and the other brandished a shortsword in one hand with a small, bronze buckler covering his left forearm. They initially tried to overwhelm her by both staying in front of her and pressing forward, but she would sidestep and use one man as a buffer against the other and so they split and tried to corral her from opposite sides.

Ernest watched on from a couple dozen feet away and eyed his little bow, debating if he should get involved in some way. He decided not to, having seen Bird fight before he was confident in her victory, and should she lose he was ready to run, and should they catch him, he had a satchel of silver strapped under his right armpit that he hoped was enough to buyback his life.

The man with the buckler was content to hide behind his little shield aside from the occasional, half-hearted swipes he took at Bird's back, and so she focused on his partner instead. They continued to maneuver and dance, her always repositioning to look for a better angle on the longswordsman, until he rushed in hard with a huge horizontal cut that Bird softened with a parry of her shortsword and then caught between the claws of her fist weapon, which slid down the blade and got tangle and affixed onto the sword's hilt. Her sword hand was still free and the man knew it, so he pulled his sword, and Bird's attached left hand, hard across his body and attempted to throw her. However, she was ready, and she flattened her left hand and tightened her fingers as narrow as they could go and, when the man yanked, the fist weapon came sliding off her hand and sent the man stumbling with the entangled weapons still in hand. She shadowed every imbalanced footstep from the man and when he finally stopped reeling she was there with her sword diving between his ribcage. As this happened the other man charged forward, shadowing her movement the same she had done to his partner. She extracted her sword from the man's torso just in time to dodge the man's swinging cut, but he followed up with a hard backswing of his shield arm, bringing the buckler hard across her face with a loud crack where bronze met bone.

She was sent tumbling to the ground, doing her best to roll with the blow and Ernest caught his breath sharply, thinking she was bested, and his despair rose when saw her gather herself on one knee and realized she had lost her sword as well. When she made no immediate move Ernest was sure she must be critically injured, but he quickly realized that the other man had made no move either and as he looked closer he realized why—Bird's sword buried half deep into the left side of his rib cage, sticking out of him like some gargantuan effigy of dark magic. The poacher dazedly reached at the hilt of the sword with both hands but he collapsed to his knees and wheezed out the last bloody breaths that his torn lung could handle and then fell sideways into small puff of dust.

It was quiet for a few moments, when it seemed even the anxious horses were perfectly still, and then a loud moan came from the second poacher with the cut face. Bird's slash got him across the bridge of his nose and over his left eye and he pressed his hands to his gushing visage, trying to stop the bleeding and ferry blood out of his vision. He saw well enough to know which way Bird was, so he stumbled in the opposite direction, blindly into the empty desert. The quiet hung in the small area amongst Ernest and Bird and the wild horses and they all watched as he stammered his way a dozen paces out into the sandy tundra, collapsed, and writhed listlessly for several moments before going still forever.

Bird stayed on her knee and gathered herself, gently pressing on the left side of her face and feeling her way around the injury as would a blind person. Ernest picked his way through the bodies of the fallen poachers and squatted in front of her within her field of vision and said, "You okay?"

She nodded and he had her follow his finger while he inspected her left eye movement and he thought it looked fine and asked if anything was broken. Under her hand her skin was flushed deep red as blood rushed to the wound, but other than a few bits of blood that dripped from her nose, there was no apparent severity to the injury.

She said, "I think it's all intact," and then got to her feet, retrieving her sword from the dead man's torso, and crouched next to him, wiping the blade clean on his cloak. When she was done she approached the wild horses—there were fourteen of them in all, separated into three groups—all tethered like a jigsaw to each other and moving their heads in sporadic motions to view the world outside of the leather blinders that had been fixed to their heads. As she got closer to the first group, the horses grew visibly agitated and pulled firmly at their harnesses, shaking the tree they were fastened to and knocking each other off balance as they tugged in different directions.

Bird backed off the nearest one and made calming gestures with her hands and spoke to them in the same manner. She said to Ernest, "We can't just cut them loose or they're gonna live the rest of their lives with those blinders on."

"What do you want to do?"

"We're gonna have to get in close enough to get them off. If you do this bunch I'll do the other two."

He sighed and muttered a reluctant agreement under his breath, but as he walked toward her she stopped him and gestured with a half-circle movement of her forefinger. "You need to do the last one first, otherwise they're going to get away all tied together."

"You're trying to get me killed."

"I don't get paid if you get killed, so I'd actually prefer it if you didn't get kicked in the head. It's the only way."

"Shit," he said.

He swung a wide arc to get behind the horses while she continued to distract and placate, and when he identified the last one in the tethered chain he crouched and stalked into its blind spot. The beast sensed him there and it started doing a skittish dance as it pulled on its tether to the other horses and they moved with it, creating an amorphous shuffle of very scared horses and one very scared man, and within all the commotion a little cloud of dust was summoned around them, all engulfing. As his vison was obstructed by the airborne sand particles, images ran through his mind of his head getting caved in by a rear-kick from one of the spooked horses and she called to him and said, "We're losing daylight quick and this isn't going to happen in the dark."

He cursed at her under his breath, getting a mouthful of sand, but he finally made his move, sidling up close to the horse's neck and moving with it, magnetically, while he managed to unbuckle and shed its bridle and blinders. The horse darted away, nearly trampling him in the process, and made its way a hundred feet southwest into the empty lowlands before stopping and turning to look back his way. It stood silhouetted against the blood red sky and peered back at him with some kind of regal confidence as he worked his way through freeing the other four horses and in time all five of them stood out in the desert where they carried on their observance.

The sun was three-quarters set into the edge of the world by the time he was done but he could still see the group of freed horses frozen in the dusk and he continued to watch them as Bird made her way through the next group in the same skillful way she did all things, and before the sun could vanish entirely she had all but one of the horses unleashed and the thirteen of them stood mustered in the declining light with their long faces looking back at the two strangers. The final horse was a foal of brown and white coloring and as if its fear had not been pushed to its limits already it now stood, bound alone with the little bald aliens and each of them leering around its vulnerable body. When she unbuckled and slipped off its bridle it sprinted into the desert among its kin, but the fourteen of them continued standing there, motionless and serene, and as the last bit of sun cast its darkness over the landscape they could just barely be seen to finally turn and together disappear in that darkness so cast and if there were any acknowledgement among those beasts of what had transpired they offered no sign of it but until the day of his death he would never forget the way they had stayed and watched on and it gave him some peace that what he believed and all that he had done—maybe it wasn't all for nothing.

***

High Commander Faidrion was a twenty-five-year-old infantry officer when Oleria invaded Eporisia in 1034. A tremendous, natural leader, he distinguished himself commanding an improbable counterattack at the Battle of Lukas Point and then grew his reputation for the rest of the war by conducting a seemingly endless number of successful coastal raids. With the defeat of Eporisia and the apparent non-threat of the Copperfoot to the south, career military personnel would spend most of the following two decades back in the highlands, waging small campaigns on resistant tribes and local uprisings. With no major war for officers to prove their tactical brilliance, military promotion at this time became more about political maneuvering and charisma, and it was in this landscape that Faidrion shone brightest. Unlike most Olerian brass, Faidrion fought and issued orders from the front lines of his battles, putting himself at the same risk as the soldiers he commanded. This endeared him to everybody that served under him and even his professional rivals found it impossible to ignore his undeniable leadership. He would be named High Commander in the year 1051 and within a month of his appointment would be called to the emperor's palace and given the instructions to wage war on the Copperfoot people and capture the Dialla Desert for the empire. Faidrion was thrilled. Even though it was the minor campaigns in his homeland that had allowed him to climb to High

Commander, he understood that a major war on an unexplored frontier offered a chance at historical immortality.

Faidrion would indeed be immortalized in Olerian lore, but for none of the reasons he dreamed. In years to come, Olerian historians would paint him to be a vain, inept tactician and obsequious general who talked his way to the top and then fumbled it spectacularly. This was far from a fair portrayal of a man who reached the height of his profession while time and again risking his life for his empire, which only served as proof that even the empire's historians bought into the myth and manifest destiny of Olerian greatness—and those that failed to live up to this greatness would always only reflect their own personal faults, and not the empire's.

Because, the truth is, when Faidrion made his biggest mistake there wasn't a single general to second guess it, because not a single one thought to first guess it. For hundreds of years, for the Olerians, summertime was for war time. Even in the temperate highlands of their origin, winters were dark and filled daily with freezing rain, and the added difficulty of keeping soldiers warm and moving supplies through mud-bogged roads were complications that could be avoided by waiting for warmer months. So long had major campaigns been launched in the late spring, when the rains began to dry up and the days grew longer and warmer, that it ceased to be a factor in their calculations. This cultural reverberation was so strong that there was not a single dissenting opinion given when plans were laid to invade the Dialla in the late spring of 1053, and it was by this way that, in a place where water and shelter were scarce commodities, the massive Olerian army invaded the hottest region on the planet just weeks before the beginning of summer.

Faidrion's opening gambit was simple—throw the entire weight of the Olerian army at the Copperfoot's nominal capital city, Camphania, and use its central location in the region as a hub for all subsequent activity. After pushing hard across the north reaches of the Dialla in an attempt to maintain a semblance of surprise, it was the Olerian army that was instead surprised, for when they reached Camphania, ready for a vicious battle, they found the city abandoned. Faidrion had resisted using scouts, so as not to tip his hand, but deployed them now in full force to discover what had happened to the vanished city. The huge majority of scouts were never seen again, seemingly swallowed whole by the warming desert, and those that reported back had found no more than smatterings of corpses left behind by the fleeing Copperfoot. Scouts on horseback returned alive at a higher rate, but horses were arguably more valuable than men and without a detailed understanding of good locations to water and rest a horse out in the desert, Olerian brass resisted using them as much as possible. Not understanding that to be gifted to the desert in this fashion was the standard Copperfoot ritual, the Olerians would use this detail to portray them as savages who didn't have the decency to bury the dead properly.

The Olerians searched for weeks for the missing people, as spring turned officially to summer, and for every three scouts that left Camphania, two were never seen again and the lucky one had little to offer by way of information. Faidrion expanded the size of scouting groups in an effort to curb the losses and then decided to split his army—keeping one half stationed in Camphania and leading the other southeast to city of Helena. It was similarly abandoned and Faidrion could continue to only guess at the Copperfoot's tactics and brood over their delay of his inevitable and glorious victory. The Olerians now had two established footholds from which to hunt the Copperfoot, and in the coming weeks their bloated scouting groups had more and more encounters in the southern regions of the Dialla. Faidrion credited this uptick in fighting with the Copperfoot growing more desperate, and so, when a scout returned to Helena with a report of having discovered thousands of Copperfoot camped southwest of the city, he did not hesitate.

After spending weeks in a restless occupancy of empty cities, and having soldiers continually picked off by the elusive desert people, Faidrion yearned for the chance to fight this foe head on and score a decisive victory that many thought would have come by now. Faidrion split his army again, leaving behind enough from his half to man Helena and marched what was left southwest into the Dialla in full pursuit. In the highlands a decision like this was one that'd be easily made and executed—fresh water over every next hill, Olerian forts within a day's march in every direction—but in the desert it was fatal. Faidrion pushed his army hard through the blazing, summer sun, and as scouts continued to confirm that the large camp of Copperfoot had yet to flee, he pushed even harder. Set at the base of the mountain range that would eventually be home to West One, this area of the Dialla was rough, uneven, full of washed-out canyons and large boulders that splintered from the leering mountain range above. Above all other features stood a gigantic butte that overlooked the area like some red-rocked, brooding colossus, and it was here, at the butte's base and near an ancient, dried-up lakebed, that the Copperfoot were believed to be hiding.

Any Olerian general with the sense to urge Faidrion to slow down was dissuaded by the fact that it was Faidrion himself who marched at the head of the vanguard, never asking of his men any more than he was willing to give. But, even driven as he was by the motivation that victory in the Dialla would mean his name would be forever etched in Olerian history, Faidrion began to falter. Dressed in full bronze regalia and traversing the rough terrain through the desert's high heat, as the Olerians neared the Copperfoot's position they were three days from their last watering hole, and, unfamiliar with the area, didn't know when they'd see the next one. The horses were parched, dehydrated. Some men's canteens were already empty and had been for a day. Soldiers began regularly dropping from heat exhaustion while others wandered off into the desert, deliriously mumbling to the hallucinations that greeted them from the sand. For those that didn't have the whisper of immortality driving them forward, it was a demoralizing situation.

For the Copperfoot, the situation was only slightly less dire than that of the approaching army. Spending a good portion of the summer on the run in the Dialla, with old and young alike, had inflicted hundreds of casualties. With enough water, they could have hidden, fled, and sniped Olerian scouts until the end of time, but as the summer season advanced and regular water holes dried up, it was clear for them that something needed to happen. Ablebodied groups were constantly making runs to the Powder River to bring back water to the people, but with thousands of thirsty mouths it was an unsustainable situation. So, when a Copperfoot scout, a young girl by the name of Bird, spotted an Olerian scout approaching the massive butte, she was under orders to do nothing to hinder him. It was time for the Copperfoot to be seen. And they would be seen exactly where they wanted to be—close enough to warrant an attack from Helena, far enough away for the journey to take its toll on would-be attackers. In their desperation, the Copperfoot would risk thousands of lives in an attempt to bait out the foreign invaders. It worked. Faidrion's army was shadowed by unseen Copperfoot scouts from the moment it left Helena, and Olerian scouts would continue to be left alone, unbeknownst to them, free to keep tabs on the Copperfoot camp. When the Olerian Army made it to within a day of the plateau, Copperfoot scouts were ordered to kill any and every Olerian scout they could find. With the Olerians once again in the dark, the majority of the Copperfoot camp moved northwest away from original camp, leaving behind only the capable fighters.

The bait had worked perfectly, but there were no guarantees for the Copperfoot. The shape of the land made traveling brutal, but it still left plenty of room for the Olerian cavalry to maneuver, and this is what they feared the most. After months of evasion, the Olerian army emerged from the mouth of a large canyon that housed the river that used to feed the ancient lake to finally see what they had spent months searching for—the Copperfoot en masse. There were more than a thousand of them in a half circle around the canyon's mouth, in the shadow of the mammoth plateau, glistening in their steel armor and brandishing their steel weapons.

For whatever his faults as a commander, Faidrion recognized the situation immediately, and understood that his cavalry was behind the infantry and would be stuck behind them up the canyon if he didn't make room for them. Dehydrated, sun burnt, dirty, exhausted, and cornered, Faidrion didn't hesitate to lead the infantry headlong into the awaiting army. High Commander Faidrion, born Olerian year 1009, was one of the first to be killed. His infantry fought ferociously but was overmatched by the skilled desert people, and the Copperfoot line held strong until the Olerian cavalry was able to escape the canyon and punch through the northern line. With fresh horses the cavalry alone might have been enough to take the field, but they were as poorly watered as the men, and fought at a fraction of their capability. Instead of moving around the field and overwhelming Copperfoot weak points, they fortified the north flank and kept its opening so that those still stuck in the canyon and the southern flank had options for retreat. Very few of them were able to do so. After over an hour of hard combat, what was left of the Olerian army consolidated just north west of the canyon entrance, with cavalry acting as a buffer and deterrent to the Copperfoot to the south, who seemed to want nothing to do with the riders on horseback.

As dusk settled over the armies, the Olerians thought maybe the Copperfoot would attempt to finish them off in the night. They set what small fires they could and every man stayed alert through the night but no attack came. In the morning the Copperfoot were still south of them, stationed in the open on the rise of the dried lake's bowl, but they were further away than the night before and difficult to discern. They searched nearby casualties and collected any extra water they could find and then, with Helena too far away, began their retreat to the north and west, to Camphania. It took them almost three days to make it there, unhindered by any Copperfoot scouts, and this time, when they marched into the city's gates, they did so in defeat. Oleria had taken defeats in battle before, but not like this one. Not only had their High Commander been killed in battle—an unprecedented occurrence—but the survivors talked of being thoroughly outmatched by the Copperfoot who not only were, man for man, more skilled fighters, but also better equipped, dressed in their hard steel. If not for the heroics of the cavalry, they were certain that not a single one of them would have made it out alive, and it was this detail that gave the next High Commander an idea that would send the Copperfoot people to the edge of extinction.

—Excerpt from Ilia's *A Brief History of the Dialla Desert and its People, 1063*

***

In the night, creatures came for the bodies of the fallen riders and whether they were at first wolves or coyotes was impossible to tell but when she saw the worried look on his face she said, "Whatever's out there wants nothing to do with this fire so you can relax," and he nodded but he did not relax. They were both awake long into the night as she fueled and stoked the fire and he tried not to listen to the sound of the nearby corpses being torn apart and contested. He said, "We should have moved them further away," and she agreed.

They managed to sleep some before the sun pulled itself from over the peaks of the Echora Mountains to east, and she went to the creek where she splashed water on her face and next to her were the four horses of the dead riders. After freeing the wild horses, Bird had unsaddled them and tried to shoo them on their way, but they made it no further than the creek where they had lingered through the night. She finished rinsing and considered the horses, and while three of them paid her no mind, the fourth one—a chestnut colored mare—looked at her in search of direction.

When she got back to camp, Ernest was sitting awake, stuffing his cheek with the dark herb he carried, and looking into the nearby trees where several carrion were already stationed and eyeing the corpses and the two travelers alike. He said, "I never knew them to have any manners when it came to eating."

"They probably lost their appetite when they got a glimpse of your face sittin there."

He snickered and said, "You know the Olerians make it a point to bury their dead?"

"Why?"

"I don't know."

"Don't animals just dig them up anyway?"

"Not if you bury them deep enough."

"Just a feast for the worms then."

"I guess it is."

She said, "The desert takes it all back either way, no matter which way you gift it."

He nodded and she offered him a biscuit and he nodded and they both chewed quietly, bathed by the rising sun, and he said, "You check their saddlebags yet?"

"I'm not robbing no dead men."

"You already robbed them of their lives, what's a few silver?"

"It's principal."

"What principal?"

"Their silver wasn't what was poaching horses."

He shrugged, rose to his feet, and walked over to the four saddles still laying in the dust next to the nearest tree where Bird had discarded them the night before. He spat as he went through each one, setting aside their food and canteens and holding various items of clothing into the sunlight for inspection. She saw him do this and said, "Please tell me you aren't planning on wearing their dirty drawers."

"No not the drawers. They had shit all for silver though."

"That's because there aint shit all to buy out here. Look around."

"A lot of types like these tend to carry everything they own with them though. Means they had someone back home to leave it with. A family," he said, and looked at her.

"Shit," she said. "I've felt guilty about killing people before but these four here don't qualify."

He spat and walked back to his bedroll and began packing up and said to her, "You could've set the horses free without killing them. Destroyed the harnesses."

"They'd just come back."

"Maybe," he said.

"You know it as well as I do. Why are you so hung up on it?"

"I don't know. It just doesn't sit right."

"That's the only way it sits out here. You don't live in the Dialla anymore, do you?"

"No," he said. "Pridipoa."

She let out a sarcastic huff of air and said, "Shit. No wonder you've gone soft. You're turning into an Olerian."

He spat and she continued, "For one who's combatting a moral crisis, you sure didn't have a problem rummaging through their shit over there in hopes of finding a few silver."

He slung his pack around his torso and fixed his cloak about his neck, wiggling his shoulders each way until the straps settled in comfortably. He said, "Carrion don't eat silver. Wolves don't eat silver. The worms don't eat it. If it finds its way down into the earth it aint going to grow more silver. It's no gift to the desert. Leaving it out here is nothing but a waste."

She rolled her eyes and finished packing and as she did the chestnut mare meandered up from the creek, looking at both of them and then out at the desert toward the riders' bodies. He looked at the horse, then at her, but she just shrugged and finished packing her bedroll before heading westward out of the camp. He followed behind her several paces while the horse looked emptily into the soft horizon. They passed under the trees and the sentinel carrion stationed in the upper branches and their cold eyes followed the two passing into the countryside and when the travelers were several hundred paces beyond the camp he turned and spotted the mare following in their footsteps. He directed a short whistle toward Bird and then gestured with his head at the trailing horse and she stopped and squinted back at the approaching mare and said, "It's following?"

"Looks like it," he said.

"Shit. What do you want to do about it?"

He shrugged and she said, "We don't want some horse following us across the Dialla."

He said, "Why don't you go politely ask him to stop?"

"Hims a her."

"Her then."

"I can't speak horse."

"Can't say I'm fluent either."

"Shit all," she said. "Let's just keep going and maybe she'll lose interest."

Bird led the way through landscapes of burnt sienna, and the two of them talked sparingly except for her to point out features of the rocky countryside or consult him on preferences for navigation. She told him they could turn north to Helena, and take well-traveled roads from there to Camphania, which was largely used by commercial wagons bringing in shipments of iron from the southeast, but he opted for the tougher, less-populous paths to the south. They continued west into the early afternoon, and when they finally stopped for a rest, the mare was still following them and it approached the shaded overhang where they sat, sniffed each of them thoroughly, and then gazed out at the rocky surrounding. Ernest pulled a dark glob of herb from his cheek and tossed into the sand where it landed with a dull thud and sent up the smallest of red dirt clouds that then settled back onto the moist herb and stuck to it, turning it the color of oxblood and then absorbing it into the earth entirely. He watched this and then looked at the horse and then at Bird and he said, "We don't have enough food for a third."

"She'll take care of herself."

"You think so?"

"Why not?"

"They get the touch of man on them and then they get soft."

Bird shook her head and said, "A horse doesn't forget how to be a horse."

The mare did manage to take care of herself, though they never knew how. It would wander from them for hours at a time while they traveled and it would vanish during most nights, but almost always making it back to the camp before they would leave the next morning. One instance, when the horse had gone for the night, missed their departure, and still made no appearance by lunch, the two thought that they had at last seen the last of it, only to have her meander into their camp the next morning. Despite never seeing it eat, the mare maintained a healthy weight and the shine of its dark brown coat only seemed to grow healthier as the days of hard travel piled up behind them. At one point, while the mare had wandered off in the afternoon, they saw the approach of two riders in the distance and so they stepped off the trail and hid in the dip of a small, nearby ravine in waiting. She perched herself near the lip to watch the two riders—typical for an Olerian patrol—while Ernest sat with his back to the rock wall, chewing and occasionally spitting his ever-present herb. She spoke quietly down to him to say, "What do they even patrol for out here?"

"It's for the wild goats."

"What?"

"In case they unite and rise up against the empire."

She shook her head quietly and continued watching and moments later cursed under her breath. He asked her what was happening, and she said, "They stopped."

"Why?"

"Shit if I know. It looks to be about the same spot we stepped off the trail too."

It was his turn to curse this time, and she continued, "One of them is getting off his horse now."

He cursed again, aggressively spat, and then started mumbling under his breath about how they weren't doing anything wrong, and how they needed to come up with a decent lie about why they were in an area so remote. He continued to talk himself through the situation while Bird watched and then interrupted his own verbal rambling with another curse, because from up the ravine, the opposite way of the riders, their mare was walking out of the desert toward their hiding place. Ernest got to his feet and crept toward the mare, putting both his hands out and urging it to stop, but it continued to mosey toward them, and he eventually resorted to putting a single finger to his lips and shushing the plodding horse. Nothing in his performance slowed the approach of the mare and when she reached him she half nuzzled him, half pushed him aside with her head. She took up a spot under the lip of the small ravine just below Bird, turned facing south, away from the Olerian patrol, and offered it a look as empty as the desert itself. He glared at the horse and then hoarsely whispered to Bird, "What's going on?"

She said, "The one on the ground is dancing around now."

"Did you say *dancing*?"

"That's all I can see. Shit, I don't know. He's getting back up on his horse now."

He waited in silence, expecting the riders to follow their tracks to their hiding spot and begin asking questions but her voice came down with an exciting pitch as she said that the riders were moving on.

"Where?" he said.

"Down the trail."

"I don't trust it."

"Let's sit tight for a minute then."

But the riders were gone. He sat in the ravine and waited while she crept east to see if they were doubling back on their position, but they weren't and she returned to him with a small shrug and said, "Nothing."

They made their way back out to the trail where the riders had stopped, and they found the corpse of a snake in the dirt. It's head and tail had been severed completely and were missing and what was left of the torso had three deep gashes in it.

He spat and said, "Here's the dancing partner."

She squatted down to her knees over the dead snake and said, "Look. He took the tail and the head like he got himself a trophy but this breed isn't dangerous, and not in the least bit poisonous." She shook her head.

He looked on without expression and then squinted into the west where the sun was beginning its descent and he said, "The Olerians are still stupid to this part of the world."

With each passing mile the terrain grew rougher, with their nominal trail constantly being obstructed by large boulders and thick growths of sagebrush that were sprouting up more often the further they traveled west.

The next day, around midmorning, a large desert butte the color of rust, that towered hundreds of feet into the air, came into view only slightly south of their direct line of travel. It loomed over them for the next day and a half until its substantial shadow passed over and then settled on them like a cool blanket against the blistering heat. They ate and she asked him, "You know this area?"

He pointed with his chin to the butte and said, "Yeah, I know it."

She nodded and said, "I want to show you something later."

"Okay."

They walked on and a short time later she stopped and looked south at a dip in the land that sloped into the side of a small canyon that branched south and then turned hard west toward the butte. She said nothing of it but gestured toward it with her hand as if wanting him to make note of the spot, which he did. The path they stayed on ran parallel to the canyon route, and after another hour of walking the entire area opened to give them their best view of the butte yet. For the first time they were able to see it from top to bottom, its circular base sloped sharply for maybe one hundred feet before shooting straight up to a sheer rock wall for hundreds of feet more before crowning out flatly to an unviewable top. Between them and the butte the earth was uniformly compressed where, several million years earlier, a large lake had thrived, but the land now was only sparsely populated with small outlets of sagebrush and cacti. On the left edge of their view—the east end of the lake—was the mouth of the canyon she had referenced earlier. She pointed to it and he nodded in understanding. The canyon's walls were diminutive compared to the plateau and much of the surrounding area—partly due to the change in elevation and partly with the millennia of erosion that sanded off many of its highest layers. She waved for him to follow her and pointed to a large outcrop of boulders just north of where they stood. He followed silently and the mare came along just several steps behind. The outcrop was a couple dozen feet in height with a handful of large boulders acting as steps to the highest point, which she immediately began scaling. He watched her and climbed it the same way she did with the mare seemingly standing watch at the outcrop's base. When Bird reached the top she waited for a moment before sweeping some sand off of it with the bottom of her foot, and then she tapped the spot with her toe before saying, "Thirteen years ago this is where I watched the world end."

He followed her gaze south across the depression of the ancient lake to the mouth of the small canyon and he said, "If you're going to watch such a thing then you might as well have the best seat."

She shook her head and said, "I couldn't agree less."

He said nothing and she said nothing and a soft, desert breeze rolled over them and pushed their hair and their cloaks behind them and he said to her, "Can you tell me what you saw?"

"You weren't there?"

"Not on that day."

"I'll tell you what I saw if you tell me where you were at."

"Why?" he asked.

She shrugged and said, "This is twice that you've gotten dodgy about it and now I'm curious."

"Fine," he said as he gestured generally west and north form where they stood on the outcrop and continued, "I was with the group that fled, just before the battle. With the hospital."

"You were injured?"

"No, not injured."

"You're a physician?"

"I was the *musician*."

She opened her mouth to respond before catching herself as confusion and then realization spread across her face. "That was *you*?"

He nodded and she looked at him, jaw dropped, as if some joyous magician had just appeared before her. She said, "I can't believe it," and then scrutinized his face carefully while he gazed awkwardly back at her and after a moment her mouth formed into a huge grin. "It really was you."

He made a facial expression of mock appreciation, but she said, "I'm not pulling on your rope here. I am being deadly serious when I say that you were incredible. What was that instrument called that you played? That big thing."

"A viola."

"A viola," she repeated it back under her breath with a soft inflection to her voice as if the word itself tasted like some fond memory from her past. "Where on earth did you get such a thing?"

"It's an Olerian thing. My mother traded for one when I was a child."

She nodded and said *viola* again and then said, "I've seen a few of them played in the cities since then, but none of them could play it like you did."

He dipped his head toward her in acknowledgement of the compliment but remained unsure if she was genuine or not, and after a moment he spat and then said, "Your turn."

She pointed east, directly up the trail from where they had come from and said, "We expected them to approach the same way that you and I just did. It's the only route that makes sense, really. The only other feasible option is through the canyon over there but nobody in their right mind would take an army into that thing—the path is more uneven, it's narrow, it's extremely vulnerable to an attack from above." She shook her head in confusion and continued, "I'm convinced now that it was just dumb luck that sent them down the canyon, but for the longest time I stayed up at night trying to figure out what they knew that we didn't."

This time she pointed to different spots in the immediate areas north and west of them before continuing, "We committed everything to these positions, so sure were we that they would come this way. By the time any scout made it back that they were heading down the canyon, we had to scramble just to get down there—if they made it out of the mouth of the canyon uncontested, it would've gone far worse for us. For those further up north it was quite a run to try to get down there, and they were winded and aching in the legs before the fighting even began."

She paused again, shaking her head subtly as the memory continued coming back to her. After a moment she took a deep breath to steady herself and continued, "Enough people made it down to initially seal off the canyon, but their vanguard was ferocious. You wouldn't have guessed that they had just got done force marching all the way from Helena. As much as I hate them and despite the bitterness that rides in me still, it's impossible not to admit that the way they fought was nothing short of heroic. We weren't in the best shape by any stretch, but you wouldn't expect an army that had just made that trip through the heat to have any fight left to them, and instead they fought like wolves. I mean, we had heroes too. I know it. And we were holding the line well enough. Until the cavalry came."

She looked at him in an attempt to gauge his reaction to her retelling but so fixed were his eyes on the distant canyon that he took no notice of her pause and his eyes remained unblinking on the spot as she continued. "The cavalry was backed up when the fighting started. Stuck further up the canyon behind the infantry. But they finally got enough of a push—or enough people died ahead of them—that they were able to get out around the north lip, there. Our line broke almost immediately at the spot that they hit and all the remaining Copperfoot had to try to reposition on the fly to keep from being rolled up all the way down the line. If the cavalry had been fresher then that might have just been the end of it, but they were conservative and hardly pushed their advantage. We gave up the mouth of the canyon as the northern parts of the line tried to swing back south without getting pinched, and mostly we did. The fight continued but any place on the field that we made progress they would send the cavalry as support and the advantage was lost. It went on like that for a bit longer, until both sides were spent—we pulled back to the plateau, they came up not far from where we are now. I was one of those that went down there in the night to help get any wounded out that we could."

She reached out toward the canyon with her palm out and then moved it slowly east about halfway across the dried lakebed and said, "The dead were all the way from here to here. A lot of the wounded made it your way to the hospital, and a lot of them didn't."

He heard her sniffling and for the first time took his eyes from the field to see her running a hand under her nose and tears building up in her eyes even if none of them fell. He said, "Thanks for telling me. Your account fits perfect with everything else I've heard."

"What else?"

"From the Olerians."

"They talk about it?"

"They keep histories that are exhaustive, especially about their military. There's a lot of different portrayals depending on the historian, but the most reliable historian is Illia, and your story is the same as hers. The funny thing about it is that even with all the same details, they are all uniform in their opinion that it was a crushing defeat for the Olerian army. Maybe their worst. They all shame the man that led them, and it's the Copperfoot that were the wolves."

"You're shitting me," she said.

"Nope."

"One of their worst defeats?"

"That's how they tell it." He spat.

"Shit. Life has been good to those people, for that battle to be measured as a defeat."

"You don't think we won?"

She shrugged and said, "Maybe. We killed more than they did, and they had to suffer the shame of retreat. But we had no answer for the cavalry, and we never did recover from it. So many casualties, so little water. Every loss that came after for us was just an echo of what happened here."

"I always felt the same way."

"How do their histories feel about it?"

He flapped his lips in a mocking gesture. "The histories are all glory to the Olerians from that point on. The empire that braved the savage desert, and through Olerian ingenuity and grit, they were able to tame the wolves that lived there."

She sighed at this last thought and ran the back of her hand across her eyes and the two of them made their way down the outcrop to the mare waiting below. They camped that night under the sentinel butte, as the glow of their fire rebounded in wild angles off the camp's surroundings and their faces alike, casting acute shadows that settled like daggers upon each. The mare perched just outside of the light in a way that only her silhouette could be seen and to Ernest, because of her stillness, looked like some predator stalking him from the darkness and crouched in the moment before striking and so unnerved was he by this thought that he looked away from the horse into the fire and when he looked back it was gone. Across the fire was Bird's huddled, sleeping form, and he snuck past it to grab a large branch to add to the flames before he too lay down. He couldn't sleep, and when a call of wolves went up in the distance he reflexively looked to where the mare stood but there was nothing and when he set his head back down to sleep he imagined her out in that darkness, roaming the old lakebed and communing with the ghosts that were lost there the same as the mare and in their communal would come to terms with what it meant to be wholly absorbed into some foreign history and forever after be a pawn in the hunt for more.

***

High Commander Ulysses Esco was an authentic military lifer. During an era when most people used the military to advance themselves politically, Esco spent his career and life with a singular focus on armed endeavors. Through this lens he made for the perfect successor to Faidrion—whereas Faidrion was perceived to be a naïve, overly ambitious glory monger, Esco, who at the time of his promotion was the oldest serving general in the Olerian army, served as Faidrion's more experienced, conservative foil. Stationed in Camphania at the time of Faidrion's fall, the fifty-five-year-old general was one of the first men to welcome back the defeated soldiers and listen to their tales of fighting the Copperfoot. Two days later, when he was sent to meet the Emperor in Pridipoa, he spent his time on the road turning the battle over in his mind and kept coming back to one thing—the Copperfoot's response to the Olerian cavalry.

It was well established to any person living in the region that the Copperfoot would not ride horses, but Esco speculated that their aversion to horse riding ran deeper than what was common perception. Indeed, the superstition was strong enough that a people, adept at fighting and living among the finest horses known to man, used no cavalry in battle. Esco deduced that either the Copperfoot held horses in a higher regard than was understood, or that they were terrified of them. In his mind it didn't matter which one it was, because, if true, both presented Oleria with an advantage that he planned to exploit.

With the emperor's full support, and no pressing ambition to satiate, Esco was content to play the long game. In his mind, capturing the enemy's two largest cities already constituted a

*successful summer campaign, and so he spent the rest of the sea-
son laying the groundwork for when the heat would eventually
dissipate. He spent no time in pursuit of the Copperfoot people,
choosing instead to pursue the region's limited water. When scouts
set out to map out significant water locations, they did so on
horseback, and in force. Esco then called in shipment after shipment of lumber from the Olerian highlands and erected small,
effective forts at any watering hole deemed significant. Here men
were stationed to repel any thirsty Copperfoot, and if any Olerian
was to engage the enemy, they were to do it on horseback or with
cavalry support, no exceptions. Though it was impossible to fortify
the whole length of the Powder River, as the summer moved along,
more and more of Esco's forts went up at major junctures. Between
the newly fortified locations defending much of the region's water,
and with riders tormenting the Copperfoot at every skirmish, Esco
had taken what was once the Copperfoot's greatest strength—the
brutality of their homeland—and turned it against them.*

*Fighting subsided significantly through the rest of the summer,
and, as far as the Olerians could discern, the Copperfoot broke up
from the large camp at the ancient lakebed into smaller groups
that dispersed to all corners of the Dialla. The Copperfoot tactics
continued to elude Esco and other generals, but they lost no ground
and gained no disadvantage by staying put, and so that's what
they did. As the fall and then winter seasons cooled the region, the
Copperfoot seemed to come alive. Fighting broke out all across the
Dialla, and it was then that Esco began to understand the strategy
of his opponent—they were highly proficient using guerilla tactics. Had the Copperfoot stood their ground in Camphania and
Helena, they would have been pitched in a shoulder to shoulder
fight against the Olerians, or had to deal with an extended siege,
neither of which would let them utilize the individual brilliance of
so many of their fighters. Even though no large-scale battle took
place during this time, a large number of casualties was racked up
on both sides. Esco was concerned by the newly displayed ferocity
of his enemy, but the cavalry remained a steady, winning force,
and even as men were killed, more forts were constructed and the
Olerian foot soldiers gained more and more comfort fighting their
opponent with each passing engagement.*

*As spring rolled around and the weather warmed, the vio-
lence again subsided. It had been almost a year and the Olerians
still did not know what to make of their situation—most impor-
tantly, were they winning the war? Esco was confident in his strategy and the Olerians were now firmly entrenched and fortified
across the desert, but he continued to only guess at the true health*

*and status of the Copperfoot. He had to consider the possibility
that they knew exactly what they were doing with their bizarre,
evasive tactics, and that it may be some time before the war was
resolved. Regardless, he and his generals decided that they would
continue through the summer with resumed emphasis on water
control. For the duration of the summer, Olerian patrols and
scouts, which were now exclusively done on horseback, hounded
bands of Copperfoot all across the Dialla while the infantry again
postured around watering sites to repel and pick off any thirsty
intruders.*

*Esco and his generals continued to guess at the effectiveness of
their approach, until one early morning just halfway through the
summer season, when guardsman atop the walls of Camphania
spotted a group of people approaching from the desert—Copperfoot leaders looking to discuss terms of surrender. They were
treated with respect, and Esco traveled with them personally to
Pridipoa so that they could parley with the emperor directly.
Negotiations were relatively simple—the Dialla Desert and everything in it was now the possession of the Olerian empire. Addi-
tionally, Copperfoot blacksmiths would have to reveal everything
they knew about steel, how to work it, and they would be forced
to accept contracts to begin outfitting the Olerian army with it
immediately. The emperor then made a demand for all historical
scrolls kept by the Copperfoot so that they could be transcribed
and placed in Olerian archives, as it was Olerian custom to add
conquered histories to its own. However, this was something that
could not be conceded, because the Copperfoot kept no written
history of its people, and though some legends were passed down
orally, these were strictly for the Copperfoot and it was forbidden
for them to be shared with any outsider. The emperor insisted that
they make an exception for posterity, but it could not be done, and
so strong was this belief among the Copperfoot that they would
continue the war if it were made one of surrender's conditions.
Though disappointed, it was not a point that the emperor would
continue the war over, and thus terms were met for peace. In the
coming weeks and months, word went out to the remaining Copperfoot that the war was over, and slowly they came in out of the
wild desert and returned to their towns and villages. Without
formal recordkeeping there is no exact tally for their losses, but the
year spent on the run had reaped a crushing number of casualties.
Many of the homes in Camphania and Helena were never claimed
after families returned, and entire villages in the Dialla's outskirts
remained ghost towns until they were later filled by Olerian citizens—those looking for remote living or a fresh start.*

*In the years to come, the Copperfoot would drift into obscu-
rity. Some among them made an effort to assimilate while others held on to the bitterness bestowed upon conquered peoples.
Their dwindled numbers and lack of cultural infrastructure made
it difficult for the survivors to organize and carry on traditions,
and with no obvious physical discernments, they often became
estranged from each other, and with more and more outsiders
moving in, they were soon strangers in their own homeland.*

*Many historians pursued the Copperfoot, looking to tell their
story, but with no luck. Around the Dialla they became rumors,
enigmas—any person seen walking instead of riding was followed
with whispers and speculation that maybe one of the mighty desert
folk breathed here among them. If only they rode horses, maybe
it was them that would conquer, and not be washed away into
history, marked only by the dusty steel armor adorned over the
hearth, or the magnificent sword caught leaning in the doorway.*

—Excerpt from Ilia's *A Brief History of the Dialla Desert and its People, 1063*

***

THEY PUT THE LAKEBED AND the nefarious butte behind them, moving
mostly north with a slight edge to the northwest. On the clearest of days,
they might be able to see the Echora mountain range to the east and south
of them, but mostly it faded away into the world until they were engulfed by
the red rock of the desert and the azure of the sky. Gone were the large boulders that fractured and rolled down from the upper echelons of the Echora,
replaced instead with red-rock sandstone that dominated a landscape filled
with jutted buttes, deep canyons, lava formations, and large arches that
roped out of the ground and strung across expanses like the ruined foundations of some ancient leviathan city. Any area not dominated by open rock
face was spotted with sage brush and yucca plants that tickled their legs as
they weaved through, the woman in front, the man in the middle, and the
mare in the rear, with its large head hung somberly as it swayed ever so
gently back and forth with each stride.

Ernest sidled up next to the mare as they walked and put a gentle hand
on her neck, whispering for her to be careful in the dangerous terrain. Bird
called back to him and said, "You're not getting attached to her, are you?"

He patted the horse's neck and replied, "This old girl might be out of
her mind, but I don't want to see her go pitching off the edge of some canyon
any more than you do."

She said, "Speaking of pitching, watch your step around here—it's the rainy season and all the flash flooding can make for some dangerous washouts. Also, keep an eye out for the snakes, Pridipoa boy."

They camped that night at the base of a giant stone arch. The air was still and warm as the sun set but they could see massive, grey rain clouds hunkered north of them and they ate as they watched the curtains of water crawl over the land. In time the sun went down and they made no fire because in the clouds, in the darkness, lightning went off in a splendid array and it pulsed its light into the blackness of the world and the air cooled and they could feel the condensation in the air coming from the storm and even the mare stood and watched. Bird eventually went to sleep and the mare vanished again like she always did, leaving Ernest to watch the storm and wonder at the nature of the thing and when it finally broke and the stars could be seen again he wondered at the nature of those too.

He finally slept and woke to discover the mare sniffing and licking his hair. Bird was up across from him, near where she slept, laughing at him, and said, "I think that's her way of saying you stink."

He cursed and pushed the horse's head away from him and then rolled up into a sitting position to take measure of the morning. He said, "Looks like the rains gone."

"Aye, it is. But it's important through here that we keep a constant eye on the sky. If one of those storms gets over us then we're going to want all the time we can get to find a good spot for sheltering."

He nodded and then, digging into his pack, he said, "Foods getting a little low."

"We're not far from Camphania now, just got to get through canyon country."

Canyon country was a regional moniker for the area just south of Camphania where a combination of elevation decline and the erosion of sandstone due to the seasonal rain torrents created a sloping labyrinth of canyons, gullies, and ravines. Blended with the red-rock and arches, it was an area that was as dangerous as it was beautiful. Their progress was slowed by the mare, as they encountered numerous rock shelves and small cliffs that the two of them could easily scale down but were impassable for the horse. However, Bird always found an alternate route and whatever appreciation was felt within the horse was forever hidden behind her long face and dark eyes. In the evening they spotted more rain clouds moving in from the west and they spent that night huddled under a huge, sandstone overhang and, as the rain cascaded in thick torrents around them and made its way forever downward, they could almost hear the erosion around them happening in real time., "Were you ever bound to somebody?"

"Once"

"What was her name?"

"He wasn't a her."

"Oh."

"Have you?"

"No."

It grew dark beyond dark and the two of them sat in silence amidst the thrum of the rainfall and Bird said,

"I hope you like this because where we're going it rains every day."

"Have you been there before?"

"Kardona? I've been there a few times back when I worked the cara-vans. It's been some years now, before things started getting really bad."

"What was happening?"

"What's that people that believe in rebirth?"

"The Samsarans."

"The Samsarans, yeah. One of them was getting everybody in the re-gion riled up—about that herb you love so much."

"Was his name Atun?"

She nodded and said, "That sounds familiar."

"What was he doing?"

"At that point, just a lot of talking. People got a taste for Kardoan herb and the price for it catapulted. There was already a big overlap in Samsarans and herb farming and this Atun thought that the overlap should be bigger—as in the Samsarans should be in control of *all* the herb farming in Kardona. He was preaching to his people that the herb was not only their rightful birthright and domain, but so was all of Kardona. He painted a picture of the Samsarans taking Kardona for themselves and, fueled by the commerce of the herb, eventually taking more—the world even."

"How did you hear about all of it?"

"Just common talk on the caravans—it was no secret to anybody. Atun talked openly about all of it in Kardona and people didn't take him serious enough. They dismissed him as some copper piece prophet trying to make a name for himself. No one understood that he was resonating with a lot of his people, and, at the time, there were *a lot* of Samsarans in Kardona. Pretty soon farmers in rural areas started disappearing. Traders would show up to farmsteads that had been in the same family for generations only to find a stranger had taken over overnight. You had farmers going out and working their fields equipped with whatever weapons they owned. Work on the cara-vans picked up—there were weapons going in and herb coming out—but I stopped taking those jobs. With the Samsarans at war with everybody in

Kardona and with the rise of the Crimson Shrouds out of the Badlands, those jobs were no longer worth the risk to me. That's about all I know on it."

"It's a world more than I knew until a few months ago"

"What happened a few months ago?"

Ernest spat out into the rain and said, "Udura Atun was killed."

Bird nodded and said, "Good riddance."

"I didn't know you had taken sides on the matter."

"Any matter that involves Samsarans will see me on the other side—seeing how my grandfather was killed by one."

Ernest flashed an expression of confusion in the darkness, "In the Dialla?"

She nodded again and said, "Something like thirty years ago? Not long before I was born. They had missionaries all over western Dialla."

"I never knew that—none of them ever came to Ibria."

"Doubt they ever made it that far east. They probably didn't convert a single Copperfoot and, even for a people with multiple lives up their sleeves, I don't think they found us or this desert very suitable."

He spat again but said nothing and the two of them sat in darkness with no sound but for the patter of the rain as it continued with the same steadiness that it had, and the world gave them no indication that it was ready to relent.

Bird then said, "So things in Kardona are getting back to normal there, then?"

"Far from it."

"What now, if this Atun is dead?"

"Now the Samsarans are reaping what they've sowed, and they've sown plenty. You mentioned the murder of farmers just to steal their farms, but once war broke out, they raped civilians, looted traders, tortured prisoners, killed physicians in the field, you name it. He broke all of the unwritten rules of war, and now that the war has turned in the favor of the Kardoans, they're taking that anger out on what's left of the Samsarans."

"Why don't they just surrender?"

"Because of the rebirth thing."

"What does that matter?"

"Let's say you're a Samsaran, and you die tonight—three days from now they believe that you—your soul—would be reborn back into this world."

"Okay."

"Well, after Atun died, the Kardoans figured that this man that had caused so much trouble would be reborn and come back to them in due time, causing the same problems."

"No."

Ernest's voice grew quiet against the sound of the rain but she still heard him clearly when he said, "Yes. It's still whispers at this point, but there are *a lot* of whispers of killing babies. Any baby they can find. And that's probably the reason why the Samsarans won't surrender, regardless of the state of the war."

"That's the worst thing I've ever heard."

He offered an unseen nod of understanding and the two of them looked out into blackness of night and listened to the falling rain in silence for several minutes. The mare lowered herself to the ground, tucked her forelegs under her chest, and, for the first time since she began following them, they witnessed her lying down. Ernest watched the mare settle in and when it too continued staring out at the dark rainfall so did he.

She readied her own sleeping situation on the hard sandstone and she said, "And you fit in, somewhere in all of that mess."

"I wouldn't call it a fit, but my boss thinks there's something that needs doing and I'm the one to do it."

"And it's all very secret."

"I can't tell you what it's about."

"I wasn't asking you to."

"Okay."

Bird settled in under her wool blanket, with her pack as a pillow, and she looked up into the black base of the sandstone overhang that simultaneously sheltered her and loomed over her like a multi-ton leviathan that with the slightest crack could fall and pulverize her out in this wilderness with nothing in the storm to bear witness except for future wanderers that might stop and offer no more than an awe-filled whistle about nature's power that caused such a rock to crumble into submission. She struggled to fall asleep for the first time in many nights and when she heard Ernest moving restlessly just a few feet away she said, "It's an odd destination for a couple of Copperfoot."

His voice came back, tired and sad, "I can't tell you what it's about.".

"I wasn't asking you to."

"Okay."

"It's just grabbed my interest a little more than the work of that cartographer."

"Get some sleep."

"Okay."

He was curled up next to the horse and Bird not far away and they each passed the remainder of the night restlessly because, to desert dwellers, the unfamiliar sound of rainfall acted more as cacophony than harmony. He woke to clear skies and Bird eating breakfast and the mare standing out from under the overhang, bathing in the morning sun. There was no sign of the rainfall from the night before except for the feel of moisture in the air but this vanished by midmorning and it felt again like the desert of their keeping. They continued moving north, steadily descending among the short cliffs and canyons at any point a trail offered passing for the mare. Just before midday, when they typically would find shade and rest, their most recent trail brought them to one of the largest canyon systems in the region. On their left, looming over them, was an intersection and opening of a small canyon inlet that ran perpendicular to the larger one that dropped more than a hundred feet below them on their right. The trail ran parallel to the large canyon, just a few paces from the rim and drop-off, and made its way across an alluvial fan of debris and huge, scattered boulders that had been washed out of the smaller canyon by flash floods. The fan was several hundred paces across, and she reflexively looked behind her at the other two to see they were stead in line behind her, each a dozen paces apart. He stopped a moment to admire the view and magnificence of the canyon below and even moved just to its rim to peer over the edge at the drop. The mare stopped behind him, disinterested, and when he got back to the trail his attention was on the canyon's beauty as much as the fatal drop that lurked only several paces away. Bird noticed the two of them lagging behind and stopped at the fan's halfway point, she too distracted by the view. Ernest saw her waiting up ahead and, looking forward to a break, locked his eyes down on the trail and increased his pace. Moments later he was startled by the mare, who went galloping past him in such a hurry that she clipped his left shoulder and sent him spinning to the ground. He cursed at it and, upon getting to his feet and composing himself, looked to see it charge in a full run past Bird and out of site on the trail ahead. She yelled back at him, "What the hell?"

He looked behind him at the spot where the mare was following from and saw nothing. He threw both hands up in an exaggerated shrug and called back, "I don't know. Crazy fucking horse almost killed . . ."

She quickly threw up a single finger to get him to stop talking and, when he was about to yell at her again, she gestured with her entire arm to keep quiet, and he did. For a moment he heard nothing, then a small noise crept up at the edge of his senses, and it sounded like a very distant stampede of large animals. His face bunched in confusion until Bird let out a blood turning scream: *Ernest, run.* He immediately began moving, even though his brain hadn't consciously registered what exactly was happening. She turned and began running too, along the same route the mare just had, and moving much quicker than him. Out of the mouth of the small canyon the first sign of the flood appeared—just a couple inches of slow moving, dirty water—as the sound of distant stampeding rapidly grew into a dull roar. Ernest fully understood his peril now and he ran like a man possessed, even managing to shake the pack off of his shoulders and the sword off his waist, in mid stride, dropping them to the ground directly in the path of the approaching water. The next time he stole a glance toward the canyon, the first surge of water, at least waist high, was powering its way toward him, no more than a hundred paces from him now and moving at a sinister speed. The water's color was a deep, impenetrable brown from all the soil it carried, and on its vanguard rode a barricade of jagged branches, trees, and vegetation that had been swept up in the flood's passing.

Bird was fast. She could make out, from the discoloration and vegetation patterns, where the alluvial ended and thus the likely extent of the flood's passage, and she thought she would make it there before the water reached her, but she knew Ernest wouldn't. She changed directions, now angling back toward Ernest and directly toward the water and a cart-sized boulder that perched, isolated, in the middle of the fan. She knew that the charging water had the ability to move such a rock, but, with no time and no other options, she leaped on top of it. She took off her pack and, on the water side of the boulder, she threw a shoulder strap over one of the rock's jutting edges and then craned her left elbow and locked it around the other strap, leaning her weight against it in an attempt to secure her and the pack's position. Ernest saw Bird change directions toward the approaching flood but was too panicked to make anything of it—his lungs anguished for oxygen and his legs ached with fatigue from the sprint and the days of travel before it. The first few inches of water finally reached him and his feet slapped loudly in the shallow water and the sound to him was the sound of doom and he knew that any moment he would be swept off the rim of the canyon into the gorge below. Blood powered through his head and he could hear his rapid heartbeat reverberating in his eardrums, but still a sound came to him and out of his peripheral vision he saw Bird, perched atop a boulder and calling his name. The flood was only a dozen paces away and Bird urged him on and he had no idea what her intention was but she turned to look at the water coming toward her then back to Ernest and her face was all fear and he knew his was the same. Mere moments before being dragged away by the murky water to his grave, he lunged forward for Bird's outstretched arm just as the forefront of the flood reached them. They grabbed one another, each by the wrist, and he quickly pulled up his other arm so that both of his hands were grasped firmly around the steel vambrace on her wrist. The water hit him and, with so much of the debris stacked at the forefront of the flood, it felt like being kicked in ten different places at once. But he held on. The water lifted him parallel to the ground and grabbed onto his cloak and clothes and, with the power of nature, pulled at him with all its force and on the other end of that force was Bird's rangy arm. He managed to roll his body slightly so that his right shoulder was taking the brunt of the force and, by craning his neck, was able to just find an angle for his mouth and nose not to be overrun with the passing water, even if almost every breath brought a bit of water into his lungs.

She had gambled with both of their lives—if the height of the water at any point went higher than the boulder, then they would both be carried away. Furthermore, if the boulder, which had undoubtedly been brought to its current position by a flash flood not unlike this one, were to be moved again by the water, then all three of them would find themselves at the bottom of the gorge. For the time being, her gamble was paying off—the rock seemed sturdy and, though water lapped up around her feet and legs, its current depth appeared to be stable. She recognized her luck immediately, but the good feeling was short lived, because she was mere seconds into her grapple with Ernest and she already felt like her body might be torn apart. She was sure he could not hear her, but she implored him to keep hanging on even as she doubted that she could herself.

They held the precarious pose for several minutes, even if it felt like hours. The water was cool in temperature, but she was poised atop the boulder, straining herself in the midday Dialla sun and she knew nothing of Ernest's condition other than that he was still holding on. Her eyes were closed both from concentration and to keep the sweat pooling on her brow form finding its way in. A passerby with no context might think her some spiritual figure deep into meditation, except on the inside she was anything but. Her right arm that gripped Ernest was somehow both totally numb and throbbing with discomfort. Her other arm around the pack wasn't any better off—the packs strap was digging itself deep into her flesh and was beginning to have a tourniquet effect on the rest of it.

She had to try something. The boulder did not offer her much room, but if she could reel him in, and even if he had to sit on her lap, it was a far better situation than the one they were currently in. She knew he could not respond but she called out to him and said, "Ernest, I'm going to try to get you in," and she began exerting her strength on her right arm—trying to curl the weight of a full grown man against the pull of the flood's water.

He did not hear her, but for the first time since being consumed by the water, he sensed her arm move and he correctly suspected that she was trying something. He kicked his feet in a swimming motion—he still could not find the ground—and attempted to pull himself toward her, but his strength was depleted, not only from his run and then hanging on for dear life, but from the abuse that his body was still taking from passing debris. She gritted her teeth and slowly she was pulling him toward her, until she heard a loud pop from inside her arm, and her arm went slack and she screamed a horrible scream and so powerful was the pain that she physically swooned and was nearly knocked unconscious on the spot. He heard her cry of pain and her grip on his wrist vanished and though he did not know what happened, he knew it was solely up to him now to hang on. So severe was the pain that her body visually trembled, and tears streamed down her face along with the sweat, but Ernest was still there and it was enough to keep her pack arm hanging on.

Time passed, though neither registered how long, each of their minds receding into the deep instinctual corners of the brain that has only one concern and one function: survival. He was deep into said corner when the whisper came to him, and it told him it was okay to let go. It told him that Bird was in great pain, and he could alleviate her pain if he just let the water take him. All the torment of his current situation and every torment in his life could be erased by simply relaxing the grip on his exhausted hands and taking a short ride to the canyon's edge where he could experience the thrill of flying before being handed a clean, painless death. The survivor in him fought back against the whisper but with each passing moment it grew more soothing and persuasive and as more water filled his lungs and he decided that it was best to let go, his foot hit something. Unsure if he was mistaken, he tried his best to whip his leg outward, and there it was again— the ground. It was impossible for him to determine if the force of the flood's pull had lessened, but he was certain that the depth of the water had subsided. Having all but surrendered his life already, he had nothing to lose by making one final play for life, and so he did. Maintaining his grip on Bird's limp arm, he rolled to his right, face downward into the water, and bringing forth a painful gasp from Bird who was caught off guard by his stunt. He powered both his legs downward in the direction of the ground, and when his toes made contact he drove his legs toward Bird while simultaneously abandoning his grip on her wrist and reaching further up her arm, just past her elbow. If at any point his feet slipped or his change of grip missed the mark, he would have been swept away, but the survivor had not surrendered yet and instead he found himself in a standing position, nearly waist deep in water, leaning against it with both hands encased on Bird's lower bicep. It took two more hazardous steps for him to reach her, pulling himself up her arm like a climber, and with almost no room to spare, he flopped his body on the boulder next to her.

She maintained her sitting position, but pulled her injured arm into her chest, contracted her body into a tight ball, and then was quiet. He caught his breath but then began hacking and coughing up mouthfuls of

dirty water he had swallowed during the ordeal. The water continued pouring off the canyon rim behind them and with each passing minute it re-
ceded a little more from its high point around the rock. He finally managed
to gather himself and turn his attention to Bird, who was still balled up,
with her arms crossed tightly and her chin tucked into her chest. He asked,
"What happened?"

She looked up at him with tears still brimming in her eyes and shook
her head, "My arm. Something happened to the elbow."

"You saved my life."

"That's why you hired me."

"My packs gone."

"We're not far from Camphania."

"How far?"

"I don't know. Maybe two days."

He cursed under his breath and her voice was frail unlike he had ever
heard it before and she said to him, "I have enough food in mine to take
care of us."

"It's not the food that I'm worried about," he said.

"What? Your herb? You can't make it a couple days without that shit?"

"I don't know."

"What do you mean *you don't know*?"

"I mean it's been years now since I went even a day without it."

"What happens when you don't have it?"

He shrugged and said, "It's different for everyone. Some people die in
the withdrawal."

"You're not allowed to die after what I just did for you."

"I wish it was that way."

She rummaged through her pack with her good arm and took out her
goat's wool blanket and, with her clawed weapon, cut a length of it off and
fashioned it into a sling.

Ernest said, "Let me have a look at it," and she showed him. It looked
unremarkable in proportion to the amount of pain it was causing, with
some minor swelling around the elbow joint and little else visible.

"Can you move your fingers?"

She managed to wiggle them, far less than their typical range of motion and he nodded in approval.

She said, "Is that a good sign?"

"I don't know—can't be a bad one."

They moved off the rock late in the afternoon, after the water was
down to ankle height, and waded down their original path. There was no
sign of the mare and they stopped for the day much sooner than usual,

so exhausted were they by their encounter. He fell asleep immediately while she struggled with finding a comfortable position and finally settled in, sitting half-up with her arm resting across her chest. He woke the next morning to the dark, brown eyes of the mare just inches from his face. After running a gentle hand from her forehead to her muzzle he pulled himself into a sitting position. Several feet away was Bird's still sleeping form and he realized that, since meeting her, this was the first time she had slept later than him. The horse seemed to read his mind and walked over to her and nudged her awake with its muzzle and she jolted awake in surprise and then cursed in pain as the motion tousled her arm. Ernest turned his thoughts to his own body for a moment and realized that in all his life he could not think of a time when his body ached as profoundly as it did now. It was as if every muscle from his waist up had been isolated and systematically tormented and now, having tasted a bit of rest, rioted against his decision to begin moving again. And Bird was worse off than him. The swelling in her elbow had tripled since they fell asleep, and as she tenderly slipped it out of the sling, he could see a deep purple color settling in on the elbow area and upper forearm.

"Shit," he said. "Your arm looks the way my whole body feels."

She said nothing, gently pressing on the swelling with her good arm and hissing quietly when she encountered particularly vulnerable spots.

He said, "You need to get to a physician."

"Like I told you, we're about two days out."

"Two days might be too long. That arm doesn't look long for this world."

"Well two days is what it is."

"Maybe with me it is. But I slow you down, even when I'm healthy, and right now I'm anything but."

"I'm not sure how much faster I can move with this arm."

"Take the horse."

She shot him a chilling glare and he threw up his arms defensively, even as it hurt his body to do so. He said, "I'm sorry. I'm just saying it might be the difference between losing your arm and not."

"I wouldn't ride that fucking horse if it meant the difference between losing my life and not."

"I shouldn't have said it."

"Have you ever been on one?"

"No."

"Me neither."

"I shouldn't have said it."

"Okay."

"I still think you should go ahead."

"You'd be out here alone."

"I've lived almost my whole life in the Dialla."

"Without herb?"

"If you could pick some up for me in Camphania, it'd be appreciated."

She stared off into the morning sky, deep in thought and then said, "What about the withdrawal?"

"Just get yourself to Camphania and then get back out here."

She shrugged and said, "I don't think it's a great idea leaving you out here, but it's you who hired me so I'll let you call it."

"It's been called."

She set down her pack between them and picked out only some of their remaining food for herself. She used her right arm to detach her shield from its perch on her back and set it on the pack and said to him, "This was crafted for my grandfather, so please take care of it. You've already seen what water can do around here so be mindful of that. When the wolves get active at night it can be a little spooky when you're alone, but there's enough cover out here to run a fire without worrying about drawing the wrong kind of attention. When you do move just keep on a line north as much as possible and I'll find you. North is that way."

"I know which way North is."

"Okay."

She adjusted her attire now that she was free of her pack and shield, and he began rummaging in his pants with an expression of concentration on his face and she shot him a look of disgust before saying, "What are you *doing*?"

He responded with a satisfied grunt and brought his hand out, clasped around a small pouch he kept hidden and, upon opening it, sifted through a handful of silver.

She said, "That's revolting," as he offered her the coins and she reluctantly took them and after she had added them to her own pouch Ernest patted his groin area again and under his left armpit and said, "There's more where that came from, so when you come back out and I'm a corpse, make sure you take it with you."

She nodded and wished him luck and he the same and, with her right arm slung tightly to her body, bounded off north. The mare watched her go and looked back at him as if waiting for him to follow and when he did not move, she sauntered off after Bird. He nibbled on one of their last biscuits for breakfast and then settled his aching body back down and slept to almost midday. When he woke again he immediately felt the pull of the herb. His brain itched at the thought of placing a pinch of it into his cheek and in turn his mouth salivated deeply. He took a long pull from his waterskin to wash it away but it returned immediately and, even though it was near mid-day, he opted for traveling in the apex of the sun's power than sit still amid the herb's whispers. After an hour he had to quit, as the heat overwhelmed him and a dryness set into his mouth now as if packed with wool. He pulled again from his water but it had no effect against his parched mouth. He looked out at his surroundings and, when he felt the origins of a headache creep upward from the base of his neck, he attempted to distract himself from the impending misery by moving. His legs wobbled as he stood and, after the feeling of light-headedness passed, the headache returned and he tentatively continued north. Squinting his eyes against the afternoon sun exacerbated the pain in his head and as his feet grew heavy and his pace slowed, he moved like the risen dead over a raptured planet. Between the heat and his labored exertion, he should have been layered in sweat, but his skin was as dry as his mouth and it was hot to the touch and his chest felt tight with an intangible discomfort and long before nightfall he curled up in the shaded corner of a sandstone outcrop and tried to rest.

***

In the Olerian year 876, living on the rainy, western slopes of the Omoya Mountains, a young farmer unwittingly altered the course of human history.

A fourth-generation potato farmer, Elio Bebin was left to work his eight-acre plot of land alone after his parents passed and his sister married and moved west to the coast. His provincial existence left him quite alone, but he was not a lonely person and he kept himself preoccupied with numerous agricultural pursuits. While most of his plot was for growing potatoes, he maintained a small vegetable garden that produced enough green beans, onions, and sweet corn to keep his meals from becoming stale. He raised goats for milk and replaced two rows of potato plants with hazel-nut trees, which was a commodity he traded with tinkers, traders, and other locals—usually for the lamb meat that so many other farmers of the area were dedicated to raising. He grew so fond of lamb jerky that he constructed a small hut on the property that he used exclusively for smoking meat.

In the spring quarter of 872, Elio was visited by a physician who had an interest in a plant—a herbaceous fern—common to the region. It was a large plant, nearly to a man's waist, and usu-ally had roughly a dozen bright, green leaves—some as large as a man's thigh—that sprouted from the main stalk in all directions.

Elio had never heard of the plant, which was unsurprising given that it served no agricultural purpose, but it also thrived at higher altitudes and was thus sparsely seen among the lower slopes where his farm operated. Had he gotten out more often, Elio may have heard the reverence that travelers held for the plant and its perceived beneficial qualities. One of these—the one the physician was interested in—was its quality to act as a painkiller. For decades, travelers passing over the treacherous Omoya's, if they were to encounter the wild fern, would gnaw on the plant's leaves as a way to combat physical discomfort. Joint pain, muscle soreness, and headaches might all be made more bearable by the plant, but its effects were mild and brief, and it was never taken seriously as a medicinal remedy. The physician was interested in changing that. Having performed numerous, horrifying surgeries on patients that were all too cognizant of having a limb being sawed off, she was looking for a way to dampen, or even eliminate their pain altogether. She would pay Elio to cultivate the wild fern so that she had a steady supply of the plant's leaves, and she, a dabbler in alchemy, would attempt to exploit, and amplify, the plant's natural, painkilling qualities.

By the end of the year, he had nearly three dozen wild ferns growing between the hazelnut trees and the potatoes. The physician returned at the end of summer, paid Elio his silver, and left again with a cart-load of the stripped leaves. When she was gone, Elio harvested the seeds from the largest, healthiest ferns and set them aside to be planted the next year, so that only the most superior genetic traits carried on. He took a farmer's pride in the quality of the plants, and in the following years he too began to experiment with its leaves, using them as a cooking ingredient, as mulch in the garden, and even as decoration in his home. He thought that maybe the dead leaves could be used as a good fire-starter, but even they were too damp to light. Aside from its effectiveness as a mulch, it seemed to Elio that people were right to have dismissed this plant as one that was largely useless to human interests, and the physician, having made no advancements in her research, was coming to the same conclusion.

However, all that changed on a summer night in 876, as Elio prepped his smokehouse with a fresh batch of lamb jerky, and he got an idea—what if he smoked the fern leaves the same way he smoked the lamb meat? After all, it was the dampness of the leaf that prevented it from lighting. He hung the leaves in the little smokehouse alongside the lamb, scaffolding and hanging them over a small coal fire he kept lit as often as he could maintain— and he waited.

The lamb meat was finished long before the leaves, and he took the meat out and added even more leaves to the vacant spots to keep the smokehouse full. The leaves stayed green for the first week, but by the second week most of them had turned to a pale-yellow color. Though he didn't know it, this reduction to the leaves' chlorophyll content not only altered their color but made their flavor much more palatable than when chewed on as a raw plant. Elio remained patient, and this continued curing of the leaves caused further chemical alterations—particularly in the plant's carotenoids—that would drastically affect the chemical makeup and potency of the leaf. By the beginning of the fourth week the leaves turned from yellow to brown, they took on the appearance of large bats, the little husks hanging motionless in the dim, ember-lit smokehouse.

He finally removed them in the beginning of the fifth week and, trip after trip, carried the shriveled, brown husks into his house. It was a late morning, the fall quarter quickly approaching, and he looked at the leaves there and wondered if he had accomplished anything other than making the most elaborate fire-starter in history. The dried leaves did not flake, like he expected, but instead had an elastic quality to them. He wrestled a small chunk off of the largest leaf and smelled it as he considered what to do with it. Eat it? Smoke it? Snort it? Since his inspiration for whatever this was had come from the jerky, he decided to treat it as such, and he tucked the piece into the back of his left cheek, near his molars, where he could chew and suck on the flavors at will.

Almost immediately, as the leaf's juices powered through his salivary glands, he was hit by the impact of the drug. He grew lightheaded and his toes tingled for a few seconds before going completely numb. As the room began to spin, he stumbled over to his chair and sat down to regain his composure. He breathed with the depth of somebody fast asleep and felt at his body as if it were not his own. Within minutes a wave of euphoria washed over him as complete as any he could imagine and though he wasn't fully aware of it, he spent the next hour staring at the house's ceiling. No amount of ale could have prepared him for this. He spent the rest of the day in and out of consciousness, and as the sun set that evening, its light glistened sweetly off of the drool hanging from the side of his mouth.

When the physician came to visit two weeks later to retrieve her batch of leaves, she was met with a smitten Elio Bebin. She was blown away by what he had discovered and paid him double the silver for however many husks he was willing to sell her—he had already stashed away more than enough for *himself. She left and within months every person in the region had heard of the physician's new wonder remedy. Every patient that got a taste of it would push her relentlessly for more, and it became quite clear, quite quickly, that Elio's smoked leaves were highly—cripplingly—addictive.*

Elio spent that fall replacing all his hazelnut trees and the majority of his potato plants to create more room for his ferns. And every day that he worked—and every day that he didn't—he had a wad of the smoked leaves tucked into his cheeks. He would've been happy to dedicate his entire farm to the fern, but the man had to eat, after all. Over the next three years he spent the rainy, winter season building a second smokehouse and clearing more land for even more ferns. It was conceivably more work than one man could handle, but he was perpetually high on his creation, and numb to the toll of the farm work. The physician began to charge unreasonably high prices for the leaf, and people continued to pay them. She was harassed constantly for her supply and it was during this time that people learned of Elio's role in the fern's origin. Late in the winter, during a torrential rainstorm so common to the region's climate, four bandits kicked in the door to Elio's house and put a sword to his throat. They demanded to know everything about the smoked leaves and how they were made and—in his drug-induced, euphoric state—he happily walked them through the method. They let him live, but when they left they did so with four of his exhumed fern plants riding in the back of their cart.

Other farmers caught on too, and Elio's property was routinely raided by people looking to grow the fern for themselves. This irked him, not because of all the new competition in the marketplace, but because the plant was readily available in the wild and he saw no reason that people should steal from him what could be taken for free. Smokehouses began to sprout up throughout Kardona, and as the winter quarter came around the next year, the wet countryside was dotted endlessly with the dim firelight of the smokehouses, like so many fireflies lost their way out in the wild darkness of the world.

As the dried leaves became ubiquitous throughout the region, Elio was given official recognition by way of the fern being renamed in his honor—Bebin Euphoris—but the fern itself and the resulting product came to be known simply, almost exclusively, as the herb. Other regions grew their own Bebin Euphoris plants and discovered that different methods of curing the leaves—sun dried, air-tempered, and sugar fermented—all resulted in a variety of ways for people to get strung out. But the Omoya Mountains remained the pinnacle of herb production and its climate and traditional smokehouses continued to create the finest herb known to man.

Elio's ending was not a happy one, and the entire region would come to regret the day he decided to smoke a wild fern's leaves. He was killed in the year 882, in the heart of the night, shot through the chest by the bow and arrow of a herb addict looking to loot ferns from his property. His end would become common to many who lived in the area, particularly after a large band of religious migrants—a peculiar people that believed they would be reborn on this earth three days after their death—moved into the area, incentivized not only by the financial potential of the herb, but by their own addiction to it.

—Excerpt from Marcus' A Modern History of the Kardona Tribes, 1104

***

Little rest came to Ernest. Despite the late evening heat that lingered in the air and on the surrounding rock, he began shivering, and the sweat that was absent earlier in the day when he needed it most, beset him now with the sun going down and his teeth chattered inside his head and he pulled his wool blanket tight around him to protect against the falling night. Curled under his blanket in a cold sweat, he closed his eyes and wished to just fall asleep as a way to pass the misery, but he was not so lucky. Years of dependence on the herb left his sober brain in a state of anxiety and even when, by way of pure exhaustion, he managed to fall asleep, he was besieged by dreams that disturbed him and startled him back to consciousness in such a way as to be a net loss for his energy. He could feel the heat of Rathalla's flame growing cold in his chest and he called out to his deity and if Rathalla's call came back to him he did not hear it. Shapes moved out in the night and he shook and peeked from under his blanket out at them, knowing if they were anything truly sinister he would be helpless, but feeling every degree of fear all the same. Wild calls that he had not heard on any other night came in out of the darkness too and echoed off the canyon walls and he suspected that these calls concerned him in some way.

He was unsure of how much he ultimately slept, but from out of the east flew a calling wren and behind it a thin tiger reef that simmered at the rim of the world and foretold of the sun to come. Exhausted, he willed his aching body to retrieve his waterskin and food from his pack and, as he ate, a red fox showed itself just a dozen paces from his position. It was no bigger than a small dog but its brilliant orange coat glowed against the grey dawn atmosphere and it measured Ernest with its ears directed forward and its shoulders crouched at the ready but Ernest went on chewing his breakfast and the fox in turn relaxed. It finally took its eyes from him to look around as if it expected more from the huddled vagrant and then looked back at him as if piecing together his story of origin. Eventually it sulked off into the waking world and Ernest passed out again and woke in spurts through the day, alternating between shaking with cold sweats and struggling to breath against the dry, suppressively hot air. Time passed and he looked dead-eyed out into the desert and night came and the urge to drink or eat left him entirely. He drifted in and out of consciousness and the mare came to him out of the wild and inspected him with her muzzle and lorded over him like some spirit animal, and he asked after the status of Bird as if the mare could respond and when he woke the following morning she was gone, and he was never sure if she was ever there.

Because some corner of his mind told him to keep moving north, he fought his way to his feet and, with Bird's shield slung to his arm, and his own bow slung across his torso, staggered over the broken land like some idol warrior made animate by the local necromancer's apprentice. The most difficult stretches of canyon country were long behind him, but he still had to navigate his way across small ravines and gullies. All human desire to eat, drink, sleep, or hide from the heat now eluded him completely. The misery of his current state became something outside of himself and he looked on at his fragile form through the eyes of the desert and the gift that his body carried with it—the soft tissue to nourish the first scavengers that would then defecate and fertilize the earth, and then the flies that laid their eggs into every orifice and fed the birds and their hatched maggots that did the same, and the iron of his blood, pulled at and soaked up by the earth and, when all gone, his disarticulated bones left among the rocks and their bleached calcium eroded and absorbed into the desert's skin with only the promise of being forgotten forever or dug up by some future prospector who would brush the sandstone off of this petrified skull and dully guess at the individual that it once housed.

Dusk came and sand blew thick across the countryside and, with thoughts of his imminent demise consuming his incoherent mind, by the time he noticed two figures approaching him from the desert it was too late. He knew of the potential danger that he was in but, with his tongue swollen from thirst and lips cracked and bleeding, he could only manage to mumble a warning out loud to himself while looking feebly for a place to hide. There was no place and the two shapes drew nearer and, with his eyes ravaged by fatigue, dehydration, and the blowing sand, he could not make out any more than their outline. All he could surmise was that the figure on the left was massive and grew larger with each nearing footstep and he pulled Bird's shield up tight into his body and assumed a defensive posture behind it with the figures just a dozen paces away.

A woman's voice came to him through the blowing sand and said, "Please don't hurt us, warrior," and before he knew it the mare's viscous tongue planted itself across his face and Bird was beside him. She had a new pack with her, but she relieved him of his and took her shield back and supported him several hundred paces away to an eroded pinnacle of rock whose surface appeared matted in the retreating daylight. She helped him to the ground with the mare watching over and Bird took a pinch of the herb from her new pack and tucked it into his left cheek. Next she took out a waterskin and poured as much down his throat as she could before he began coughing and pushing her away with a series of inaudible mumbles. She dumped more water over his head and covered him with her blanket and he fell instantly asleep with her sitting next to him at the close of day and the mare vanishing like usual into the night.

When he woke again the next morning Bird sat across from him and he lay with his eyes trained on her before saying, "Are you there?"

"I'm here."

"I thought you were a dream."

"You're not the first to say that."

"How is your arm?"

She looked down at her arm, now cradled in a fresh sling that she didn't have when she left him and she said, "The physician called it displaced. It hurt more going back in than it did coming out but he said there shouldn't be any long term damage. How do you feel?"

"Like death."

"That's good. You got to be alive in order to feel like death."

"Then what does *real* death feel like?"

She shrugged and said, "Fear. Confusion. Relief."

"You sound like you've done it before."

"If I have then I am just a dream, and you've died along with me."

"You'd be right about the relief."

She looked into his eyes, steady and unnerving, and she said, "It's always in their eyes. Yours is confusion."

"And yours?" He asked.

"Fear."

She rolled the shoulder of her injured arm forward and winced in pain while Ernest sat up and changed out the old herb in his cheek for a new pinch and she said to him, "If that shit makes you feel any better, we could make Camphania by the end of the day. We were closer to it than I thought."

He said, "I'll do whatever it takes if it means sleeping in a bed tonight."

"I thought you might feel that way."

They came out of canyon country to a landscape much like the one on the first leg of their trip, except that the sand here favored the color white more than the previous region's red. The land and the horizon were mostly barren and the sloping decrease in elevation helped move their wounded bodies along to the north toward their destination. Ernest's body still felt ravaged, but the power of the herb absorbed into his body where it kissed and soothed his nerve endings and the calming presence it held within his body and the thought of sleeping at an inn by the end of the day was enough to push him along.

They stopped briefly at midday to hydrate and eat and, as he looked out across the empty desert he said, "You've been paying attention to what's behind us too, right?"

"What's behind us?" She said.

"Like if we're being followed."

She tilted her head to look past him, over his shoulder toward the south and out at the desolate landscape behind them that on certain rises allowed visibility for miles on end, and then looked back at him and said, "Nobody is following us."

"You're sure?"

"I'd know it."

"And nobody has, at any point, up to now?"

"I would've mentioned it if someone was following us."

"Okay."

"From the moment that we first met outside of Helena, we have not for an instant been followed by anybody or anything other than that batshit crazy horse right there."

"Okay."

They pushed on through the afternoon and, for the first time during their travels together, they continued walking after the sun went down. A sliver of the moon hung up in the black sky and sent out a dim, colorless light over the world like some god's night light meant to buffer against the immutable darkness. They moved quietly across the eerie landscape, tailed only by their subtle moon shadows and the mare, that for once did not leave them at the coming of night. Exhaustion became them, but shortly before midnight small dots of orange light appeared out in the distance and, with the Powder River reflecting the moonlight and revealing its snaking form approaching from the east, they had reached the outskirts of Camphania. The typically white outer walls appeared grey under the moon and in many places the sun-dried brick was dilapidated and crumbled out into the desert to the apparent care of nobody. They could see the familiar image of spears poking above the sections of the wall that had yet to decay, giving away the presence of Olerien soldiers standing watch—sentinels looking out endlessly into the night here and along how many other walls as if the darkness itself were their charge and it was the darkness itself that threatened them and as the two travelers and their horse passed through the southern gate they were not stopped or hailed. They made their way through narrow streets of dirt, weaving through dull brown, single-storied adobe structures that populated the city. As they penetrated deeper through the sleeping city's dirt streets they could hear the steady murmur of the Powder River grow louder and they could feel its moisture on their skin and they could taste it on their lips. He named off a handful of inns that he could not be seen in and she nodded and led them to the east section of the city to a small inn named The Goat's Horn where they were tended by a sleepy-eyed keeper who took their money to stable the mare and showed them past a low burning hearth to a small, dark, and empty room. The innkeeper lit a candle for them in the room and left and Ernest immediately collapsed into one of two small beds in the room and was asleep within minutes without a word.

Bird delicately unslung her injured arm and then used her shoulders to shed off her cloak before reaching, with her good arm, to pull her shield up and then off her back. She leaned the shield in the corner and then purpose-fully removed her armor—a series of four leather latches that ran up her left ribcage from the waist to the armpit, revealing her linen tunic underneath. She slipped out of the armor and added it to the corner next to the shield and then removed her belt with the fist weapon on the left hip and her sword on the right and then laid it down in a flat line at her feet. Next were her sandals and when she had them off she sat cross-legged in front of her weapons and closed her eyes in a state of meditation. After many minutes she rose to her feet and went through the same series of poses that she had at West One and when she was finished and finally lay on the floor, with her head on her pack and covered only by a wool blanket—no different than the way she slept in the wild—it was only the sound of Ernest's snoring and the dim flicker of the candle that accompanied her to the dream world.

PART II

The Caravan

Ernest awoke late the next morning to the sound of an already awake city outside the room's walls. He struggled just to sit up on the bed's feather-stuffed mattress, which had allowed his body to relax in a way it could not sleeping out on the desert floor, but also made him feel the aches of his body more acutely. Bird was nowhere to be seen and the room's lone candle was spent, but a couple of rectangular slits cut into in the outside wall of the room allowed thin rays of light to seep in along with occasional scraps of fresh air. He slid the small bow over his shoulder, and under his cloak, and walked out into the dingy hearth room where Bird sat alone at small wooden table eating breakfast. After plucking up a small sausage from her plate and nearly swallowing it whole, he tucked some herb into his cheek and asked her about the plan for the day.

"I think it's a good idea to sit tight for a day or two and get rested."

He shook his head and said *no time* and she said, "Okay. Then we need to get to the marketplace and hope to find a caravan that we can get on with. If there's nothing going out then we might be stuck here a couple of days waiting anyway, or we head it alone. I don't know if many are going to Kardona these days but there's still enough heading to the Great Plains that we can go along with as far as we want."

"And you think that's a good idea?"

She said, "You haven't been clear on who or what you're trying to avoid, but the caravans are mostly just merchants and whatever security they've hired. There's always a handful of civilians that pay to ride along but common etiquette is that everyone minds their own business."

"Security is for the Crimson Shrouds?"

She nodded and said, "It is now. Used to be for the typical raiders and robbers, but once the Shrouds showed up a few years back, they've been a huge threat to the caravans."

"What do you know about them?"

"Next to nothing. Same as everyone else. They're holed up somewhere in the Badlands and they take whatever they need from caravans no matter how much security gets employed. The Olerians have gone in after them several times but with no results."

"Have you ever fought them?"

She shook her head and said, "No. I don't do caravan security as much as I used to though. They're more of a recent nuisance." She stood from her spot on the table and said, "You coming with me to the market?"

"You go ahead." He gestured with his chin to her now empty plate and said, "I'm going to get me some of that."

Bird slipped her good arm up under her cloak an undid the knot on her sling, causing her injured arm to go slack, and as she slipped the sling into her bag she caught his quizzical expression and said, "Gotta have two good arms if you expect anybody to hire you for protection."

She went out the same door they had come through just several hours before and he was left alone in the dark hearth room for several minutes before the innkeeper entered from some dark backroom and took his order without a word and vanished again and in the silence he could hear his food being cooked in the neighboring kitchen. When the dish came out—eggs, black beans, and two sausages served with a couple of corn tortillas—he devoured it in a matter of minutes and left a single piece of silver on the table before he walked out into the bright morning and into the city of Camphania.

The sound of the river now was covered by the bustle of a living city—and it was bustling. Given its location, Camphania was an obvious and natural trading hub for the entire region. Surrounded by an easily traversable landscape, and positioned along the Powder River, it acted as a two-way gateway between the east and the west. Even as the capital city of the Copperfoot—a trading averse society—it was a natural pit stop for the area's merchants, and with the ascension of the Olerian empire in the region, the city's economy and importance increased tenfold. Smaller road systems came in out of minor Dialla to the east, working in tandem with the Powder River to bring in iron ore out of the Echora Mountains. Stretching to the north east and due west were its major road systems, running a line to Pridipoa and the Highlands with the western road connecting the Great Plains and Kardona. Along these roads traveled wagons and carriages of ever-increasing sophistication—primarily constructed of wood, but accented with sturdy iron mechanics. Wagons out of the Highlands were packed with barley, potatoes, soft fruits, and lumber. Out of the Dialla came beans, onions, iron, and wool products. Kardona traded with the best herb in the world, but was also rich in wheat, fine fabrics, barley, and grapes. And the Great Plains, in addition to growing and trading more corn than all other nations combined, was famous for its barley, cotton, and soybeans. For emissaries and wealthy civilians and merchants, there were elaborate carriages that provided the most comfortable ride available, however most travelers had to settle with riding and sleeping atop their wares in the wagon, or with the security and hired hands underneath on the ground. Roads were busy year-round, and many people traveled them alone, but the preferred method for traders and merchants was to group up, split costs on hired security, and hope their large numbers were enough of a deterrent against highway robbers and, in recent years, the Crimson Shrouds.

Ernest made his way to the stables where the mare's giant head perched over its stall door, unflappable as ever. He sat on a small hooving stool in front of the door and reached up to stroke her muzzle while he launched dark globs of spit onto the stable floor that was already dirty with stray straws of hay and horse manure. At the sound of a short whistle he looked up to see Bird jogging toward him and, when she was close enough, she snapped her fingers and said, "Let's get on it."

Ernest said, "You find something?"

"A caravan left early this morning. The master said if we can catch up then there's room for two more security."

"Shit then. Let's get this girl out of this sty and get going."

"Not yet. We need to get to a smith first. They were full up on civilian spots so we're travelling as security and you got to look the part if they're gonna take us."

He stood from his stool and held his arms wide to each side as if to say *this isn't the part?* and she rolled her eyes and said, "All you got is a cavalry bow and you don't even ride a horse."

"This bow was your idea."

"They don't hire amateurs."

"Isn't that going to be a problem. For me?"

She shook her head and said, "They don't try you out for the job, so you just need to look like you know what you're doing."

"And how do I do that?"

"We get you some armor and a real weapon and then you do what all you men do—just strut around, swinging your dick, acting like the world and everything in it belongs to you."

"That's it?"

"That's it."

For the moment they left the mare and Bird led the way west, into the heart of the city, through dirt roads the color of chalk and structures the color of wet mud. They brushed shoulders with numerous town folk, most dressed in cream-colored togas set over linen tunics, with the occasional Olerian soldiers manning cross sections of streets in their defining wine and gold cloaks. When Bird checked over her shoulder to see that Ernest still followed her she noticed his cloak pulled up over his head, obscuring his face. After several more streets, the smell of charcoal flitted through the air and a thin chimney of smoke twisted opaquely in the morning sun and Bird gestured with her head toward the building and led them through a heavy wooden door, reinforced with iron bands, and into a dark room that was warmer than the temperature outside. The forge was set in one large space that was the entirety of the structure, and the sun rays that came in from the cut-out windows were swallowed by the artificial ember light within the hot darkness. The heavy door thudded to a close, leaving the two of them blinking their eyes in adjustment as a voice offered an ineligible greeting from the area of the hearth, which could just be seen glowing on the far side of the room. The sound of scrap metal rattled on the floor as the voice made its way through the dark room toward them and Bird whispered back to Ernest that he should take down the hood of his cloak, and he did.

The blacksmith did not look much like his prototypical namesake. He was small, wiry, beardless, with only the layer of soot covering his gray-ing hair to give away his profession. With eyes already adjusted to the dark room he sized up the two strangers quickly and, in a raspy voice born of harsh fumes he said, "Is there something I can help you with?"

Bird said, "We'd like to see what you have for sale."

The blacksmith shook his head and said, "I send all my stuff to market. The only things I have here are repairs."

She said, "We don't want anything fancy. Maybe you have some prac-tice pieces lying around, or some stuff that an apprentice has worked on?"

It was an odd request, and it made the blacksmith reconsider the two of them. As he did his eyes were drawn to the bit of Bird's armor that was visible between her overhanging cloak. He eyed it just for a moment, thoughtfully, and then said, "Aye. I have an apprentice. My niece. She's got some talent but still has a lot to learn. You don't look like you'll be needing any armor though."

She leaned her head toward Ernest and said, "He'll be needing some, though. And a weapon. Something simple."

The blacksmith shrugged and then gestured with his hand for them to follow him to the far corner of the room. He said, "We can take a look at what she's done." As they shuffled past various tools and workbenches the man looked back at Ernest and continued, "You know, I've had some armor repairs brought in that I fixed and then the people never showed up again to get them. I think one piece in particular might be just your size."

When they reached the forge area they found various armor pieces heaped in piles, along with weapons hung up on iron hooks along both walls. The blacksmith said *this is her station here* as he sifted through one of the armor heaps and tossed a leather based cuirass at Ernest before saying, "Try this one on."

As Ernest ditched his cloak and began wiggling his way into the armor, the blacksmith brought Bird to the neighboring wall where the weapons were. "Most of these are repairs that I expect their owners will be coming back for. But here's something that my niece crafted. One of her more recent ones that might be suitable for your friend."

He handed her a drab-looking arming sword, and Bird took a step back before putting the sword through a series of twists and cuts. When finished she set the sword's hilt in the open palm of her uninjured arm and made a sour face to which the blacksmith said, "I know. It's got about as much balance as a drunken goat, but the steel is strong and the craftmanship is good. Like I said, I send my quality stuff to the market."

Bird nodded and said, "Okay. I'll take it." She glanced over at Ernest who was fidgeting with the armor but appeared comfortable enough and she said, "We'll take the armor too. How much for both?"

The blacksmith appeared unsure for a moment and said, "Lady. I don't want to be rude, but I'd be willing to part with the unbalanced sword and that unremarkable piece of armor if you allow me to have a closer look at what's underneath your cloak. I've been doing this for over thirty years and I could spot the quality in your armor from across the Dialla."

Bird was amused by the man's offer, and she extended her uninjured arm toward the man and they clasped wrists, making it a deal. "If you like the armor, wait until you see what else I have underneath this cloak."

They moved back toward the entrance to the largest workbench in the room, followed by Ernest, who was fidgeting with the latch on his cloak as he attempted to settle it over his new armor. At the bench, Bird swung the body of her cloak around into her healthy arm and unclasped its latch from around her neck, removing it cleanly in one motion and setting it on the bench in a bundle. The blacksmith made an audible gasp at the full sight of the shield and weapons hiding underneath, and he watched in quiet shock as she lifted the shield off her back and, along with the sword and fist weapon, set it on the bench next to the cloak. She said, "I'd prefer to leave the armor on, since it can take some time to get on and off," and the blacksmith nodded dumbly as he stepped over to the shield first. He bent down to eye the shield at its level and then ran his rough hand over the surface, feeling out the minor nicks and scrapes across its sloped surface and, talking half to himself and half to Bird, he said, "I don't believe it. Is this a Satas?"

Bird said, "It is. That and the armor both are. I grew up near his work-shop but the shield and armor were made for my grandfather."

Ernest crept up behind Bird and watched the blacksmith from over her shoulder and he said, "A Satas?"

The blacksmith continued his inspection and never took his eyes off the shield as he spoke reverently and he said, "Satas was the greatest armor-smith ever to live. We call him the father of steel. He wasn't the first to work it, but he whispered to the steel and it whispered back to him and it told him its secrets. His works are not only flawless, but, so perfectly are they crafted that some people believe that there was some magic or enchantment used during their creation."

"Do you believe that?"

"Blacksmiths only believe in iron and steel. You say the armor is one of his as well?" The blacksmith asked as he shuffled over to Bird and began moving around her like a predator, scrutinizing the armor. He muttered affections under his breath at every element inspected and Bird said, "My mother said I was a spitting image of my grandfather, and that's why it fits so well."

The blacksmith said, "It fits perfect. A westerner then?"

"That's right."

"The greatest smiths are always from west Dialla. Always curious to me that those born furthest from iron come to understand it best."

He ran a finger over the latches on the back and asked, "And he customized this here for the shield to hang? It's beautiful. Satas must have admired your grandfather very much to create such a work for him."

Bird shrugged, "He was the best warrior in the area."

The blacksmith went over to the sword on the workbench and picked it up by its bone handle and, like the shield, brought it up inches from his eye as he worked his way around the blade. He let out a soft whistle of appreciation and continued to mutter compliments to the weapon as if it were a token of some higher deity he prayed to. He said, "I'd guess this is either an early Belmonte or a Maxmillian."

"It's a Maxmillian. That and the fist weapon both were made by him during his apprenticeship with Satas."

The blacksmith nodded and eventually moved on to the fist weapon, treating it with every bit of reverence as the previous three. Its frame shown dull in the ember light of the forge, but its claws, even the darkness, glimmered as if the light came from within and the blacksmith said that he had never seen such a weapon and continued, "It looks like an ornament. Do you use it?"

"Often."

He gestured with his head to the two steel vambraces around her wrist and asked, "And those?"

She smiled and said, "I bought these in Pridipoa."

She slid her left hand into the weapon and showed him the knuckle ridge that was designed to catch or parry incoming blades and he nodded and acknowledged the length of the weapon's base and how it went just beyond the bend of the wrist, further supporting the hand and arm. Ernest suggested that it was time to go, and both the blacksmith and Bird agreed. The blacksmith watched as Bird swung the shield into place on her back, followed by her cloak and finally the weapons. With better lighting in the room they might have seen the shallow gleam of tears build in the man's eyes as he watched each piece take its place upon Bird's body and as they said their goodbyes the blacksmith said, "Lady, these are four of the most magnificent pieces of work—of art—that I have ever witnessed in my long life. And to see all of them in the custody of a single person—well, you must be a marvel among marvels."

Bird dipped her head to acknowledge the compliment and Ernest, upon clasping the man's wrist, forced a handful of silver into his hand asked that he give it to his niece, for the sword. They stepped back out into the city's streets, this time their eyes having to adjust to the brightness of the waxing sun. Bird said, "I think you should head out of the west gate and get going. I'll go get the horse and we'll catch up. I still need a new cloak and we need more food." He nodded, pulled the hood of his cloak back over his head, and moved through the city with the sun at his back. The sound of the great market preceded any sight of it, as if an oversized beehive hung around every corner, and when finally he turned the last corner, and moved out of the tight streets, he saw it. Occupying a huge portion of the northwestern side of Camphania, the market was a mix of open-windowed adobe stalls, and wagons that were pulled in to sell wares straight from their beds as merchants and consumers alike bartered noisily over food, seed, furniture, armor, weapons, agricultural tools, livestock, jewelry, clothes, and countless other perceived assets. He pushed his way through the crowds, turning his shoulders and forcing his way through the masses when he needed to, and made his way toward a statue, twice the size of a normal human, that, upon its pedestal, towered over the market goers. The statue was of a short-haired man, older, dressed in Olerian military garb and pointing an unsheathed sword toward the east, and the rising sun. With his cloak still pulled over his head, and with little regard to the people around him, Ernest approached the base of the statue and, upon the plaque of carved marble that was headed with *Ulysses Esco, Conqueror of the Wild Dialla*, he spat a mouthful of herb and saliva so that it splattered across the name and ran down across the inscription before dripping rhythmically into the sand below.

Minutes later he slipped out of the busy west gate, outside of the city's white walls, and began walking west along a well-worn road that had been rutted out by ironbound wagon wheels in a display of erosive force more powerful than any in nature. His body ached and he moved slowly, with Bird and the mare catching up to him while Camphania was still within sight behind them. She said, "You okay?"

"I'm okay."

She took the lead and set a quicker pace and, just after midday, they crested a small rise to see, stretched out ahead of them, a single-wide line of over twenty wagons of various sizes. They descended the rise and heard a sharp whistle come from the area of the last wagon and were greeted by a single woman before they were able to catch up with the end of the line. She was a large woman with short, dark hair, with a bit of armor protruding from under her linen top and a cloak of similar fashion to Ernest and Bird's. The caravan continued crawling ahead of them while they talked and the woman said to them, "Are you two looking to get past us? Do you know about the laws against trailing a caravan?"

Bird said, "We're not looking to pass or trail. We're looking for the caravan master."

"You found her."

"Little man back in town said you could use some more security."

The caravan master eyed the two of them, and Bird pulled her cloak back from off her hips, prompting Ernest to do the same. The master nodded and stepped off to the side of the road where she sat down in the dirt, pulling a satchel from under her cloak and digging into its contents. She spoke as she did so and said, "I wish there were more than two of you, in that case. But fewer security means a better rate for you." She stopped rummaging in the satchel in a second to look at the saddleless mare and asked, "You Copperfoot?"

"Yes."

"Okay. Some caravans pay more for that. We don't."

"That's fine."

The master finally fished out a couple of small linen purses that jingled with silver from the bag and gave one to each of them. "This is one third of your rate." She then handed them each a small piece of cloth that was dyed red and yellow with an odd symbol and continued, "You take this to our building in Torriton to get the rest, once we make it. The symbol there is specific to *this* caravan, so there's no use in running off and trying to reclaim it later. Lot of people try that. Your meals are covered by us. One in the morning and one at night, at the fourth wagon from the front. Water is there too. Your horse is your business, but there's lots of animals here and plenty of merchants will be happy to sell you feed at a fair rate. Where you sleep is also your business. Head of security will come around about the night watch, if he needs you. I have no more spots in or on wagons, but if you prefer to sleep under someone's wagon, you take it up with them. Otherwise, again, that's your business. A group of people is going to do a large fire near the front at night, but if you want to make a fire, make a fire. If there is an attack of any kind and you're seen to be doing anything other than defending this caravan like your life depends on it, it's punishable by hanging. You two look seasoned enough to understand that an attack on this caravan is an attack on your life, anyway—there's no reason to take prisoners all the way out here. Either of you have any questions?"

Bird shook her head and so did Ernest.

"Good. Once we catch back up just take your places among the back few wagons and let's hope for an easy trip and some easy money."

She clasped wrists with the two of them and they caught back up to the final wagon, with the caravan master continuing up ahead and disappearing among the front of the train. Two security on horseback trailed the end of the caravan and gave a wordless nod to them as they walked up next to the third wagon from the rear and settled into the caravan's pace alongside it. It was a medium sized cart, drawn by two horses and owned by two men, a father and son. The father had wild, grey hair sprouting from underneath a wide-brimmed leather hat, with a beard to match, and he explained to the two newcomers that his son was asleep on top of the wares, unseen under the canvas cover. It was a nice wagon—ironbound wheels, springs under the seat—because the man made his living in it. He told them how he had grown up in the Great Plains, but for the last decade had virtually lived on the trade roads between Camphania, moving goods for merchants.

"Little village called Gehane. My wife still lives there. Most people where I'm from grow corn, but I got a soul that likes to move. I've replaced every piece of wood and iron on this wagon—some pieces a couple times over—but it's still the same wagon I started out with over ten years ago." He continued, "I can be a bit of a talker, if you don't mind," and Bird said, "As long as you don't mind that I can be a bit of a mute."

"No, I don't mind that," he said. "It's just the way some people are shaped. My wife tends to be that way, and our son back there probably got more of her in him than me. They say I talk enough for all three of us, but I really can't help it. I like to befriend as much of the security as I can on these caravans—hoping I'll get preferential treatment if things go sideways." He looked at Bird sideways out of his eye but failed to judge any reaction from her. He pointed to the two horses drawing the wagon, left to right, and said, "This here is Fiona, and that one's Buddy. Buddy's been with me since the start, and I got Fiona here as a foal, couple of years back. She's three now and does most of the work as far as I can tell. Buddy's going on thirteen, which means he should still be in his prime, but he's gotten lazy since Fiona came on. Either one of them could handle the wagon alone, but I think having the two extends their work lives. Plus, a lot of the better contracts require you to have two horses—it's a reliability thing. Hell, the contract that I have now requires a two-animal wagon, and you *must* travel with a caravan. That's how you know it's important stuff."

He waited for her to ask, but she didn't, so he said, "It's weapons. Steel by the looks of them. Armies out west are still trying to upgrade from the bronze they have. Hasn't been a lot of steel going out until recently though, because the Olerians have been outfitting themselves with it ever since their fight with the one folk." He snapped his fingers as he tried to come up with the name and she finally spoke and said, "The Copperfoot."

"That's right. The Copperfoot. Always thought that name was funny for them, seeing how they were the lords of steel who have made copper obsolete."

"It's just a nickname."

"How's that?"

"A nickname. They walk everywhere so their feet are always dirty with sand and desert—the color of copper."

"Huh. I never understood that. But I don't like it very much, as far as nicknames go. Is that your horse there? She's a pretty one—could be related to Fiona if I didn't know any better."

Ernest pulled himself away from the talkative driver and began making his way up the lumbering caravan line, having never seen one up close before, and what he saw was a linear migration of commerce and humanity. Wagons varied in size from nine feet in length to twice that, with the smaller ones being pulled by goats and donkeys, and the larger by horses and the rare oxen. There were little schooners packed with single families and all that they owned, looking forward to a new home or running away from an old one. There were minor merchants with overpacked carts, noisily jostling down the rough road. And there were large carriages, too ornate for the use of canvas, crafted out of iron and wood from the bottom up, that housed the wealthiest civilians and merchants.

Between many of the wagons were people that shuffled along on foot and in stride with the moving caravan. They were not security—he and Bird appeared to be the only ones of that class that were not on horseback—and they were not merchants either. Instead, they looked to carry all that they owned in large, canvas bags strapped across their backs and, with their heads dipped against the heat of the sun and whatever sand was kicked up by the wagon wheels ahead of them, Ernest suspected that their lives were stories that could illuminate the human condition but would never be told. Among those walking, there were at least twenty people with a different look than the downtrodden migrants. They moved along in a tight, circle formation around three donkeys that were laden with supplies and they all wore the same linen robes dyed a fiery orange color. He walked parallel to them, across the caravan row, and watched them for several minutes, but other than their peculiar garb, they did nothing more that was interesting, and he moved on. Apart from the orange robes, the same details repeated themselves time and time again over the course of more than two dozen wagons, until he neared the front and saw the caravan master, high on a spring seat, from the lead vehicle. He stepped off to the side of the road, sat on a rock, and drank from his waterskin until Bird and the final wagons rolled by. The old man with the wild hair was still talking—about the best foods in each region—with his son now sitting next to him in the driver's seat.

"Ah, there's your friend. Told you he couldn't have gotten far. Listen I need to get down and stretch my legs, if one of you needs a break and wants to take my seat up here for a bit."

"That's not necessary," Bird said. "I should be having a look around."

Ernest didn't hesitate. He said, "I'll take it."

She stepped off the road, followed by the mare, and the two of them walked south, away from the caravan, where they paralleled and shadowed its movement from within eyesight out in the desert. When they got more than a hundred paces out, Bird stopped for a minute and donned the arm sling and she walked on in hot silence for the rest of the afternoon. As dusk settled in, she heard a loud whistle come from the front of the caravan and saw the line come to a slow halt. Bird gestured to the mare with her head toward the caravan and as they walked back to it she went to the front and got them food. She filled her waterskin too and made her way back to Ernest and the old man, who had gone with his son to the front of the caravan for their own food.

Ernest was sitting up against the wheel of the wagon and offered an appreciative nod to her as she approached with the food. She sat next to him and he said, "I never knew a man to talk so much—and the questions."

"What questions?"

"About being Copperfoot."

"Like what?"

"Nothing. I think he was just messing with me."

"What were the questions?"

"Just the usual shit—wanted to know if a Copperfoot was allowed to ride things other than horses. Like donkeys or some other animals he was making up.

"What animals?"

"A camel? Something like that."

She laughed and said, "A camel isn't a made up animal. I've seen them in the far south. Beyond the Great Plains."

"Now you're starting up with this?"

"He wasn't messing with you, you knave. A camel is a real thing."

"Yeah? Then what's it look like?"

"It's like the size of a horse, but it's furry-looking instead. They got these big humps on their backs."

"Hell, that's exactly what he said."

"Because that's what a camel is."

"So you two are in on this together?"

"Are we in on knowing what a camel is? Shit, I guess we might be."

"You two got a real sense of humor, picking on a guy like me."

"The only thing that's funny is you knowing about as much about the world as a farm goat."

Ernest shook his head, unsure of the truth, and he said, "Anyway, enduring all the old man's talking paid off—he said that we could sleep under their wagon if we prefer. Him and his son sleep up top. Either way it'll be a good spot to rest and eat. Just don't start talking to that old camel or he might just talk us through the night and we'll never get to sleep."

"Don't worry about that," she said. "I'm a real natural when it comes to disrespecting the elderly."

They ate in silence until he said, "Do you know of any group, religious maybe, that wears orange robes? A rope tied around the waist?"

"Orange robes? Doesn't sound familiar to me. Why?"

"There's a bunch of them with the caravan. Almost twenty, maybe more, all walking."

She shrugged and they split up as they neared the caravan, with her heading toward the mess wagon and him and the mare toward the caravan's rear. He exchanged nothing more than a wordless nod with the talkative driver before ditching his pack to the dirt and finding a seat, leaning up against the wagon's back wheel. The mare sidled up to where he sat and dipped her head toward his, allowing him to stroke her muzzle while they waited for Bird to return.

With all the ingredients still fresh from Camphania, the food was good—tortillas, beans, corn, and masa—and they drank so much water that, with the sun going down, Bird walked back to the front in the darkness to refill both of their skins. When she returned with the water, she also carried a bundle of wood underneath her good arm and he asked her, "What's that?"

"One of the merchants down there sold me a fire. And I saw the master and she said that one of us needs to take a graveyard shift tonight at the rear. I got no problem doing it, so if you wake up and you don't see me, you'll know where I am."

They ate with a speed that revealed their true level of hunger, and the sun went down and Bird stacked up the lumber in a cone several feet from the wagon and the two of them sat against the wheel, watching the birth of flames while the mare disappeared into the darkness. He was too tired to sleep and he quietly stared into the fire as time dragged on and his eyes and mind grew drowsy. Bird rose to add wood to keep it alive and looked down the line and mumbled something and Ernest said, "What?"

"I said the master wasn't kidding about the fire they make at the front. It's burning taller than me standing here."

"Might be that somebody down there is afraid of the dark."

She sat back down, and the full dark of night set in on the world and the fires along the caravan shown like a simple, tiny constellation. He continued to drowse from his sitting position and was just nodding off to sleep when he heard a figure shuffle out in the sand just beyond the fire's light and, when he noted Bird was unalarmed by the figure, he relaxed to see one of the orange-robed figures breach their illumed circle. The newcomer offered them a nod and then squatted to sit on his heels with his elbows at rest on each of his bent knees. He was hairless except for his eyebrows with an unusually pale complexion given the daily intensity of the sun in the region. He introduced himself as a disciple of some religion they had never heard of before and they both acknowledged his introduction but said nothing and he waited for several silent moments, expecting more from them, but they gave nothing. He invited them over to the caravan's large bonfire, but Bird spoke up to decline his offer. She told him that their own fire performed well enough. The disciple agreed that it did and then asked them if they knew the origin of this world and the gift of the sun from Koomakul. They did not, and without further prompting he told them: many eons ago there were two planets that orbited each other—this planet and its twin sister—both shrouded in absolute darkness, but if not for Koomakul, the god of fire, who brought magma up from deep in the earth and, by way of its fire, gave to humans their first light. For the first time in their existence, they did not have to flail blindly through darkness, and color was given to their previously colorless eyes. Koomakul was generous in this way, only asking in return that the humans worship him accordingly, and they did, for a time. As generations passed, however, the unanimity with which Koomakul was revered began to wane. False gods were created by the humans and attributed with the gift of fire, and some went so far as to claim that there were no gods responsible for any of it, and that the fire was brought up from the earth by its own natural mechanisms. This happened on both planets, for it is the nature of the human to behave this way to deities, and Koomakul, though a god, did not understand this yet. War raged among the humans on both worlds. Every sect and spinoff thereof, killing in the name of so many names, and killing in the name of no name at all. On this planet, deep in the ancestral past of every living human, enough of the chosen people lived to carry on the devotion and truth of Koomakul that this planet was spared. But this was not so for the twin sister. On that planet, those that carried the truth of Koomakul lost the war and were killed. With no vessel to pass on the truth of his greatest gift, Koomakul turned his attention to the planet in a fury. He summoned the magma again, until every volcano and every crack in the world exploded with fire and, even as the surviving humans with their false prophets fell to their knees at the display, Koomakul's anger only grew hotter, until the entire planet was consumed by fire and rage, and our sun was born.

The disciple said, "Our own world baths in Koomakul's light now because of the faults of our sisters and brothers. Every day is a reminder of Koomakul's mercy, and every night a reminder of the darkness we were born in."

He looked between their expressionless faces and Ernest spoke for the first time to say, "And you and your people walk the caravans, telling this story?"

"Not at all. Me and the other chosen people that I travel with are on a blessed sojourn to Mount Ucari in Kardona."

Bird said, "That sojourn sounds more cursed than blessed. Do you know there's a civil war going on in Kardona right now? It's not exactly a safe place to do a pilgrimage."

The man nodded his head and said, "Pilgrimages are about doing what is necessary, not what is safe. Of course, we know about the war. Human armies waging war with each other over false gods? I believe this civil war is the reason for Koomakul's anger and thus why the mountain wakes. If we don't make it to the mountain then this entire world might go the way of its sister."

Bird rolled her eyes when Ernest stole a glance at her and he said, "Assuming you make it there, you just toss a couple of sacrificial people in and save all of our lives?"

"We have no intention to hurt anybody. We will perform some rituals on the mountain to show Koomakul that his children are alive and well in this world and continue to work to glorify his name and what he has done for all people. The more people that do this, the more pleased he will be. Therefore, I'm talking to you now and to anybody else that will listen. Will you come to the mountain with us?"

"It's a nice story, friend, but we have a different place to be."

"Very well. If your circumstances change, you will find us on the southern face of Mount Ucari."

He stood from his crouching position and retreated into the night from which he came, and out of the halo of the light, his skin, his robe, his features, were all swallowed by darkness and he looked like any other human might look, blindly voyaging through the world's shadow on his way back to the superfluous bonfire at the front of the caravan.

Ernest was asleep within minutes of the disciple leaving, still sitting up against the wheel and snoring softly. Bird stood long enough to take her shield off her back and then crawled under the wagon to sleep. She laid on her side with her head on her pack, using her cloak as a blanket, and then set the shield so it leaned on and covered her torso. She watched the dying fire for a little longer before drifting off, and she dreamed of angry fire elementals that worked tirelessly in the heart of some planet, pushing their fire forever to the surface, in the hopes of consuming the little creatures who stole it from them.

She woke in the middle of the night to find Ernest exactly as she left him, and their fire reduced to a small pile of embers. After crawling out from under the wagon, she put her shield back in its place and slunk off into the dark night to do her watch. The air was dry and cold, with a steady wind coming out of the southeast and pulling her cloak tight against her body and her slinged arm. Understanding how rare night attacks were—no sane person liked fighting in the dark—she did one lap, at distance, around the caravan and then found a perch to sit and watch, while she massaged her injured elbow for the rest of the night. The sun rose out of the east, announced by a deep purple and then a smear of orange that came like a small fire set at the edge of the world. She watched it until the horizon turned a hazy grey and the sun's orb rose, visible, like some reflection of itself and she returned to the caravan for breakfast.

The mare was already there, and they ate and the three of them took their place along the caravan again as it rustled to life. It was a windy morning, with the majority of people pulling their cloaks up over their heads to protect from the biting sand, but there were reprieves too, on the downslopes of the landscape as it rolled gently west, like a faintly tousled blanket. By the afternoon the wind had abated, and the road flattened out briefly before, for the first time, they caught sight of the Badlands.

Unlike much of the Dialla, where sand gusted and settled haphazardly across a surface of hardened rock, the Badlands were predominately a sea of sand. As if a world's worth of beaches was dumped into one region, the Badlands nestled itself up against the Omoya mountain range on the west, and the former Eporisia empire on the east, the waters of Koos Bay to the north, and spilled out along the trade routes to the south. Offering nothing in the way of resources and being brutally inhospitable, even by Dialla standards, the Badlands had, through history, never been properly claimed by any of the region's powers—a perpetually ignored and discarded area. However, it was this reputation that made the area appeal to cutthroats and highway robbers alike, and various, notorious gangs had taken up residence in the canyons and caves that were rumored to exist somewhere in the heart of the dunes. The most recent, and deadly, of these gangs was known by the moniker the Crimson Shrouds. Their early criminal activity suggested nothing special—a small band of men and women, on foot, that would hide along the trade routes and ambush passing wagons. But their tactics matured, and when one of their early scores contained a wagon full of fine, red, silk cloth, the next time they attacked a wagon they did so in uniform, wearing the silk as shrouds around their heads. The desolated state of the Badlands didn't matter to them, because they took all that they needed from passing traders and disappeared into the dunes with it. In time they had stolen enough horses to do raids on horseback, and as their reputation for debauchery grew, so too did their numbers. Merchants rarely decided to travel trade routes alone anymore, often deciding to pay the fees to join a caravan, but the power of the Crimson Shrouds had grown enough that even a caravan of thirty wagons was reasonable prey. As Oleria continued to ignore the problem, not willing to sacrifice Olerian lives to protect merchant profits, traders tried to take the matter into their own hands by organizing even larger caravans and pitching in on professional security. The frequency of attacks went down, and most agreed that the large caravan co-ops were an effective deterrent, though many suspected that the Crimson Shrouds had amassed such a wealth that they no longer had the need for frequent raids.

The edge of the Badland's came up just paces away from the road, its golden sand starting off in smaller dunes that, as they extended north, grew larger and larger until they loomed like an ever-morphing mountain range above the caravan. An intangible silence came over the wagons in the shadow of the dunes, all of them understanding the danger that they signaled, and Bird and Ernest kept their spot near the rear of the caravan and the talkative driver. Just after midday they heard the same sharp whistle come from the front of the caravan and in a few moments the whole line slowed to a stop. A nervous murmur of voices echoed down the line to their wagon, and the talkative merchant sent his son off the wagon to relay the message down to the end. Ernest spoke up to him and said, "What's going on?"

"There's a caravan coming from the other way."

"What's that mean?"

"Means we got to make way. Roads not wide enough for both, so we'll do one wheel on, one wheel off, and they'll do the same. Slows us down a little but it's not an issue. Happens all the time."

It took some time to offset the entire caravan line, coaxing the animals to awkwardly straddle the hardtop of the road and the drifts of sand just off it, but soon enough they were crawling along again, at a much slower pace. When the front of the other caravan began passing Ernest and Bird, it looked to them like a mirror image of their own, only dirtier. At points the animals passing each other in such close proximity caused a hiccup in the caravan's movement, as drivers worked to calm their startled animals, but the other caravan was small—almost half the size of their own—and it wasn't long before the last wagon in their line moved past and was gone without a word. As the drivers directed their animals back onto the road they were held up again, and Bird, standing off to the side and looking up the line, said, "Ah, shit."

"What now?" Ernest said.

"I can't tell. Some wagon up there is all cockeyed off the road. Looks stuck maybe."

"Do they pay us for that?"

"No, but this is a bad place to linger."

"Okay."

It was one of the smallest wagons in the caravan, drawn by a single horse, and captained by a single merchant who, as they approached, was whipping and cursing at the frustrated animal from his seat. The problem was with the rear wheels that had been caught in a drift of sand when the wagon had apparently gone too far off the road, and from the handful of people mustered around the wagon, Ernest and Bird gathered that the horse had been spooked by a snake. It took some time to get enough people behind the wagon to push it out, while the driver, in his anger and embarrassment, whipped the panicked horse relentlessly. With the wagon finally back up on the road, the angry driver—a tall, thick man—stepped down to check the integrity of the wagon's mechanics. He finished by inspecting the rear axle and, when he walked to the front to take his seat again, he was met by a pair of dusty strangers—an athletic woman with dark hair, and behind her a man with peppered hair and ill-fitting armor protruding from under his cloak.

"Yeah?"

The woman said, "I was just taking a look at your horse here," and gestured to the strokes of red, agitated skin where it was whipped.

"And?"

"It's only natural for a horse to be scared of a snake."

"It's nothing but a stupid, fucking animal that deserved every lash I gave."

"Listen to this one, Ernest. He's got a hand like an ogre and a tongue like a serpent." She took a step closer to him and before the man could register her movement she had a sword in her right hand pointed at his heart and with her cloak pulled back he could see the wicked fist weapon hanging from her belt on the other side. She spoke in a low voice to him and said,

"Listen here. If I see you needlessly whipping that horse again, I'll cut off that fucking hand of yours and I'll plunge it so far down your fucking throat that not one honest person walking this planet will ever hear that nasty tongue of yours form another word."

The man was visibly shaken, but he stood his ground and his lower lip bulged out in defiance of the young woman and, with a twinge of shaking in his voice he said, "It's *my* horse."

She said, "Aye, the horse is yours, but if there were any justice in this world, then no musty goat turd such as yourself would be allowed to own any property, let alone a living thing. And since the only thing you know how to do with that property is abuse it, I'm going to be that justice. I'll be watching you. And you can go tell the caravan master and whatever security it is you got, but if there's ten of them, you'll think there's twenty of me. I'll cut off every shriveled cock that stands between me and you and I'll make you hurt, and I'll make you bleed, and after I've stuffed that vile hand down your throat, I'll harness you to the front of your own wagon over there and whip your sorry ass until you're dead."

She spat at the man's feet before sheathing her sword and walking away from him. Ernest let her go without saying anything and then he pointed at the man for just a moment before turning and following Bird back to the rear of the caravan.

That night Bird built another fire for the two of them, encouraged by the caravan master who wanted as many fires as possible, hoping to swell their strength in the eyes of any Crimson Shroud that may be watching from the darkness. Even with a night watch ahead of them, the two stayed up in the presence of the fire, long after the mare had disappeared into the night and the wind died down and the stars above shone through the polluted light of the fire as if it wasn't there at all, and the sound of him spitting being the only sound.

"You know," he said. "I hired you to protect me from enemies—not create a bunch of new ones out of every son of a bitch that crosses our path."

"What enemies?"

"Those horse poachers."

"They're all dead."

"The driver earlier, with the horse."

"A man like that is only dangerous to those weaker than him, and we don't qualify."

"Chances are that there will be more."

"Which is why you hired me."

He shook his head and spat directly into the flames of the fire while their reflection danced lucidly in her dark pupils. The figures of other security and more of the orange-robed zealots passed by in the night outside the range of their fire but nobody stopped and nobody talked to them. They sat on in silence, except for the sound of him spitting, and eventually he dug the spent herb out of his cheek, flung it into the night, and went into his bag to replace it with more. He snapped the saliva and herb residue from his fingertips and, looking at Bird sitting across from him, he said, "I have a serious question for you."

"Okay."

"I'm serious."

"I heard you."

"It takes some build up."

"Just get on with it."

"Okay. Our people have a reputation as great fighters. Even now among the Olerians and in Kardona and toward the Great Plains—the word is out and all are in agreement that they wouldn't want to come face to face with a Copperfoot warrior." She nodded and he continued, "It wasn't until I was an adult, and the war was over, and I lived in Pridipoa that I realized that all those years I was living among real masters. And it made me think back to the people I've seen fight over the years and to the two times I've seen you in action—at the fort and then with the poachers—and I'm sure I've never witnessed anybody fight the way that you do."

"That's not a question."

"Okay. You're not going to bite—are you the best?"

She arched both of her eyebrows in an expression of surprise, though he didn't know at what and he said, "Is that an offense to ask?"

"No. I'm just surprised at the question."

"Why?"

"I've never thought about it."

"Really?"

"Really. But I'm thinking about it now and I'm not sure I could explain it."

"I'd be interested if you could."

"Okay, I'll try." She was silent for a few more moments and more figures skirted the darkness around them and to the south a distant howl of wolves sounded in the distance. She looked reflexively for the mare before remembering she was out for the night and then she started talking. "For most skills, being the best is a matter of consistency—a lot of people can be good, but the person who can be good, more often, ends up being the best. The best general doesn't have to win every single battle as long as they win the war. The best merchant doesn't have to be profitable in every transaction as long as they come out ahead in the big picture. The best farmer can lose a crop and, though it makes times hard, can make ends meet to see another season. Almost all talents and skills survive by a code of consistency. But in the warrior code, consistency means nothing—only perfection. This is why your question is so difficult to answer."

She held up both of her arms parallel to the ground, one at chin height and the other at her torso and when she shook the shoulder-high one she said *this is perfection*. And she shook the torso one and said *this is death*. "Everything in between these two is the infinite variations of consistency that most live by—terrible, bad, decent, good, better—but for a warrior there are only two things: perfection and death. You can't have a terrible warrior. A terrible warrior is just a dead warrior and thus no warrior at all. So, through this view there can be no best in this world because every person right now who lives by the sword and is still alive is perfect. We're all perfect up until we're all dead. We're all the best otherwise we wouldn't be here."

She paused here and he said nothing and she continued, "If I were going to try to answer your question more directly, maybe in the spirit in which it was offered, I would ask myself if I've ever fought anybody that I was afraid of. I know that if I'm feeling fear then I'm feeling the possibility of death—that I need to be perfect."

"And have you?"

"Yes. There have been a few times that I've been afraid of the person I was up against. I felt the fear, but it is fine to feel fear so long as you don't let it talk to you. Once you let it start talking then it becomes a distraction. Much more often I don't feel the fear though, only the focus. And even those that were perfect enough to scare me? Once I settled in it was only my focus that I felt and it was me that walked away alive and not them, and so, to answer your question in this way: Yes, I am the best and I've never met anybody better than me."

He nodded and spat and then thanked her for what he called a *thorough* answer. She found a place under the wagon like the night before, and he stayed out next to the fire again until the wind picked up in the middle of the night so much that he crawled under too, looking for cover. She woke him with the sky still full dark and wind howling and told him it was time for their watch. "I'd let you sleep and take care of it myself, but I think tonight we should take no risks."

He agreed, wordlessly with bloodshot eyes, and packed for travel. She told him to just stay close to her and led them into the sand dunes where they patrolled the north and east sides of the caravan. They only spoke once, with her instructing him not to skylight himself on certain rises and passed an uneventful early morning until the purple sun rose like a spell out of the east. The wind calmed when they returned to the caravan and they had breakfast, joined by the mare, as the sky blossomed into sapphire and settled sublimely over the world. The caravan came to life and began to move with the same anxious atmosphere as the day before and, like before, they settled in beside the wagon of the talkative driver who spent the morning mumbling some endless monologue to his son next to him. As if the wind the day before had blown all excess matter from the sky, Ernest noticed the Omoya mountain range to the north and west for the first time, stretching away from them to the where Koos Bay collided with the Great Water. Today's was a crystal clear heat, dry and empty as if the desert itself were the untouched pagan soul of some being that spent the eons of its existence in conflict with moisture.

Ernest continued looking at the distant mountains as he walked. The Omoyas didn't hold the elevation necessary to have the year-round snow coverage that many of the peaks in the Echoras did, but they were still formidable in size, and their dense vegetation on the rainy, west slope made life difficult for travelers, though there were few. Running into the coast, flanked by the Badlands, and stretching only a couple hundred miles south, almost all travelers from the Dialla area opted to stick to the trade roads until bypassing the entire range at its southern tip and then going into Kardona north, up the coast. Understanding how plush with vegetation and life the west side of the range was, Ernest marveled at the visible east side, in all its barren glory, towering above the even more sterile Badlands below.

It was as Ernest looked distractedly at the mountain range beyond that something in his peripheral caught his attention. Atop one of the larger sand dunes, between his line of sight and the mountains, he saw a lone figure on horseback. The figure was far enough away, several hundred paces north of the caravan's line, to cloud any details and he walked on a few more steps, his brain telling him it was one of the caravan's many security. Walking just a couple of strides behind Bird and the mare, though he could not put to words what was wrong, alarm bells began sounding in his head. He stopped walking and said, "Bird."

She turned around and waited for him to continue, but he only gestured with his chin toward where he was looking and she stopped too, along with the mare, and followed his gaze to the top of the dune. Just as her eyes found the distant figure, the lone rider donned a bright red headpiece and was joined by a handful of other riders, in matching attire, that appeared from behind the crest of the dune to take their places next to the first one. It dawned on Bird what was happening just as the sharp whistle came from the front of the wagon and she muttered, "Oh, fuck."

A bell began ringing from the area of the front wagon, and then a horn blew from the same place, bringing the caravan to life with their sound. Two wagons further up the line pulled out of the formation and attempted to race west into the desert, with the first one disappearing from Ernest's sight in a cloud of dust and the second moving too fast off the road, tilting the wagon until it flipped on its side and sent the driver and his goods crashing to the desert floor, along with the two goats that were still awkwardly harnessed to the yoke. The attackers now appeared in force, at least fifty riders perched at the crest of the large dune in a single, horizontal line, parallel to the caravan's own. Every one of them donned a headpiece of crimson color and they were all of them still for several moments, like a predator eyeing prey that had caught a trace of its scent. Without a sound, they started their descent down the face of the dune in unison, all riders sending neat plumes of sand in their wake until the plumes merged into one massive smog that followed the riders and their crimson crowns down the dune like a scene out of some pagan religion's origin story.

Merchants scrambled around their wagons—some arming themselves and others hiding among their wares, waiting for their fate to be decided in the battle to come. The mare galloped south into the desert, and Bird darted over to Ernest, snapping her fingers under his nose to redirect his attention from the approaching attackers and said, "Hey, hey. Listen."

"Huh? Yeah."

"Pack on the ground, now. Water down too. Keep your cloak on as long as you think it doesn't hinder you."

He scrambled to follow her direction and she continued, "Get your bow out. Arrows are good? You can reach them quickly? Only use the sword as a last resort. I've seen you fight."

He nodded, shedding off his supplies and gear until he had only the small cavalry bow, its quiver on his leg, and the unbalanced sword held in his belt. She said, "Just south of the road, up ahead, you see it? The rocks? Get as high as you can. Shoot that fucking bow if you think you can help, otherwise just hide. You'll get yourself killed trying to do much more. You got it?"

He nodded and she said *go quick* and he ran toward the outcrop of rock as the Shrouds neared the bottom of the large dune's slope and began their approach, with only a couple of small, wavy dunes standing between them and the scrambling caravan. Bird had shed her nonessential gear along with Ernest, ditching her cloak along in the sand with their packs, giving her access to the shield latched on her back. Her left arm was still swollen and aching, but the rush of adrenaline began to work its numbing effect on it. The son of the talkative driver was in the back of his wagon, with a sword lying at his feet and struggling to slip on an iron cuirass while his dad was at the front of the wagon with the horses, working to keep them calm.

Bird approached the son on the wagon and spoke quickly to him, "You guys are hauling weapons, right?"

He shook his head at her and said, "We can't do that."

She responded with the nastiest scowl she could summon and he nodded back and said, "You're right."

She jumped into the back of the wagon with him as the first sound of battle echoed from the front of the caravan, archers on horseback from both sides sending their first volley at each other, followed closely by cries of war and pain in equal parts. The weapons in the wagon were wrapped in canvas bundles, and she tossed aside some of the smaller bundles on top to reveal ones underneath that were longer than she was tall. She slipped her sword out of her belt in one smooth motion, cut a line down the wrapped canvas, and sheathed her sword again before falling to her knees to tear the canvas the full length of the wrapped weapons. It was a bundle of six well-crafted poleaxes, with polished ironwood shafts a head taller than her that were capped by iron that was crafted into a broad axehead on one side and a serrated mallet on the other, topped with a dague the length of her forearm. She shook one free and handed it to the driver's son who said, "I don't know how to use this."

"Just swing it at the bad guys. That sword of yours isn't going to do shit all against horseback."

Bird jumped off the rear of the wagon and pulled the bundle of poleaxes after her, making them land in the dirt with a puff of sand. "If you don't want to fight, then try to get these in any pair of usable hands that you can find." She grabbed one of the long weapons for herself and jogged toward the front of the caravan line, opposite the oncoming attackers, while looking for Ernest in the rock outcrop, but she did not see him. She made it three more wagons down when the attack reached the caravan, a loud metallic crash rang out as the line of riders arrived simultaneously. Those attackers that weren't met by security or an armed merchant, shot through gaps in the wagons, passing to the other side and immediately creating guerilla chaos. The sound of the melee grew louder until it encompassed the front half of wagons, where the yelling was constant and a cloud of dust and sand, kicked up by all the commotion, enveloped the caravan like an unwashed fog. The unarmed civilians that were on foot came out of the haze, retreating past Bird in various stages of urgency, and behind them came her first real look at one of the crimson-hooded warriors.

Riding on the back of a stout draft horse, and with a head completely shrouded in a bright red wrap, Bird could only guess at the gender of the warrior. The rider was thin, with a long, scimitar styled sword, and the dull glint of iron armor showing from under a loose fit tunic. Bird thought she

may have lost the element of surprise, but the rider appeared wholly focused on running down the fleeing civilians, occasionally leaning off the
horse's saddle to hack at those in retreat. Bird used the distraction to slip in
between the front and back of two of the wagons in the caravan, watching
the rider charge up the line in her direction, and she shifted the poleaxe
in her grip and bounced it lightly on her palms to find the weapon's balance. The rider never saw her. Closing hard on another fleeing victim, the
rider was leaning toward the caravan, sword arm drawn back, when Bird
stepped from between the wagons and, putting her entire body—including
her lame elbow—behind it, swung the mallet side of her weapon into the
rider's chest. Not even the rapid collision of iron weapon on iron armor
was loud enough to cover the sound of the rider's torso shattering under
the force of the blow, that, with a sickening crunch, sent the rider spinning
violently into the dirt. A shot of pain fired through Bird's elbow at impact
and she checked it to make sure it hadn't displaced again while she stood
over the broken body of the fallen warrior, who wheezed out their final,
painful breaths at her feet. More migrants flooded past her, and on the other
side of the caravan another Shroud rode up the line, firing an arrow at her
that went quivering like a taught string into the side of the wagon between
them. She was nearly run over by the next rider that came charging out of
the dust cloud, and she had to determine whether or not it was worth it to
keep using the poleaxe, understanding that reinjuring her arm now would
be a death sentence. Before she could decide, yet another horse was bearing
down on her and she hoisted the weapon, leading with its dague, aiming it at
the charging Shroud. The rider leaned away from her, avoiding the skewer,
and just narrowly missed trampling her. She darted back into the wagons,
and, as another arrow thudded into the wood just inches from her, she could
feel the situation spiraling out of control—she could feel the fear. More caravan migrants retreated past her, most bloody and dirty, one collapsing near
her position between the wagons with two arrow shafts protruding from
his lower back. One horse, coal black, raced by riderless and trampled one
of the fleeing merchants. At the sound of another approaching horse she
braced herself, but it was one of the caravan's security, gashed at the neck
and slumping on the galloping horse for a dozen more paces before sliding
off the animal's back and landing dead on the ground.

Feeling like a wild beast getting corralled to the slaughter, Bird turned
desperate and did something she never imagined that she would. When the
next rider came riding up the line she made no attempt to snipe the rider,
but instead swung the axe-side of the polearm horizontally, cleanly cleaving
through the horse's front, right leg, sending horse and rider crashing to the
ground.

The horse let out a sickening squeal, as a bright red spout of arterial blood shot from its amputated leg. The horse shuttered for a moment before trying to get back to its feet, sending it plunging back to the earth in a bloody mess. Bird dropped the poleaxe to finish off the dazed rider with her sword and then turned her attention to the flailing horse. With tears in her eyes she picked up the poleaxe and brought it down mercifully on the horses neck, further darkening the immediate ground with its blood. Even with the threat of imminent death, she lost the focus. Hard as she tried she couldn't keep tears from coming to her eyes and her elbow felt on fire again and she stalked further up the caravan with the retrieved poleaxe in hand, eventually hurling it at rider, taking them cleanly off their horse. She pressed on toward the main bout with only her sword drawn in her uninjured arm— her other hanging limply from her shoulder. A shrouded figure danced out of the dust cloud on foot, and she put him through a series of motions with just the sword before driving it into his left lung. Dust flew into her eyes, further obscuring her vision, and with her mind clouded by images of the horse slain by her hands, she barely registered the approaching shadow, and the charging horse that it signified. The animal's muscular breast made full contact with her right shoulder and head, sending her flying half a dozen feet into a wagon, where she crumpled into the dirt, and everything went black.

ERNEST SAW ALMOST ALL OF it. He made it to the rock outcrop before the wave of attackers made first contact, where he let off two poorly fired arrows before their skirmish with the caravan's security made the area too messy for him to shoot at. Without bothering to notch another arrow, Ernest leaned up against the east side of a large sandstone slab and looked for Bird back where they separated. His leg jittered nervously as he filtered through the distant figures, unable to find her, until he saw the passing crimson rider get unseated by the violent mallet swing. He pumped an excited fist and said out loud to himself, "Where in the shit did she find that?"

With the enemy warriors, in their shrouds of crimson, being so easy to discern from the caravan's security, Ernest could tell at a glance that the fight was not going well. His flight instinct urged him to run, but Bird was still alive, and with his water and pack back with the caravan, the reasonable part of his brain was equally pessimistic about retreating. He continued to follow Bird as she moved up the caravan, holding his breath each time a rider went charging past her. When she stepped back between the wagons again, he could hardly see her and thought that she was hit by one of the many stray arrows. He was momentarily relieved when he saw her step out again, until he saw her slay the horse.

"Oh, shit."

He closed his eyes as her killing blow descended toward the horse's neck, unable to watch, and when he opened them again, even with the distance between them, could see that she was not right. He continued speaking out loud to himself, urging her to move, as she stood like a scarecrow over the horse's corpse. When she finally did, he said *good girl, now get out of there,* but he knew something was wrong. Her sword was out, but she didn't reach for her shield or for her fist weapon, as she should, and instead lumbered toward the heart of the battle unprepared. All of the kicked-up dust made it hard to see her, but he saw the horse charging toward her and his breath left him as he saw her figure thrown violently into the side of one the merchant wagons. *No.* Her body didn't offer one sign of life and, as though in a trance, he stepped from behind the slab, staring at her fallen body and instinctually moving toward her to help. More of the crimson riders appeared in the area around her body, as the battle appeared settled in favor of the attackers, with only small pockets of resistance still being put up by the merchants and their security, and any chance at a rescue appeared impossible. He decided to return to the outcrop, hide, and figure out a plan from there, but as he turned back he glanced east, down the caravan line, and saw a pair of crimson riders idling on their horses, with one of them appearing to look his way. They were too far away for him to tell if he was spotted, so Ernest darted over to the outcrop and peeked out in the direction of the two riders. The one was still looking his way and now the other pulled his horse so that it too was facing him.

"Shit all," Ernest said.

He pushed off the rock and started running as fast as he could, south into the desert. It became quickly apparent why the road had been established where it was, as the land quickly devolved from the level, solid pathway to a landscape of discarded sandstone slabs and minor gullies bedecked with cacti and numerous species of palo verde that demanded a detour every dozen steps. It was not favorable horse country, and as he pulled himself, sweating, over the lip of one of the gullies, narrowly missing planting his hand in a cactus plant, he held out hope that the riders would not bother following him in. Too afraid to look back, he pushed himself southward into the heat, and he checked the position of the sun in vain, knowing that darkness was too far away and time was no ally. When he encountered another small gully he got sloppy in his haste, and went tumbling a dozen feet down its gravel slope. He felt a pain on his left hip and looked to see that the fall had jammed the end of one of his quivered arrows into his upper thigh.

There was a small spot of blood from what he could see, but he just cursed, and his adrenaline and fear fueled him forward.

When he crested to the next low anticline he hunched over with his hands to his knees and breathed loudly into a wind that settled in headlong from the east. The layer of sweat that covered his body began taking on the dirt and the dust of the living land until it dried and cracked upon him like a fragile and limitless armor, and there he breathed like some golem newly risen out of the earth coming to terms with this sentience. Before his breathing could settle the two riders appeared on the ridge behind him, not more than a quarter mile and they froze at the sight of him and he too, the loose ends of their shrouds being tossed by the new breeze. He still didn't move, unsure of what they could see, but after a moment they descended the near side of their ridge and made toward his position and he ran again.

The land remained uniformly rough. The leather sole of his sandal steadily scraped over rocks and loose gravel as he navigated his way around even more dense shrubs and cacti. The small leather quiver began to rub on his outer thigh as he pushed on and when he stopped again for another rest he removed the bow from across his chest and tested its ability to act as a walking stick. Its short length made it too awkward to be effective. When he hung the string back over his torso, he did so as he looked back at the top of the hill from which he had just descended. No riders yet. He removed the quiver completely this time to reveal that his pants were blood-stained from the hip to the knee, the injury sustained in the fall appearing more serious than he understood.

He tossed the quiver into some nearby sagebrush and removed his linen pants. The blood came from a cut from high on his thigh where the fletching-end of an arrow had lodged itself briefly. The penetration of the cut appeared shallow, but the exertion of the chase had moved an amount of blood through the wound that belied its minor nature. The location of the wound made it difficult for him to figure out any kind of effective wrap in the short time and so he left it exposed. Because he was overheating anyway, he kept the pants off and instead cut into them with the tip of one of his own arrows and tore away the bottom half of the pant legs. He kept an eye to the hill behind him while he deftly removed his sandals, wrapped his feet in the torn linen, and got the sandals back on over the makeshift socks. He took what was left of his pants and loosely tied them around his neck and carried the remaining arrows—five in total—in his left hand.

He pressed on, several times checking the empty air that floated absently between the sun and the rim of the planet that would bring with it darkness and a chance to hide from his pursuers, and he shook his head. Not enough time. No night to hide in. No cool breeze. He moved on and when he peaked atop the next shallow hill, he saw the two riders again. This time they didn't stop when they summited but instead moved down its slope and purposefully toward him. He looked around him and he hung his head in a pose of those conquered. Who knows what moisture he had left in his body, but enough to cry. He made no noise but the tears ran down his dirty face, and when they revealed the skin beneath, it was as if his face was some lost map containing rivers and perils and treasures of no land yet seen. He looked back again and saw the riders coming deliberately across the rough terrain, and they were getting close enough that he could make out details of their person. This was his last chance at the high ground, but he continued his retreat and moved down the hill's backside to the south.

There are some that would call it a clearing if it had anything to be clear of. If all the hills around him were the rim of a bowl, then he positioned himself in the low center of it. The slopes around him were shallow, and many who had previously passed this spot mistook it for nothing more than a small valley. He descended to the low point of this meeting of hills and near the center was a small patch of dried yellow grass and there he sat on the ground and caught his breath.

He removed his bow and adjusted the linen scraps that were stuffed into his sandals before wiping away the dry dirt cover of the ground next to him and deliberately stuck his remaining arrows, tip first, into the cold clay underneath. The world his quiver. Five arrows in the ground like some ancient, or inevitable, burial marker. He looked at the one he held and the blood from his leg that had dried onto its fletching. He rubbed the fletching between his fingers, fanning the feathers, and the dried blood flaked off onto the ground where it disappeared into earth like how much blood before it and how much blood still to come and would any prospective person understand that their whole world was built on this very thing they were all made of?

He was still sitting on the ground, pantless, with his cloak bunched behind him, when the two riders summited the lip of the last rise. They looked as if they were going to press forward as they had thus far, but they froze at the sight of him sitting directly in their path, facing them down. They were still fifty paces out and they watched him for a while to see if he were even alive and when they determined that he was they leaned in and exchanged words. As they conversed, Ernest stood on legs that wobbled and shook from dehydration and exhaustion. He steadied himself and notched his first arrow and they watched him quietly for a minute longer. The sun now nearly touched the rim of the planet and he had one last, longing thought of *if only* as it turned the world all the color of deep orange except for the dark circumscriptions of he and the two riders.

When it became clear that this half naked barbarian had no intention to shoot them where they had stopped, they finally moved. Without either of them taking their eyes from him, they swung in opposite directions of each other, each keeping their respective distance in a half circle with him at the center. Ernest attempted to spit onto the palm of his right hand but was unable to summon the saliva to do so. Instead, he wiped his hand, particularly his fingertips, onto the discarded pant legs that still hung around his neck and then tested his grip on the string of the bow. He nocked the bloody arrow and drew on the rider to his left, who coolly pressed his body to the horse, making himself the smallest possible target. Ernest saw no scenario where he could use all five of his arrows and so he exhaled and let this one heave out of pure desperation. It landed a full body length short of the rider and skipped off the ground with a handful of dull clacks. He muttered a string of self-deprecating curses and retrieved another arrow from the ground, nocking it and drawing it again on the same rider.

He slowly slackened the string without firing and turned his head to see the other rider had stopped when he saw Ernest prepare for fire. The second rider relaxed, and they both moved again until they were on opposite sides of him like some ritualistic dance performed by the three of them and revolving around Ernest in the middle. The rider on his left had cleverly aligned himself with the setting sun and Ernest was forced to strain painfully with his eyes in order to keep track of him. He could tell now that it wasn't just the difficult terrain that had slowed the riders' chase. The horses looked no better off than he was. Their steps were tentative and their breathing strained, and he could see dirt crusted to the outside of their nostrils and their lathered chests that visibly heaved the world's oxygen, in and out.

Both riders startled their horses within moments of each other and charged ahead. Ernest didn't hesitate to draw again and release an arrow toward the western rider who stormed out of the sun at him like some monstrous photon sent by the very star itself to strike down this sorry fragment of flesh ignorant enough to stand before it. The arrow struck the horse at the base of the neck and before he could see what happened further, he pivoted on weary legs and grabbed the base of another arrow from its clay quiver. He let fly on the other rider who was only a dozen feet from him by now, but the shot was errant—this time the arrow flying high as he aimed for the rider instead of the horse. The rider's right arm reared back, sword in hand, and prepared for the killing blow, but as he brought it down it was met with nothing but air.

After his failed shot, Ernest knew there was no time for another and so, as the horse bore down on him, he let his left leg go limp, using the falling momentum to roll away from the second rider and just inches away from his swinging blade. The horse's velocity caused it to almost collide with the first rider, who was in the process of trying to calm his panicked, wounded steed. Its head reared over and over again as a guttural howl emanated from its pierced throat. Its eyes rolled wildly in its head until it pitched and collapsed violently to the ground with its rider still attached, heaving and flopping loudly in the dirt. By this time the second rider had his mount turned and was charging toward Ernest again as he got to his feet and attempted to get back to his planted arrows. He reached the last two arrows but as soon as he got his hand on one of them, he knew it was too late. The horse was nearly on top of him when he tried to roll away again, but this time the upper front leg of the horse clipped him and sent him spinning half a dozen feet where he landed unceremoniously hard.

He wanted to get back up and continue to fight, but he had nothing left to give. Between the ambush on the caravan, his exhausting retreat to this spot, and being trampled by a thousand-pound animal, his body had reached its physical limit. He reached around blindly for his bow and possibly the last arrow but neither of them was around, and he resigned to stare dazedly at the dusky sky and waited for the killing blow. Through his concussed senses he could still hear the wounded horse wheezing out its final breaths and he could hear the voice of the man pinned under the animal—he sounded worse off than Ernest—crying for help.

The fallen rider stopped wailing long enough for Ernest to hear the two riders talk briefly before total silence, and then the sound of feet shuffling toward him. The remaining rider stood over him, blocking the sun, leaving Ernest squinting up at a crepuscular silhouette that held in one hand a long, curved blade that released an irregular drip of blood into the sand next to him. Ernest willed his fogged brain to deliver some final word of defiance in the face of his certain death, but his breath was stolen from him as the rider drove his knee into Ernest's torso, removing his sword and tucking it into his own belt, before binding his hands with rope. The knots were firm and the rope dug into the skin on his wrists, and when he was finished the rider removed his red hood and stuffed it into a satchel on his waist to reveal long, dark hair and thick beard, shining with perspiration. The rider stood and put one foot onto Ernest's chest and took out his water skin, drinking from it deeply and pouring some over his head. Without a word he put his water away and returned his attention to Ernest, stringing the rope down from his wrists to his ankles, intending to hog tie him.

Ernest finally gathered himself enough to speak and said, "If you're not killing me—please don't put me on that horse."

The man stopped and turned to take full measure of the pantless, waterless, bleeding form of a man before him and, of all possible requests he could have in this circumstance, it was this one.

"Why?"

"Just please. I'm a Copperfoot."

The rider was quiet for a moment and then shrugged, unspooling the rope from around Ernest's ankles and walking it over to the horse, where he tied it on to the saddle. His voice was deep and emotionless and he said, "I'm going at my pace, even if that means dragging you."

Ernest struggled to his feet and the man walked back over to him, giving him his waterskin and allowing Ernest to drink. As they headed out, back north, they walked by the dead rider and horse, and the mahogany of the bloodstained sand, where Ernest saw the rider's cut throat and the horse's eyes still open and untamed, even in death.

The rider led them to the top of the bowl, and then a shade west of the route of Ernest's retreat, finding some ground that was easier to pass. It took all Ernest had to keep putting one foot in front of the other at the aggressive pace set by the rider, further complicated by the setting sun and the waning light that made it even harder to find sure footing on each step. By the time they had retraced their way back to the caravan and the site of the battle, those that were still in the area moved like shadows between the wagons, loading up horse-drawn carts of their own with stolen goods and sending them north, into the dunes. Ernest's captor took his hood out of his satchel and pulled it back over his head as they approached the caravan, and Ernest noticed how, though they all wore the same, crimson-colored headpieces, there was no uniformity to them—some were hoods, some wraps, some cowls, some veil-like—all with unique stitching patterns. The rider dismounted without a word to Ernest and left him tethered to the horse and he walked over to another Shroud unloading food from one of the caravan wagons, and the two of them talked out of earshot, pointing to Ernest occasionally. He came back and Ernest said, "What?"

"What nothing," his captor said, who looked back at the caravan, "You just killed his brother and I thought he had a right to know."

Ernest spat nothing but dry air and said, "You're the one that cut his throat, all I did was shoot his horse."

"I told him the details." The man mounted again and said, "How is it that you won't be hogtied and made to ride on a horse, but you're okay with killing one the way you did?"

Ernest didn't respond and the man led them into the dunes as night fell and a quarter moon hovered up in space, making the world pale. Unable to walk anymore, he fell to the ground, using his cloak for protection, and riding atop the cloak, allowed the horse to pull him along the sand dunes like a makeshift sled. It was uncomfortable, but effective, and he drifted in and out of consciousness for an indeterminable amount of time before the rider stopped. The sky was dark enough that stars accented the moon and the rider stood over him again and kicked him gently with a sandaled foot not unlike his own, "You alive down there?"

Ernest groaned and the man untied his wrists and, leaving the horse behind them, led him into a cave entrance. The air was stale and smelled like a campfire, and he was dragged, stumbling through a series of tunnels similar to those at West One, to a large wooden portal with a torch smoldering dimly at the entrance. Another person was there and he heard the sound of wood scraping on wood as the door opened up and he was pushed through into absolute darkness as the door closed behind him and left nothing but the softest bronze light illuminating the edges of the portal.

He stood still, hoping his eyes would adjust, when a hand grabbed his wrist and he jumped, but the voice of a woman came back to him from the darkness and said, "It's okay. It's one of the new ones. You can sit here." She led him just a few paces away and sat him down on some cool, hard clay, with a wall behind him of the same stuff.

"Are you hurt?"

"Nothing too serious, I don't think." He could barely talk, given the state of his hydration, and the woman called for some water before pressing a metallic cup into his hands. He drank it all and she called for another and he asked her who she was and she said, "I'm nobody now, just like you."

He passed out for an indefinite amount of time, eventually waking to the same dense blackness at his arrival and his first thought was of his missing herb and he ran a hand down to his wool underwear where the small leather pouch of coin was still hidden and secured. His body hurt and he could feel his mind thirsting for herb. He pulled three cactus spines out of his lower left leg and used his left hand to prod at the hip wound made by his own arrow. The wound was dried over and he let out a grunt of pain and he wished the unseen lady with the water would find him out again.

He could hear the breathing of other people in the dark space, but could see nothing and didn't know how many there were, so he offered a harsh, loud whisper into the darkness saying, "Bird. Bird."

It wasn't her voice that came back to him, instead near on his left came back the aged and deep voice of a man who said, "What's that you're saying there?"

"I'm looking for my friend," Ernest answered.

"Well, there's no need to be discrete in here. You can't be in any more trouble than you are right now." The man then spoke loudly into the darkness and said, "Do we have a Bird here?" And when no answer came back he said, "Doesn't sound like your friend is here, but that don't mean a lot. This aint the only room they got people in, so don't let your mind go racing to the worst scenario."

"Where are we?"

"Somewhere in the Badlands. They got a whole system of tunnels in here. Seems like their home from the little I've seen, but they got rooms like this one where they keep prisoners too."

"How many rooms?"

"I don't know that."

"And people?"

"I don't know that either."

"How many are with us now?"

"You make eight."

"How long have you been here?"

"Tough to say in the darkness. I'd guess just over a week if you put me to it. Was coming up from the plains with a small caravan when they took us."

"What do they do with you?"

"Nothing evil, yet. Been generous enough with the food and water."

"What do they want?"

"Haven't told us anything—lining up slave buyers if I had to guess."

Ernest thought about Bird and the last time he saw her motionless form discarded in the dirt, and he fell asleep again to restless dreams of her death and his own. The sound of scraping wood woke him some time later and his eyes burned at the site of a torch lit at the entrance of the prison, held by a dark figure who stepped into the room. The light allowed Ernest to catch brief glimpses of the cell that was illuminated by the fickle flame—it was oblong and he saw the feet of some of his fellow captives stretched out on the ground as they sat along the wall in the same position as he did.

The torchbearer said, "Where's the new one, without the pants?" and when nobody answered he stepped further into the room until the light settled over Ernest and the man said, *come on.*

"I need help."

The man motioned with his free hand that wasn't holding the torch and he pulled Ernest off the ground, where he swayed uncertainly before walking to the entrance of the cell with legs that wobbled like a fresh born calf. Ernest pulled his cloak around him, covering himself as much as he could while his captor walked closely behind him with a hand on his shoulder, guiding him through the tunnels. They remained underground, but eventually came out of the tight tunnels to a large chamber, where the air was dense, smoky, and smelt of burnt oil.

In the middle of the chamber was the dark silhouette of a finely crafted wooden table. In a chair paired with the table sat a dark figure that cut and pulled at a charred cut of beef that oozed blood and juice as the figure's knife cut into it. The man that brought Ernest in sat him on a small, wood crate after placing his torch in an iron holder near the chamber's entrance. His legs were too tender to prop up at the awkward angle required by the crate, and so they lurched out in front of him as they would for a spent fighter. The man that retrieved him from the cell removed Ernest's cloak and gestured for him to take his shirt off and Ernest said, "What?"

"Your armor."

Ernest shed his shirt and then fumbled with the leather straps on his armor before the man stepped in and just pulled it off over his head. The pouch of silver he kept fastened under his armpit fell to the ground and the captor smirked, picking it off the ground and tossing it to the side along with the armor. The captor stepped off to the side as Ernest pulled his shirt back over his head along with his cloak and he sat in silence and watched the man at the table eat—his skin was sun tanned and dirty. His hair was short and dark—he was young—with facial hair that was thick and neatly trimmed, and as he chewed on the meat Ernest could see thin streams of grease run from the sides of his mouth. He chomped on another bite and then wiped his hands on a dirty, wool towel that sat in his lap.

"What is your name?"

"Ernest."

The man spoke to the side of the room and said, "Get Ernest some pants," and then to Ernest, "Are you frightened right now?"

"I'm resigned."

"Resigned to what?"

"To whatever you're going to do to me."

The man chuckled and stabbed the piece of meat he was eating, held it up to eye level and said, "Even if it's this?"

Ernest maintained an expressionless face at the grotesque suggestion and the man smiled to himself and said, "I'm kidding. I like a resigned man. A resigned man has no need to lie."

"Lie about what?"

"About who you are."

"I'm Ernest."

The man nudged his plate to the side of the small table and pointed his knife at Ernest, shaking it, "That may be your name, but that's not who you are. My man told me you wouldn't get on his horse."

"I'm Copperfoot. I told him as much."

The man nodded and said, "And of all the hired hands with the caravan, it was only you and one other that didn't ride."

Another person shuffled in the darkness at the edge of the chamber, and a figure stepped into the light briefly to set on the ground Bird's armor, shield, and belt that still held her unmistakable weapons. Ernest inhaled sharply at the site of them and said, "Is she alive?"

The man from the table stood from his chair, leaving his knife behind, and walked over to Bird's arsenal. He crouched next to it and turned her steel claw gently in his hand and said, "Who is she?"

"My friend."

"Your friend. And she is Copperfoot too?"

"Yes."

"Of course she is. Look at what she wore. Look at my men that she killed, and my men are not easily killed."

"Is she alive?"

The man looked at Ernest with dark eyes and said, "She's alive, and it's up to you to keep her that way."

Ernest let out an audible sigh of relief, even as he understood that there was no reason to take this man's word as truth.

"How?"

"By telling me the truth—about you two."

"What truth?"

"The truth about what you are up to."

"We were hired security for the caravan."

The stranger was firm when he said, "Lie to me again and she dies."

"That's no lie. Somewhere in all the shit you stole you'll find my pack and my token for payment from the caravan."

"Okay," the man said and he walked over to Ernest on the crate and squatted in front of him and looked into his eyes. "So, you fooled some amateur caravan master into giving you a free ride, but the misfit armor, the child's bow, and the piece of goat shit sword that was balanced by a toddler you carried in your belt—they give you away."

"It's a cavalry bow."

"A cavalry bow for someone forbidden to ride a horse."

"It's all they had."

The man leaned his head toward Bird's belongings and said, "Your friend there is overqualified for caravan security, and you're not qualified at all. So what are you two doing?"

"Why do you care?"

"You lie, she dies."

Ernest anxiously massaged his legs with his hands and a woman walked into the dim light of the chamber and tossed a pair of sturdy, linen pants onto Ernest's lap, where he was using his cloak to cover his beaten legs. He managed to stand and slip each leg through the pants and sat back down on the crate, pulling them up to his waist and clasping his cloak in its place around his neck.

The man watched in silence and said, "I can see that brain of yours working. You're going to get your friend killed."

"I have no reason to lie to you."

"Tell me then."

"I'm not a warrior, but I am Copperfoot. I hired the woman as a bodyguard and guide to take me to Kardona."

"What for?"

"I work for an Olerian Elder who has important business there."

"What business?"

"Herb."

"Which Elder?"

"Kira."

The man raised his eyebrows and his eyes darted to the side of the room at the sound of feet shuffling in the darkness. He said, "An Elder dealing in herb, even though it's outlawed by the emperor—thus your discreteness."

Ernest acknowledged that his observation was true and the man said, "How much does your friend know?"

"She knows about the discreteness, and nothing else."

"I can understand why you haven't told her."

"Because I'm not allowed to."

"Because you know that no self-respecting Copperfoot would do something for the benefit of an Olerian Elder. Especially Elder Kira, whose own father was central to the Copperfoot defeat a decade ago."

"Bird's a professional."

"Is that what you call yourself, as you run around for some Olerian like a whipped dog?"

Ernest brushed off the question and asked again, "Why do you care?"

"I've always taken an interest in any Copperfoot that passes through."

"Why?"

"Because I am one."

Ernest couldn't help but let out a small gasp and he reflexively shook his head and said, "No."

"Yes. Almost all of us here are—The Crimson Shrouds. Another bad nickname, but the Olerians have always lacked creativity."

Ernest continued shaking his bewildered head, "I don't believe you."

"You would rather we go by the true name of our people—the Mey-Anki?"

"Don't speak the name."

"Why? We're just a couple of Mey-Anki here, having a conversation."

"You're not," Ernest said.

The man tapped the tunic on his chest, just over his heart and said, "I carry Rathalla's flame right here, just like you."

"No."

"You don't believe? How else then would I know the true name of our people—the Mey-Anki—and not that condescending, filth title, *Copperfoot*? How else would I know of Rathalla, for whom we carry the flame? How else would I know of the seven sisters? Of Beauregard's last ride?"

"Stop," Ernest snarled in anger, but he tempered his voice and his emotions. "Just stop. If it's true, then you are worse than any of our enemies. You've spoken Rathalla's name out loud after riding horses. After riding horses *into battle, to their deaths.* You've worn your masks to terrorize, murder, and rob innocent people, and call yourself Mey-Anki. You've earned whatever filth title gets bestowed on this pathetic company."

The man chuckled with mock sadness and said, "I understand your anger and I expected it. You're not the first Copperfoot to pass through and spit in my face after learning the truth. But this is about the survival of our people now, and while you and the old guard are content to give up the fight and go extinct, there are some of us still able to carry Rathalla's flame."

"You can't carry it—not on horseback. It is a known tenet."

"You can now. The world has changed, and it is time that we change with it. Fifteen years ago the Copperfoot could have stood toe to toe with any force in the world, but because of this one precept—tenet as you call it—that disallows the riding of horses, we stood no chance. Even a child understands that one man on horseback is worth four on foot, maybe more on a desert terrain. It is not the will of Rathalla to see his children defeated by a lesser people, simply because of this single, misunderstood tradition."

"I don't imagine to understand the will of Rathalla."

"Then don't imagine that his intent is to have us spend the entirety of our existence on our feet, while the world passes us by on the horses stolen out of the Dialla. It was your generation that lost the war to the Olerians by running and hiding—most of us here were just children then. Now it will be my generation that takes back what is ours. We won't be left to wander our haunted homeland, like ghosts. Unseen, unheard, unable to act on the physical world, and carrying with us only the pain at what we used to be, or what we could've been. Are you a ghost, Ernest?"

Ernest didn't respond, dropping his eyes to the dark floor, while the man walked back to the area of his table and paced back and forth quietly. Ernest pulled his legs into himself on the crate, then watched the man nod to himself at whatever thoughts ran through his mind and then the man stopped and stared absently into the darkness for several moments before pacing again. Eventually he grabbed the chair and moved over to Ernest so that he sat directly in front of him, only a pace away. He pulled up his left leg, crossed its ankle over the top of his right knee and assumed a casual posture with his hands resting on his raised shin.

"One more thing," he said. "How old are you, Ernest?"

"Thirty-eight years."

The man nodded and then said, "Thirty-eight. You would've been in your prime age thirteen years ago when Oleria invaded, so how does a non-warrior survive the war that killed so many of his more capable kinsmen?"

"I was lucky."

"Lucky in what way?"

"I never had to fight."

"No? You were the physician? The cook?"

"The musician."

"Ah, very good—that is lucky. What can you play?"

"Anything with strings."

"Anything with strings. Very good."

The man used a single finger to summon a figure out of the darkness from the side of the room. The figure bent an ear to the man who whispered briefly, and then was waved away with the same hand. He uncrossed his legs and stood before Ernest, "I'm not going to kill you, or your friend. If you lied to me today, then you lied well. Though, since I too am being truthful, I wouldn't have killed either of you anyway. Not a Copperfoot."

"I suppose I got lucky again."

"There is one condition, however."

"What?"

"You must play us a song."

ERNEST WAS BROUGHT BACK TO the initial, dark cell where he fell asleep again, and he was woken at a later time with the same ceremony that got him the first time. More tunnels, more torches. He walked for some time, and he began to wonder if he wasn't being led in a circle, to confuse him about the true scope of the tunnels. He tried to keep oriented, but his brain was fogged with the lack of herb and he trekked onward, sullen and miserable.

Eventually they reached another wooden door, identical to the one of his cell, and, when he was led inside, his eyes were met with the first natural light he had seen since being captured. It was the dragon's hoard. The room was still part of the tunnel system, but a large skylight was bore into the roof of the room, allowing a thick beam of sunlight to pierce the center of the room and cast a pallid gloom on the rest of countless objects that filled the chamber. Furniture, armor, weapons, chests filled with silver, piles and piles of fabric, leather sandals and boots, and that was only a fraction of the practical objects. Ernest saw urns, mosaics, figurines, silverware, mirrors, brooches, ingots of bronze and iron, and jewelry.

The guard with him pointed in the direction of some of the fabric and said, "Take whatever you need, and make yourself look better than a busted drifter. I'll show you to all the packs taken from your caravan and you can find you and your friend's. The music stuff is somewhere in that back corner—you're to play tonight."

"Is there any herb?"

The man rolled his eyes while his hand disappeared under his cloak and revealed a small leather pouch, much like Ernest's own, and allowed him a hefty pinch. The man sat down near the door and another guard came in, taking a seat too, and the two of them conversed disinterestedly while Ernest waded into the room's treasures. His cloak was still in good shape, despite the stress of being dragged across the Badlands, but he made his way to the stash of fabrics and found himself a pair of pants that fit better than the ones just given to him. He secured them with a belt and replaced his sandals along with a new linen shirt before picking his way through the room to the area with the instruments. Their mistreatment was evident at a glance—harps of all sizes tossed haphazardly in a pile, as if their value was known, but not understood. There were lavish wooden cases and Ernest opened them to find lyres, violins, guitars, lutes, cellos, and basses. He inspected a handful of these before unsheathing a three-quarter cello and moving it out of the heap to an uncluttered area in the chamber.

The instrument was smaller than the full model he grew up with. Other than two scuffs to its large, maple body, it was in pristine condition. One of the guards noticed him from across the chamber and told him that most of the instruments had been recovered in a raid just months earlier, but nobody knew how to play any of them. Ernest ran a hand over the maple back of the instrument, with its smooth surface providing a stark contrast to the roughness of his dried and beaten skin. His hand continued to explore the instrument, up to its spruce top and ebony fingerboard. He gave some exploratory plucks to the strings and closed his eyes as he listened to the low hum of the summoned notes. When he opened his eyes again he asked the man where the bow was.

"What bow?"

Ernest said, "They typically have a stringed bow with them. To play with."

The man looked confused for a moment, but he nodded his head and slipped out of the chamber. Ernest continued to pluck at the strings and twist the four knobs on the instrument's head. It was badly out of tune. The man returned with a bow and gestured to Ernest with it, who nodded his head. The man said, "We were wondering what these were for."

Ernest pulled a wooden chest out of the clutter to sit on and took the bow in his hands. It was the length of a long dagger and he held it at eye level as he inspected it. It had a fine ivory heel, and the wood was one that he did not recognize. The bow's ribbon was horsehair. Ernest smiled. There wasn't a part of his body that still didn't ache from the journey, but he gave a shimmy and then straightened his back into rigid perfection. The cello lay angled into his open lap, with the ebony stem whispering into his ear. He cocked his bow hand perpendicular to the strings over the instrument's fat middle and his other clasped claw-like onto the ebony arm. He settled the ribbon of horsehair over the thinnest string and pulled a long, sweet note from the belly of the instrument. His claw hand explored different chords along the neck and he worked through several scales to feel out the instrument as much as to explore the limits of his pained body. He ended the final scale with a timely drag across the fattest string, which issued a deep echo in the chamber. Ernest set the bow in his lap and flexed both of his hands open and closed.

The guard said to him, "I didn't know it could do that."

Ernest said, "That was nothing."

He continued to play, and soon the fingertips of his dried hands began to bleed from places where calluses were once prominent but had faded in the years of their disuse. It ran down the neck of the cello as if the instrument itself were injured, and the guard watched on with concern. Ernest stopped to wipe the blood off on his leg and in the silence the guard said, "Does it hurt?"

"A little."

He kept playing, and he continued tuning the instrument when he stumbled into notes that didn't sound as they should. While he practiced, songs rose out of his consciousness and he began replicating them with all the capacity of a lucid dreamer. He could see the bars of music that his mother would sketch into the sandy ground around their home. He could see her dirty hand pointing to the small divots she made with her thumb and explain to him how each divot represented a note, and how there was a proper way to play those notes. There were octaves and accented beats. There was vigor and measure. There was allegro and adagio. There was double time and triple time. She showed him how to pluck the strings to create up-tempo rhythms. When he was fourteen, she gifted him his first sheet of music, a ballad written by an Olerian composer, Raymond Vin. The complexity of the piece enchanted him, and over the next years his mother continued to collect any written piece of music that she could. He memorized every one.

When war came he suited up with tools of violence, but his small contingent insisted he would be more effective if he brought his viola instead, and so he did. At night, he'd play around the fire if they made one, and if they didn't, then he'd play in darkness. When the fighting picked up and they joined with a larger contingent, he found a place in the field hospital, where he would play through the night as the physicians sawed off infected limbs, stitched lacerations, and dug arrowheads out of the living and dead alike. These would be reused. It became his duty to play in the hospital tent every night until the war was inevitably lost. After the fighting and the running stopped, he attempted to find solace in playing music, as he always had, but he could not. Every chord he played was accompanied with the smell of injured human bodies. Every note was associated with agonized screams and the images of mutilated limbs. Music was blood. It was pain. His music was the soundtrack for the worst that people could do to each other.

So he stopped playing.

It was night and their faces were shaded in the fire light. His people. Somewhere between sixty and one-hundred of them sat on a steeply bowled, arid hillside at the base of a tunnel entrance. It was mostly men, but there were women too—no children—with their crimson hoods pulled down around their necks like a scarf. It was his first time outside of the tunnels since his capture and he breathed deeply from the trove of fresh air. The absent moon allowed for a full expression of the stars and he was immediately able to orient himself to the cardinal directions.

He walked with the cello tucked under his right arm and with the bow gripped tightly in his left. The crimson congregation sat facing the bottom of the slope where a single metal brazier burned on a spacious landing. He was escorted by a single guard and the two of them skirted the settled crowd and made their way to the fire. This was his destination. The guard gestured to him as if this was where he was going to play and he looked around with some confusion. He told the guard that he needed something to sit on. The guard gestured with his chin into the crowd and then the two of them stood silently for a minute before a man came forward from the darkness with a three-legged stool. Ernest nodded and the man placed it next to the fire.

The stool was lower than he would have preferred, and it wobbled on the uneven ground, but he shifted his weight appropriately and leaned the upper part of the instrument into his chest while he steadied it between his knees. As the nearest person to the flaming brazier, it made the left side of his body uncomfortably hot, and he couldn't see through the smoky darkness except for the first row of faces that hovered without expression before him. Their eyes were dark against the flames and their mouths were cowled by the night's shadows. There was no sound except for the aggressive cracking of wood being consumed by flame.

Ernest spoke quietly when he said, "This song is called Copperfoot Hills."

It was one of the first songs he had ever learned, and it was one that sounded best accompanied by a harp. He felt the music falling flat among the crowd, making him nervous, and so his already rusty fingers tripped over simple chords and he stumbled to the end of the piece through a dozen errors. There was no sound from the audience when he stopped playing. He told himself that probably nobody had noticed the mistakes, but he held no confidence in it. He took a deep breath and let the instrument lean into his chest like a great, wounded mammal and he flexed his hands which cast strange shadows by way of the firelight. A figure approached from the darkness and tossed a log into the fire pit. Its impact sent a flurry of orange cinders into the blackness where they twisted and faded until they became part of the night like all else.

Ernest took his position with the cello again, but his head was lowered and for a moment he stared at the ground between his feet. It occurred to him that he might never leave this place, as he had no reason to trust to the word of the leader and he saw no reason why the man would let him go. The prospect of death made the cello feel fresh in his hands and briefly he felt again an emotion toward the instrument that he hadn't felt since before his time at the hospital had forever tainted it. For a moment it was like a long and lost friend had come to visit on the eve of execution. It whispered to him and his racing heart grew calm. He thought what else to do with a friend in such a dire setting than to remember a time when life seemed perfect. He steadied his breathing and then raised his head to speak, and when he spoke this time it was loud enough for the crowd to hear and he said to them,

"This song is called Early Spring, but every time I hear it I think of my mother. Maybe you will think of your own mothers as I play."

Ernest pulled the instrument into his left ear and began to play the best rendition of Early Spring he had ever played in his life. That had ever been played in *any* life. In that world and in that moment his single instrument transcended what an entire orchestra could deliver. He summoned from the instrument an elegant, but alien, sound that contrasted starkly with the austere ugliness of his position. The brazier. The rocks. The shrouded faces. The violence. The empty and despotic land echoed the music back as if refusing to absorb any of its beauty into its own hard self—a beauty that it feared brought softness where softness cannot be afforded.

But he played anyway. He played with the precision of a man in his final moments of life, and, although they didn't know it, he played for them a piece written by none other than Raymond Vin—the Olerian composer. But neither the setting, the song, the song's origin, or the perfection with which he played it, ultimately mattered. It only took a few moments before Ernest was true to his word and the song came with a rush of memories of his mother, and many persons in the crowd also began to think of their own too. They had made themselves hard like the land but they had something the land did not—a mother. The world had never come weeping into existence, wailing against its vulnerability, like every fool in the crowd had spent their life pretending against. What the music could not break down in the earth was broken down, briefly, in each listener's heart.

Lost in the spell of the song, Ernest did not hear the restless murmur build within the audience. He did not hear the stifled sobs, though they were audible. He could hear his mother's voice on each note as she ran her hand through his hair to calm him, sick in bed. He heard her laughter. He could see her do the same for his sister. He remembered how she would listen to him play for hours on end and fell into spells of her own as she listened to each practice session.

He was roused from the music's incantation as he played the song's lengthy, final chord. The neck of the cello was messy with blood and sweat, and his eyes stung from the smoke of the fire. Unsure of how much more he was supposed to play, he was relieved when the guard came to him and pulled him up from the stool. He was told to leave the cello and the man pulled him up the slope of the bowl toward the tunnels, and Ernest caught glimpses of the faces in the crowd—those who didn't have them buried in their hands were laden with tears.

The guard escorted him back into the tunnels, to a different dark cell that, this time, was empty except for Ernest. There was nothing said between them and Ernest curled up in the darkness, falling asleep almost immediately. There were no bad dreams this time. He was shaken awake by a pair of strong hands and they slipped a dark hood over his head before leading him back into the tunnels. When he felt a breeze push the hood up against his cheek, he knew they were outside again, the dim light suggesting it was very early in the morning. The voice that talked to him was a woman's, "I'm gonna tie you off to my horse. Keep your head down and you should be able to see through the hood well enough to stay on your feet."

Rope was tied around his wrists again, this time more generous than when he was brought in, and he followed the dulcet tones of the horse's hooves on hard ground before trespassing soundlessly into the soft sand dunes. He walked for a couple of hours, straining to see through the thin fabric of the hood, and it wasn't until they hit a stretch out of the dunes that Ernest heard the sound of another horse following behind him. They stopped long enough for the rider to slip a waterskin under his hood, allowing him to drink, before moving on in silence to midday. The next time they stopped, he shuffled nervously as the rider unbound his wrists and removed his hood, leaving him squinting uncomfortably in the light of the noontide sun. His captor moved back to her horse and he watched her discard some stuff from the back of the horse, saddle up, and trot off in a direction different from where they came. He turned around to see the second horse nearby, with Bird tethered to it the same way as him, and they went through the same rite as he and his captor, with the hooded rider also exiting without a word.

Bird shielded her eyes against the blowing sand and squinted toward the departing figures as they melted into the bronze horizon. They didn't move or speak and he watched them too until long after they were gone and even then the two continued to watch. Finally, she said, *Is that it?* and Ernest shrugged and she said, "I thought it was over."

Ernest went to where the rider had tossed his gear into the dirt, to find not only his pack, but some armor and a sword that he did not recognize. The first thing he checked was his pack, for herb, and let out a sigh of relief as he found it and pinched some into his cheek. Upon seeing the strange sword he was reminded of Bird's weapons and he looked over at her gathering up her supplies and said, "Is it all there?"

She nodded as she flipped the shield over her shoulder and said, "I didn't think I'd see any of it again, but it's all here."

He picked up the armor he had never seen before and spun it around— it was leather, sleek—and he pulled it over his head and his shirt to find that it was a near perfect fit. He picked up the sword and had no way to judge its quality but it had a simple lip sheathe that he threaded through his belt and then moved it just off his hip. Bird saw this and said, "Not only are we alive, but they sent you with gifts?"

"He said that the other ones gave me away."

"Who said that?"

"I don't know, their leader."

"Why should he care?"

"I don't know."

They were still in Badland country, though not the sea of dunes they were taken into, and, with the Omoya range protruding ahead of them, it was easy to get oriented within the bigger picture. He walked over to a nearby jut of sandstone, sat down, and drank lightly from his waterskin with his cloak pulled up over his head to protect from the sun. She walked gingerly to join him and he saw dark bruises underneath both of her eyes.

"Did they hurt you?"

"Yeah."

"I'm sorry."

"It wasn't you that hurt me."

"I know it."

"Then you got nothing to apologize for."

"Still," he said. "If it weren't for me you wouldn't be here."

"If I weren't here then I'd be somewhere else, and there's no place in this world that isn't filled with men who are ready to hurt a woman."

They said nothing of their plans or what they intended to do moving forward, each of them content to sit still, and quiet—resting on the jut and watching wisps of sand blow and reshape the minor dunes around them.

"Are you gonna make me ask or are you going to tell me?" She asked.

"Tell you what?"

"I guess you're going to make me ask it then."

"What?"

"Why did they let us go?"

"You know why."

"For the life of me, I don't."

Ernest pulled the stopper from his water skin and smelled inside and then put the stopper back. He said, "Because as good as you are at your job, I'm every bit as good at mine."

"I don't even know what your job is."

"Talking. I'm a professional talker."

She said, "Here I was, ready to believe anything that you said. Tell me honestly. I think I'm owed it."

"I was going to tell you honestly," he said. "But the truth is even harder to believe."

"I doubt that."

"What if I told you that I played for them a song so beautiful that they felt they had no choice but to set us free."

She looked blankly at him. "You played them a song?"

"That's right. They found out I knew how to play music and they took me to this room full of all the stuff they'd stolen. They had the best collection of instruments I've ever seen and not one of them knew how to play. Gave me this shirt and these pants too."

He sipped again from his water and she looked him up and down and said, "We get captured and are held by the most feared outlaws in the region, and somehow you come out looking better than how you went in."

"Did they talk to you at all?"

"One of them did—asking me to join them—and I spit in his face. Right in the eye." She pointed to her bruised eyes and said, "He did this to me and that was all the talking there was."

"Did they keep you with anybody else?"

"No. Couldn't see much but the cell was hardly big enough for me alone."

"And when they asked you to join them, they didn't say anything else about it?"

"No. What else is there?"

"Just the worst part."

"What?"

"They're Copperfoot. They're Mey-Anki."

Her jaw dropped and she looked at him in search of some punchline but there was none and she said, "No."

"Yes."

"Who told you? That leader?"

"Yes."

"It's a lie."

"I'm sure it's not. He used the ancestral name, we spoke of Rathalla and the seven sisters, and he acknowledged Beauregard's last ride."

"But they ride horses," She shook her head in disbelief. "Heretics. Heathens. Traitors. Why?"

"They want to take back the Dialla."

"At what cost?"

Ernest didn't answer and they rested in silence before he said that he didn't think that he could go any further for the day and she agreed to camp for the night. They stayed around the jut, with no fire, for the rest of the day, and he remembered her elbow and asked how it was and she said it that it was doing better. As the sun went down they each set out their blankets and she discovered that her pack had a new blanket with it, along with food and a fresh pair of clothes, which drew a look of disgust from her, though she kept it all.

They both lay quietly in the darkness, waiting for sleep to come, when he heard Bird begin to chuckle, and then the chuckle turned into a full belly laugh. He asked what was so funny but she had trouble catching her breath to tell him, and when she finally did she said, "I actually believed it when you said that they let us go because of your stupid song."

"I stand by it."

"You know damn well it's because we're Copperfoot."

"That's your take on it."

"It's the right take, too."

"You just didn't hear the song."

HE WOKE THE NEXT MORNING to the sound of her stirring next to him, digging some wheat bread and seasoned chickpeas out of her pack and saying *you know this is the shit they just stole from that caravan.* She ate while he took inventory of his body—the wound on his hip still heavily scabbed over, but closed, his wrists raw, but healing, and then the invisible soreness throughout his entire body from being dragged behind the horse. Lastly, he looked at his hands and the tiny trauma on his fingertips that came from playing the cello, and as he looked at them he could hear the music of Early Spring and it played in his head as Bird walked a dozen paces away from the jut and went through her morning exercises. When she was done she walked back, flexing her elbow experimentally and said, "What now?"

"Nothing's changed."

"I don't know exactly where we're at, but it's a long way off the trade routes."

"Then we'll find our way back and keep going."

"I got a different idea."

"What?"

She pulled her head to gesture to the mountain range risen behind her and said, "We go over the Omoyas."

"You think?"

"You said your contact is on the western slope right?"

"Yeah."

"Well then, why not? Going is a little tougher—steeper—but it's not exactly scaling the Echoras, and the season is right for it."

"Okay."

"The better idea you have of where we're going the better route we can take."

"I got no idea at all. We need to find a small village over there by the name of Bontu and I'll know where to go from there. That's where we'll meet my contact, who'll connect us with the Samsarans."

"What Samsarans?"

"They're the ones that supply the herb."

"What?"

He tried to talk past the reveal like it was nothing but knew that it wouldn't work. He couldn't keep it hidden forever, and as he remembered how she had told him that Samsarans had killed her grandfather, a great pain shot up in his chest and he regretted his decision deeply. His voice was somber as he said, "They're just suppliers. It's just business."

She nodded but her eyes maintained a distant look as she pulled off a chunk of wheat bread from her bag and chewed in silence while he packed up and prepared for departure. When she was finished eating, she packed up too while he slipped a pinch of herb and he stood, ready to go, waiting for her. When she was done she slung the pack over her cloak, but she faced toward the rising sun, east, instead of the mountain range at their backs.

"I think I'm going to turn around. Back to the Dialla."

Even though he expected her to say it, his stomach still dropped. He quietly said, "Please don't."

Her lower jaw flexed to bite back the lump in her throat, but her voice was steady and clear as she talked. "You know, I started taking on any work I could find immediately after the surrender thirteen years ago. I've worked private security for merchants, caravans, elders, and free lanced as a scout and guide. And you are, in those thirteen years, the first ever Copperfoot to hire me. It's like we got swept off the face of this world and any person able to avoid the broom is shut up in their home, waiting to die. It was fun to haggle silver with you, but I honestly would've taken this job for free, just so that I could, for the first time in more than a decade, use my ability to help one of my people."

She shook her head and continued, "And you work for an elder? That's fine, everybody does now. And so what that this elder happens to be the daughter of Cevrias, the man who pushed the Olerians into war with us? I don't know this Kira and I'm not going to hold a grudge against her because of the actions of her father. And then the Crimson Shrouds—the worst of the killers and looters—are actually our own people who have forsaken our core beliefs in pursuit of revenge and power? And finally this, that our bidding will not only be for the benefit of this Kira, but by some sickness of fate, the benefit of the Samsarans, who not only came into the Dialla and killed my grandfather, but are, in every corner of the region that I've visited, cast as an ignorant and violent bunch."

She nodded her head sadly, still not looking at him and she said, "I don't see how I can reconcile that. I'm sorry to leave you here like this, but there's no fit for me on this errand anymore."

He leaned back up against the jut of rock as she talked, posed like a sagging scarecrow. When she was done talking he said, "Everything you say is the truth, and I don't blame you for any of it. But there's a larger landscape that you don't understand, and I'll tell you everything I know if you'll walk with me for a bit, because I think if I sit down now I won't want to move again for another day."

Indecision showed on her face and he pressed on, "Just walk with me for a bit and I'll explain, and if you still feel how you feel then you can head back, and you won't be much further out of the way than you are now."

She said *okay* and they walked, side by side, toward the base of the looming mountain range. Unlike the Echora Range to the east, with its angular, granite peaks that inched closer to the heavens with each passing year, the Omoyas were on the decline. With their days of granite peaks millennia behind them, the forces of nature trimmed the range's tops until they were uniformly rounded. The east slopes were typical of the desert motif, dry and sparse, with moisture from the Great Water being blocked and hoarded by the lush slopes and land west of the range. The north end of the range was capped near the bay by the impressive Mount Ucari, the northernmost and largest in a series of active volcanoes that stretched the length of the continent and beyond. On a clear day the two of them could have, with a good vantage point, looked far south and spotted the cratered top of Mount Macka—the next nearest volcano that erupted the same year that Bird's grandfather, murdered by a Samsaran missionary, turned four-years-old.

"How much do you know about how the Olerian Empire works?"

"About as much as you know about camels."

"This is going to be harder than I thought then."

"I'm a smart girl."

"Okay."

He talked as they walked and as his diatribe progressed, he surprised himself with his own knowledge as he said, "At the top of all things in the empire is the emperor. This person—currently a fourteen-year-old girl—is divinely selected to their position, and so their judgment and wisdom is taken as infallible. If you're wondering about the novelty of a fourteen-year-old girl as emperor, then you're perceptive. She is only the third woman to ever be granted the position while also being the youngest. Quite the little knave of a prodigy. But, despite being infallibly wise, the emperor tends to be pretty hands off. Almost every aspect of the empire is run by elders, with the emperor acting as an overseer. These elders are almost all exclusively wealthy business persons who control certain major aspects of the empire's economy, and profit hugely from doing so. For example, the elder who has sent us here, Kira, makes most of her fortune from the iron mined out of the north Echora Mountains, which she inherited from her father—who you also know, Cevrias—that profited from the Olerian bean and blacksmithing industries before the war with us. Because Cevrias was the elder who brought the idea of a Dialla invasion to the emperor, and because the iron ore spoils meshed so seamlessly with what Cevrias already controlled, he was rewarded by the emperor after their victory with the main ore supply. Now, almost every bean and piece of iron that comes out of the Dialla eventually ends up as silver in her pocket."

He stopped talking, giving her an opening to say something, but she just nodded to acknowledge that she was listening.

"But it's important to understand that all elders serve at the pleasure of the emperor. Because of the infallible judgment thing, the emperor can name a new elder or have another one relegated with one simple order. And if such a thing occurs, the elders have no safeguards against this happening—whatever the emperor says, goes. Now, any such shifts in power are carved out cleanly for one simple, beautiful reason—the emperor controls all aspects of military power. When Olerian soldiers take their oaths, they don't swear to protect elders, Olerian civilians, or even fellow soldiers—they swear undying fealty to the emperor and nothing else. What can a disgruntled elder do against a divinely inspired emperor with unchecked military authority?"

"Probably nothing."

"Nothing is right. You are a smart girl."

"Is this supposed to clarify anything?"

"I'm trying, but it's complicated. Do you want me to keep going or not?"

"Sure. I love hearing how our people were decimated so that some old lady could be the world's pre-eminent bean farmer."

Ernest smiled to himself and continued, "So the way it works is that elders aren't allowed to have anything more than a handful of private security. Elders pay hefty taxes and the emperor essentially loans soldiers and armies out to elders based on territory size, volatility of the natives, resource presence, and things like that. Like I said, the emperor is responsible for big picture stuff, so elders are allowed to use these soldiers however they see fit and the emperor moves soldiers and armies around should the empire be stressed elsewhere. Remember our stop at West One? That base and several more are all under the direct supervision of Elder Kira. The Dialla Desert is one of the largest and resource rich regions in the empire and so she is, in a sense, one of the most powerful people."

"Sounds like you picked the right boss."

"Can we stop for a minute?"

"You okay?"

"Yeah." He spat and then rummaged through his pack for another pinch of herb.

"For the elders, it's hard to explain, this whole system is almost a game for them. A very high stakes game. They are always looking for ways to consolidate and expand their power and wealth. Within the empire as a whole are more than a dozen mini empires that are all competing every way that you can without using military force. Each of them has more money than they can spend in one-hundred lifetimes, but they all crave to be at the top of the list as one of, if not *the*, richest and most powerful. *The* most influential. And at any moment the emperor can take it all away from them. The tiny culture they've created encourages them to climb and power grab at every possible opportunity, but without ever doing something that angers the emperor."

"Does that happen often?"

"That the emperor gets angered?"

"Yeah."

"Not *often*. And when it does it's almost always because the elder is trying to bribe vendors, short-pay laborers and merchants, or maybe they underpaid on taxes to the emperor. All things that, in their view, are harmless crimes. They get a slap on the wrist—a fine that's tangible effect barely qualifies as punitive. But some other things—such as kidnapping, or arson, or assassination conspiracies—get taken much more seriously. Just last year an elder was denounced and relegated for attempting to start fires in rival-owned workshops. He'll be spending the rest of his life in a labor camp for that. But the worst thing an elder can do is to meddle in foreign policy. That's the realm of the emperor and nobody else."

"What do you mean by foreign policy?"

"I mean anything to do with a nation or people that is *not* the Olerian Empire."

"Even just talking?"

"Even that. Hell, especially that."

"It seems pretty harmless compared to kidnapping."

"It can be. But it can also be much worse. From our end, as Copperfoot, it may seem like the empire is a limitless war machine ready to take on the whole world at once, but it is much more delicate than that. So much of the empire's military power is perpetually preoccupied with simply keeping what already exists of the empire in line—never mind taking on new outside threats. Part of the double-edged sword of being the imperial conqueror is that your empire is made up of people that you have done great wrong to in the past. When you have dozens of elders, each with their own agendas and economic interests, you can understand how messy things would get if each one were allowed to freely dialogue with foreign nations. A cultural dispute here, a trade disagreement there, and before you know it you're fighting three wars on three different fronts—a sure recipe for disaster. And so, like the military, this aspect of the empire also is the duty of the emperor and nobody else. This is especially enforced when it comes to trade. Any trade outside of the empire's borders requires special approval from the emperor. Sometimes it's granted, sometimes it's not." He spat. "Remember the wagon we walked next to on the way out? The father and the son with the nice weapons? Wouldn't be surprised if those were going to find their way into Kardona, and if you were able to trace the money back all the way to its source, you'd probably find an elder making unapproved trades to a rival nation already at war."

"Kira?"

He snickered, "Probably. But I don't know and it has nothing to do with why we're here."

"Your boss being a powerful criminal isn't a selling point for me staying, and we're just getting further away from where I intend to go."

"I'm sorry."

"If you're just trying to talk, uninterrupted, until this errand is done, I don't think you can do it."

They reached the base of the lowest foothills of the Omoyas, making them begin their climb at an angle imperceptible to them as he continued, "I'm not trying to sell you on the virtues of Lady Kira. I can say I've been around Pridipoa long enough to understand that, in her world, as backwards as it can appear from the outside, she is as principled, cunning, and ambitious as they come. The reason that I'm here is to help my people, the Copperfoot people, and that's my selling point for you to stay."

"How does any of this benefit the Mey-Anki?"

"Because Kira is the unofficial patron of the Dialla. I told you that I'm a professional talker, which is true. My job is—was—to travel around the Dialla, as a personal agent of Kira's, and figure out ways to help the Copperfoot. She's put countless amounts of silver back into the pockets of our people and ensured that we have a place in the new empire. You say that you've never been hired by a Copperfoot? That's because she goes to lengths to employ every one of them within her elder ecosystem. They're out there—we're out there—as miners, foremen, farmers, messengers, blacksmiths, traders, teamsters, and she wants to keep it that way. If you think there's some shame in this, then ask around when you're out in other parts of the empire about what happened to the native people there. Systematic death. Slave labor. Maybe we don't have it as good as we did thirteen years ago, but it could be so much worse. If something were to happen to Kira and a different elder became the steward of the Dialla, things could go rotten for us, fast."

"If she really is so great for us, then why are you going along with this task that could have her stripped of her power and sent to die in a labor camp?"

"Because this task is part of a bigger vision that she has for our people."

"What vision?"

"To militarize the legendary Copperfoot warriors. I believe that she's gathering her own army, and that she wants the Copperfoot to be the infantry of that army."

"And do what?"

He shrugged, "Take Oleria for herself, or maybe carve out an empire of her own. I'm not sure. What I'm sure of is that she needs more money, more power. She needs Kardona's herb."

"She told you all of this?"

"Shit no. But I've been working for her for a decade and I'm not an idiot."

"I need to stop," she said.

"Are *you* okay?"

She nodded and turned around and sat down on the gentle incline of the foothill, pulling out her water and taking measured sips from it as she squinted back toward the golden Badlands against the sun that inched toward its daily apex. He was quiet and opted to pace back and forth behind her in silence.

Some time passed and Bird spoke to him behind her, "Is she responsible for the Crimson Shrouds? Is that what it looks like for her to weaponize our people?"

"I don't believe so, but it's possible. She's shown nothing but respect toward our beliefs."

She said *I don't know* to herself and he stayed silent while a soft breeze came out of the east and then he said, "If I could go back in time and make it so that the Olerians never came here, and our people could be the caretakers of the Dialla forever, then I'd do it. But there's no mechanism for that, and time moves on and the world moves on and I'm going to do whatever I can so that our people are there when it does. It's a lot to take in but nothing's changed for you. I'm here to break the rules, and you're here to keep me alive so that I *can* break them. You're my personal security and you can't, and won't, be held responsible for anything that I do."

"Which rules exactly are you breaking?"

"Just the worst ones," he said. "I'll be using threats, possibly bribes, to enlist a foreign party to supply an unlawful substance through unlawful trade with the purpose of potentially overthrowing the sitting emperor."

"I never knew the job of a talker was so treacherous."

"It's not. The last dispute I worked on for Kira was negotiating with a Copperfoot teamster that earned five silver a week, and he wanted six."

"That's what you do?"

"Most of the time."

"Then what on earth are you—are *we*—doing here?"

"I wasn't the first option. Kira has other people that take care of these sort of things, and, of the three envoys she's sent, none of them have made it."

"What happened to them?"

"We don't know. They vanished. It's a dangerous journey, but it's unlikely that three envoys, to a man, became typical Dialla casualties."

"So what do you think happened?" She asked.

"Almost certainly it's another elder, maybe more than one, sabotaging her efforts. Kira isn't the only one that understands that Kardona's herb is the next frontier, and not the only one willing to take the risks to establish a supply."

"And she thought that you'd succeed where they failed?"

"I suppose so. I'm unorthodox. Anybody who has been paying attention to her operation would've known about the other envoys, but they'd have no reason to pay attention to me and the single hand of freelance security that I hired. With West One being as distant and remote as it is, we could be sure that if there was anybody in Helena following me when I hired you, that they could not continue to do so out there."

"Okay," she said. "One last question. Kardona has been around my whole life, so why now are these elders in a race for its herb?"

He nodded and said, "The civil war. Kardoan herb has been trickling into Oleria and the Dialla your whole life, but now that the empire has gotten a taste of the best herb in the world, a trickle isn't enough. It's time for a flood of the stuff, and the civil war causes instability, and with instability comes opportunity. If these elders can get into Kardona, and line up their own suppliers for when the war is over, there's hordes of silver to be made. As it happens, Kira's connection in Kardona is familiar with the Samsarans in the area, and so that's our in."

She said nothing while he paced in silence as the day grew stale and hot. Ernest figured that it was a good sign that she hadn't left right away, but he still started to think through the reality of going on alone and what it meant for him and his mission. He stopped pacing and looked up at the mountain range above him, measuring its climb of thousands of feet in his mind, and feeling his body ache at the idea. She said something that he couldn't hear and he said *what?* and she said, louder, "I don't fucking believe it."

He had the sinking feeling come to his chest again at the realization of her leaving him and his head hung in defeat and he shook it and said, "I understand. There's no hard feelings from me."

She stood up, still looking south and east, "No, Ernest. I mean I don't *fucking* believe it."

He turned around to see her facing away from him, and he shuffled a couple of paces to better angle himself for where she was looking. It was still far out in the distance, a dark fleck against the canary-colored landscape, but as he looked at it, confused for a moment, the distinct, lumbering approach of the mare became unmistakable. He was breathless, and his face twisted from a face of delight, to one on the verge of tears, as he watched the horse drag her way toward them. When the mare reached them, Ernest saw a look on Bird's face—one that he hadn't seen before—of such pure joy that it made him wish he had known her in a different life, or in a different time. The horse went to Bird first, nuzzling her torso as Bird ran two soothing hands down the side of the horse's neck, and then to him, nearly knocking him off his feet when she pushed him with her muzzle. He smiled and tickled the velvety hair between the animal's eyes and then stepped away from her to see that she appeared as healthy and whole as the day they first saw her.

Bird ran the back of her hand over her eyes and then said, "I have to apologize to you. You hired me for a job and here I am, thinking about leaving you high and dry in the Omoya Mountains. Thing is, we both knew this was going to be difficult, so really we're exactly where we expected to be."

"That's a way of looking at it."

She nodded and he said, "I'm glad you're staying."

They got moving again, in their customary line with the mare in the rear, creeping their way up the base of the range, and, with no natural shelter, getting no reprieve from the punishing sun for the rest of the afternoon. They stopped at dusk, exhausted, and instead of vanishing into the night per usual, the mare settled herself gently to the ground and fell asleep sideways like a spent dog. They didn't bother with a fire and as she was laying out her sleeping space Bird said, "If I decided to go back, who do you think she'd follow?"

He said, "That's a cruel question to ask," as he laid out his own blanket and collapsed on top of it, pulling his pack under his head to use as a pillow. "Of course its me."

The next day the going only got harder, with the incline of the mountain growing steeper with each step. He asked to rest often, but she kept pushing them, worried about their lack of supplies and worried about foraging in such an unfamiliar landscape. They trended north but, in the afternoon, came across a large wind gap running east and west and they walked its base the rest of the day, camping that night with a fire made from the scraps of acacia trees that had found a home in the more sheltered nooks of the gap. The following day they spent most of their time inching along a granite shelf that was dangerous, but circumvented a detour of untellable distance. At the top of the rise they found themselves on the eastern end of the Omoya's high plains that stretched flatly before them like a twilight plane spotted with acacias and stunted black pines with one more rise of mountain tops promising themselves on the other side. They made their camp near the lip among a bunch of sagebrush plants and a hawk circled overhead, insouciant among the high mountain winds as if lost. It was cold in the night. The darkness elemental at this altitude. He woke earlier than usual because of the cold—dark still—like deep water, but just the whisper of the coming sun was enough for the night to loosen its grip. Bird was nowhere to be seen, the mare either, and he looked east off the lip and at the sun rising below him and when its light kissed his face he knew that the flame was in him and the flame was in Bird and if they were indeed the ghosts they were accused of then they were the kind of ghosts to be reckoned with—the kind that could glide through this shadowland, across the borders of men and nations, carrying the will of Rathalla in their hearts, and the tongue of Rathalla in their mouths, and those that would listen might be haunted, and those that resisted would be done violence.

PART III

The Bird and the Wolf

He was an alien here, looking out from behind the naked base of a massive red cedar that was taller than any tree he had ever seen by a hundred feet. Behind him, the mare grazed the forest floor where the grass, in places where the canopy hadn't stolen the sunlight, grew in a shade of green that all other greens were made from. Everything was wet—he experienced more rainfall in their one and a half days in Kardona than a decade in the Dialla and it appeared that the fine leather of his pack was the only thing able to hold up against the water. They were down range from the Omoya peaks, endless overcast skies, and they were out of food and also cold at that elevation with the constant moisture and no experience or method for dealing with it. They had seen no one else and had passed two slanted, mud-roofed structures up to now, when the grumbling of his stomach pushed him to demand a stop at the third one. She said that it wasn't a good idea for armed strangers to approach a lone farmstead in a country at war, but she was hungry too and they decided that she alone would be less intimidating.

He watched her approach the house from the south side, through a field of stubby, large, leafed plants, past a small chicken coup and an outside overhang that covered a single chewing cow tethered to a wooden crossbar. She knocked on the door of the house and walked back a dozen paces before putting both of her hands into the air above her head. He saw the door open but could only see the silhouette of a person and their voices carried strongly through the humid air, though he couldn't make out what they said. By and by Bird let her hands down and went into the house and Ernest watched anxiously as the door closed behind her and time passed. When she came out she angled away from Ernest's hiding place, and he hissed at the horse to get its attention and then skirted the forest's edge around the farm to find her crouched in the trees over her pack.

"How'd it go?" He asked.

"It's a good thing you sent me."

"Why's that?"

"Because she had stew in there. Hot as a forge."

"Sard off."

"Just vegetable, but it was damn good stuff."

"I'm going back."

"You can't."

"Why not?"

"Because it's a lone mother and her daughter in there and they don't need to be traumatized by some armed, strange man knocking on their door, asking to come in. Plus, I ate all the stew."

He mumbled a string of curses and she pulled something from her pack and said, "I did get something for you though."

"What is it?"

"She gave this to me to dip in the stew, but I kept it for you."

"The fucking dip bread?"

She held it out to him and raised her eyebrows at his outrage before he begrudgingly snatched it out of her hand, and with a mouthful of the hard bread he said, "I hope you burnt your tongue."

"I didn't. And I found out about that little village you mentioned —Bontu."

He half choked on the bread, "Is it near?"

"Pretty damn near. She said if we keep going north from here we'll run into a river. All we have to do is follow it down range and we'll come to a bridge and village, and that village is Bontu."

They strafed along the mountainside the rest of the morning, making north and west as it was convenient to them, before stopping midday in a narrow valley spotted with trillium and fireweed, where they attempted to air out their soggy clothes using the few sun rays able to penetrate the grey skies above. As Ernest shook out his cloak and looked at his feet, wet and cold, sticking out of his sandals, he said, "How do they live like this? I feel like a piece of soggy bread. Dip bread."

The frail sunlight vanished in the afternoon, bringing with it a slow, light drizzle that tapped the canopy and the underbrush with such life and such unceasing noise that it sent a shiver up his spine unrelated to his temperature. The mare seemed unmoved by the change in climate, and just before nightfall the three of them encountered a massive elm tree so robust that the featherlike dirt at its base was as dry as the Dialla itself and they made camp for the night. It continued to rain, and his brain, conditioned to the hollow silence of his desert homeland, stirred him awake constantly in alarm of this noisy new environment, and he heard Bird shift next to him and knew that hers did the same.

They woke the next morning to continued rainfall that didn't so much fall as exist, void of gravity, in an atmosphere held together by water droplets and only by walking through the static moisture did it contact their faces shielded under their hood-drawn cloaks. The mare grazed and Bird exercised, and they all moved on through the wet forest of vine maples and spruces and salmonberries and duckfoot and near midday they came across a shrub of red huckleberry.

"You can eat these," Bird said.

"Is it better to be poisoned than starving?"

She pinched one of the bright red berries between her pointer finger and thumb and snapped it off the large shrub and slipped it into her mouth. "I don't remember much about Kardona, but I remember these."

They spent the better part of an hour picking berries. Eating many of them and stashing the rest away in their packs before moving on. Not long afterward, the sound of a large, quick moving body of water came crashing through the forest, and they discovered their sought-after river, being fed from the mountains above by a thin waterfall that sent water plummeting hundreds of feet from its lip. It was as loud as it was gorgeous—white mountain water cascading in freefall over granite shelves all covered with a skin of slick moss while low junipers and countless shrubs grew at impossible angles out of cracks, fighting upward for the sun's light. He said *wow* underneath his breath and when she said that they should move on, he said "I think we should stay."

"You've never seen a waterfall before?"

"Not like this."

"Okay. I'll have a look around."

He made himself comfortable at a rock base around the trunk of a big cedar and watched the waterfall, snacking on the red berries, while Bird and the mare disappeared into the undergrowth. She came back just before nightfall with an armful of dead, dry branches underneath her arm and started a fire under the cover of the skyward crowns. A fire made in that land of water. He watched the waterfall until it became too dark to see and when he fell asleep that night he was not bothered this time by the noise of the strange land.

At this elevation the river was narrow, deep, and quick moving. When he woke the next morning, Bird had finished her exercises, and she sat at the river's edge, looking across, while the mare drank. When he joined them she said, "Can you swim?"

"No. You?"

"Sounds like were going for the bridge."

They followed the river down mountain, shadowing its swift waters as close as they could. Smaller cliff faces appeared with smaller waterfalls, and they were slow in detouring around the steep, slick descents for the rest of the morning. That afternoon they came across another wooden, mud-roofed structure with a wisp of grey smoke coming from its small chimney and they quietly passed on. The makeup of the forest changed the further they descended, with the majority of spruces and firs swapped out for red alders and more dwarfed cedars and thickets of aspen and the occasional willow. They stayed that night underneath the curtained branches of one of the willows, and the rain let up for a night and they slept. The following day she found another plant populated with dark blue berries this time and they ate these too as they picked them.

In the afternoon the elevation leveled off greatly and they came to the forest's edge, and several hundred paces beyond an open field of bleeding heart and asper, they saw the bridge. She motioned for Ernest to stop and the mare stopped behind them and the two of them snuck up the front line of trees, crouched behind a salal shrub and looked out. The bridge was constructed of a dark wood and looked just wide enough for most wagons— worn tracks ran its length, at least two hundred paces, along with a thick guard rail on both sides. Beyond the bridge, toward the horizon and just within sight of their position they could see a small clutter of rooftops that signaled the southeastern end of the village of Bontu. They turned their attention back to the bridge and the sitting figures of men that were stationed at each end, five in total, with two on their side and three on the opposite. Bird said, "Kardoans."

"How do you know?"

"The cloaks."

"What do you want to do?"

"I'm thinking."

"Okay."

"Let's watch for a bit," she said.

"Okay."

They watched for over an hour and nothing happened until one of the guards from the far end of the bridge left the other four behind and walked toward the distant village. The lone guard returned awhile later and they saw him distribute food among the other four and they were all motionless again as dusk approached. Ernest said, "What're you thinking?"

"I'm thinking I wish that someone would come travelling along this road so we could get a look at how these guys behave. But since that doesn't look like it's happening today, I'm thinking that, unless you're anxious to get going, we wait for nightfall and hope that they're uninspired or unprofessional, and abandon their posts for the night. It's unlikely, but it could save us a lot of trouble if they do."

"Let's wait then."

He made himself more comfortable and soon drifted off to an early sleep. He woke periodically through the night as a light rainfall blew over and saw her in the same position as when he first went to sleep. He asked if they were still there and she nodded and then he asked if she wanted him to watch so she could get some sleep and she waved him off dismissively. Another light drizzle settled in just after he woke the next morning, and his stomach ached deeply as he ate more of the foraged berries out his pack.

She ate too and they looked out at the bridge where all five guard were still stationed, their cloaks pulled up over their heads to a man.

He said, "What now?"

"Now is when we wish we knew how to swim."

"Not a lot of opportunity for it where I'm from. I don't know about you."

She chewed on the inside of her cheek for a moment and then said, "They might be actual, professional Kardoan soldiers protecting a supply line or protecting locales, and that'd be great for us—with a couple of lies we could be on our way. They might be deserters too. A group of them flees from the heavy fighting on the warfront, bands together, and maybe they shake travelers down for bridge fares or charge locales for their protection, knowing that all the able-bodied men are off fighting and they have free reign. That wouldn't be so bad—they'd hustle us for some silver and we'd be on our way. But they could be cutthroats—those cloaks aren't hard to come by—and they're posing as soldiers while they take the lives and belongings of anybody that passes through."

He retrieved a pinch of herb from his pack and worked it into his cheek and spat. He said, "How do we figure out which one they are?"

"Without anybody else passing through, we can only guess. And if I were of the cutthroat variety and I was in their position, what I'd do with two travelers like us is I'd let them pass, let them get halfway down the bridge, and then have the other guards come from the far side. Trap them in the middle of the bridge. My chances against five of them are not great, but trapped between five of them on that bridge, with no place to move, is a death sentence."

"I wouldn't have thought of that."

"I guess I'd make a better cutthroat than you."

"Shit," he said. "I guess you would. You got any ideas on what to do about it?"

"Not any good ones. We could go around, keep following the river, and hope for another bridge, but we're likely to end up in this same situation as we are now, with all the time lost. We could get up there and I could have the two of them on the near side dead before the other three even got close. It improves our chances but seeing how you are with the ethical killing and all that, I'm guessing you don't like that option very much."

"You're right."

"We could assume they are good guys—professional soldiers carrying out a boring assignment—but I'm not stepping a foot on that bridge with two at my back and three in front of me. I didn't make it this far to throw my life away on the optimism of five strangers, and neither did you."

"So what are we left with?"

"Let's get over there and you talk first," she said. "If that doesn't work then I'll talk."

"Okay. But can you move that weapon of yours out of sight. And maybe put on your extra shirt over that armor."

She did what he suggested, sliding the fist weapon back along her belt buckle so that it was positioned out of sight and she buttoned up her linen shirt so that her armor was covered completely when her cloak was pulled up over her shoulders. She centered her pack on her back, covering the lump of the shield and he nodded his approval. With a short whistle to the mare, the three of them walked out from the tree line, across the field of wildflowers to the road and headed north toward the bridge. Getting out and away from the dense forest allowed them an unobstructed view of Mount Ucari—directly north of them and positioned just west of the main Omoya spine, it was more wide than tall, and perfectly conical in its shape, with a dull, snow covered peak. Ernest looked east, back up the range from where they came, and saw the dense, endless forest that ran the entire elevation of the range and wished he had more time to look at it as the bridge and guards came into view and Bird spoke out of the side of her mouth to say, "Whatever you're going to say, don't try to intimidate in anyway—no veiled threats or anything ominous—I want them to underestimate us."

"Okay," he said, and then spat.

"And if there's a fight, don't try to kill anybody. Get that sword out and defend yourself. Keep your feet moving always away from whoever comes at you. Sidestep any rushes. Use your fundamentals. If I die, then your best chance is to run for the tree line and hope your stamina is better than any of theirs."

He swallowed thickly and responded with a grim nod as they approached the bridge and they saw one of the guards hit the arm of the other to get his attention and the two of them stood up, sentinels to the bridge's portal. Ernest held up a hand in greeting and the three of them stopped a half dozen paces from the two guards and he said, "Something wrong with the bridge?"

"Aint nothing wrong with the bridge." The guard on the left spoke. He was close to his third decade of life—filled out form, a thick, blonde beard—and he spat into the road's dirt when he finished talking.

"In that case, we'd like to cross it."

The guard on the right spoke this time. He was short, thin, with a patchy beard and roughly the same age as the first. They could see his lower lip bulge with herb and he pulled from a leather waterskin that, even from their distance, reeked of wine. He was looking at their feet—the open-toed sandals so out of place in this country and said, "Who are you?"

"We're nobody."

"Yeah? What's nobody doing here trying to cross my bridge?"

Ernest raised his chin to gesture to the mountain behind them, "We're on a pilgrimage to Mount Ucari. To worship and please the god, Koomakul, before he devours this world."

The guard with the beard shifted anxiously on his feet and rested his left wrist upon the hilt of the longsword in his belt. He said, "You're not wearing the orange robes like the others."

"We were converted on the Iron Road, out of the Dialla."

The thin one spat and said, "Good for you."

"So can we cross?" Ernest asked.

"It costs."

"How much?"

"Three silver coin per," the bearded one said.

"Six silver?"

The man offered an obnoxious smile and said, "It's a nice bridge."

Ernest looked at Bird and saw her eyes narrow in anger at the absurd toll and, wanting to act quickly to avoid any conflict, he quickly pulled out his hefty pouch of silver to move things along. "We have the money. Thing is, there's a great superstition where we're from, and one can't cross a bridge with people on each end without bringing a lifetime of bad luck upon themselves."

The thin man spat. "What's that mean?"

"It means that we'd need you to walk to other end of the bridge there, and allow us to come across with all of you on just the one side."

"What kind of superstition is that?"

"The same as the rest."

The thin man drank again from the wine in his skin and looked, with bloodshot eyes, at Ernest's bulky sack of coins and Ernest knew that he had erred as he slipped the purse back under his cloak, out of sight.

Ernest said, "I've got the six silver right here. If we can agree on everyone sticking to one end of the bridge."

The thin man said, "It's eight silver."

"Eight? You said three per," Ernest said.

"Three per and two for the horse."

Bird spoke for the first time, "The horse pays a toll now?"

"Horses are hard on bridges."

"What's it supposed to pay with? All the silver it comes by honestly?"

"Not my concern."

Ernest could hear the anger in Bird's voice and he intervened, "How about we do seven, and we get on our way?"

The drunk one pulled his cloak off of his left shoulder to reveal the longsword sheathed on his belt and he said, "How about we just take the eight, and anything else that we want?"

Ernest held up both hands and said, "We don't want that kind of trouble."

The one with the beard brought his left hand to his mouth and let out a shrill whistle, causing the three on the other end of the bridge to look their way and start walking the bridge. Bird looked the drunk man in the eye and said something and the man said, "What did you say?"

"I said *you killed yourself*."

She pushed forward off her left foot, dipping her head and shoulder in the same motion to shed her pack to the ground before drawing her sword during her next step. The drunk man's eyes grew wide at her approach, and he dropped his wine skin and was able to draw his sword before she arrived, but only had time to offer an awkward parry. When Bird reached him she put her momentum behind a hard, horizontal cut that sent the man's longsword out wide and then plunged her shortsword into his torso, and the man collapsed under her with a long, pneumatic sigh.

The man with the blonde beard hissed, *you bitch*, and drew his sword, rushing at Bird as she wrestled her blade out of the other man's chest. She got it out in time to dance backward, away from the man's undisciplined charge, and she looked sideways out of her eye at the other three coming across the bridge, who were nearing the halfway point. Even with her fist weapon pushed behind her on her belt, Bird was able to slip her left hand into it as she retreated, and when the man ended his flurry with a hard overhead chop, she sidestepped it and brought the steel claw down on the sword, pinning its tip into the ground. The man's eyes widened as she brought her shortsword around hard on the man's wrists. The cut was powerful enough to sever both wrists completely, but her blade contacted the long pommel of the man's sword, stopping her blade halfway through his left wrist. With his ruptured right hand falling to the grass, and his left hand dangling off his wrist like a stage prop, he took two shaky steps backward and sat abruptly on the ground, in a state of shock.

Bird checked the three oncoming soldiers, nearly across the bridge now, and she sheathed both her weapons in order to unclasp her cloak, sending it in a heap to the ground, and unbuttoned and removed her extra shirt, revealing her slatted steel armor. She pulled on the latch for the claw-like weapon so it was once again positioned just off of the left side of her pelvis, and then pulled her shield off over her head, sliding her left arm through its leather strap and into the firm steel grip. She bounced the girth of the shield on her healing elbow and felt no pain or resistance come from the healed limb. She drew the shortsword again in her right hand and spun it one time while the blonde man recovered from his shock and wailed pathetically for his last minutes of consciousness before the blood loss took him.

Bird was watching the three newcomers come to the end of the bridge but looked at the wailing man briefly and said, "You should've taken the seven," and he blubbered incoherently while Ernest, watching on with the mare, took off his pack and reached for the sword given to him by the Crimson Shrouds.

"Put your sword away, Ernest. I'll pull them away from the bridge, and you can go across behind them. If I go down then you should have enough of a head start."

The three guards made it to the end of the bridge, longswords drawn and breathing heavily—they were dressed in the same leather armor and forest green cloaks as their other two comrades who were now deceased at their feet. It was two men and a woman, all of them young, and with dirty faces and angry eyes they looked at the innocuous Ernest and the mare and then toward Bird, who was crouched in a defensive posture just paces away. All three of them removed their cloaks and they looked at Ernest one last time before, without a word, beginning their assault on the lone woman. Bird immediately began a measured, backpeddling retreat into the open field of ankle-high grass and wildflowers behind her, as the three guards constantly moved and worked to get her surrounded. Their attack wasn't flawless, but they were experienced fighters who handled their longswords with aptitude.

Ernest looked at the bridge and knew that he should be on his way to carry on his errand, with or without Bird, but he couldn't take his eyes off the conflict before him and his right hand itched at the thought of taking up his sword and, in whatever way that he could, join the fight. However, after another handful of moments of watching the skirmish, it was clear to him that he could only get in the way, and the dance that Bird performed was as if it was choreographed beforehand by both parties, or that some unseen oracle whispered into Bird's ear every move before it happened and she reacted to every whisper with perfection.

The two-handed swings that weren't met with a *whoosh* of air, sounded off of Bird's steel sword and shield with the kind of fine, metallic acoustics that resounded through the wildflowers and off the forest line and carried on their waves the kind of reverberation meant for a world of death, and not this place so teeming. Their dance went on, and the occasional horizontal cut would send the heads of decapitated wildflowers spinning to the grassy floor, and the mare beside Ernest watched the spectacle with her head lowered and her dopey eyes as if their task was a mundane one, and this performance before was no more interesting to her than when a handler cleaned out a trough or brushed the dirt out of her fine coat. Ernest could see in Bird's movement the exercises she did every morning, and how she could slow the movements down or speed them up whenever she needed, but she never rushed. With less room to work, against three opponents, she would have been put into positions of high risk and high danger, but out in the field she was limitless, and she was conditioned, and she looked to Ernest like she could have fought twice as many enemies as she did, forever.

They half circled around the field, back toward Ernest, until they were near enough that he could hear their breathing and a flurry ensued that his eyes could not follow and, when it was over, one of the guards pulled up from his assault as if confused. Bird and the other two continued on, the guards now slower and more measured with one of them down, and Ernest saw the third one drop his longsword and sit at the edge of the field with a hand pressed to the inside of his thigh, where his dark brown trousers blossomed with fresh blood.

Bird handled the two that were left with the same strategy she employed against the poachers back in the Dialla. She let the guards get on each side of her, pinned in the middle, before feinting toward the man just enough to get him on his back foot and then spinning hard to launch a vigorous attack at the woman. The guard was overwhelmed by Bird working from behind her shield, thrusting half a dozen times and connecting with four of them, and by the time the guard lost her footing and rolled backwards into the field, she was three-quarters dead. Bird did a quick half-turn, using the momentum to fling the shield off of her arm and at the head of the charging man and—completely caught off guard by the move—the man's nose was shattered and his eyes filled with tears as he swung his sword half-blind in an aimless defense. He was dead moments later.

Ernest exhaled and he watched Bird checking the bodies of the dead guards before he turned his attention to the injured one, who still sat, cross-legged and head hung, with both of his hands pressed down on his wounded thigh. Ernest approached him and tossed the man's longsword further out into the field. Bird finished her round and stood with the mare some paces behind Ernest, who sat on his heels in front of the man. The blood that came out of the man's leg was plentiful, and dark, and Ernest could see that he was too injured to be dangerous.

The man spoke quietly and said, "Will you help me?"

"No, friend. This is as far as you go, but I'll stay with you if you don't want to be alone."

The dying guard nodded his head with an air of solemn understanding and tears welled under his eyelids and his voice was soft. He asked Ernest, "Are you Samsaran?"

"No. Are you?"

"No. But I wish now that I was. I wish I got another chance at this world. I'd be a nicer person." His sad voice cracked with emotion. "I'd be nicer to my mum."

Ernest forced a smile and nodded, and the man continued, "What happens to me now? I don't believe in anything."

"It's okay," Ernest said.

"No," the man shook his head weakly. "I should've believed in something. I should've done something. And now I go into darkness."

"Nobody knows what's on the other side."

The man nodded and he cried and the color left his skin completely and he began to shiver so violently that Ernest could hear his teeth chattering. The man said he was thirsty and Ernest offered him his own pouch in this land of water and the man drank deeply until all of it was gone. He then looked past Ernest at Bird and he said, "You're an incredible warrior. I felt like I was trying to hit a ghost." Bird dipped her head to acknowledge that she heard him, but she said nothing.

The man looked toward the bridge and the bodies of the first two guards and he said, "What happened?"

Ernest said, "The one there on the right wanted a toll of eight silver for crossing, and then got mean when we didn't want to pay it."

"Eight?" The man winced. "What an asshole." He looked down at his thigh and his brown trousers soaked through top to bottom and the pool of blood that he sat in and he said, "Will you bury me?"

"No."

"The animals will come for us."

Ernest nodded and said, "It's your gift."

"I'm scared."

"It's okay."

"I'm really scared."

"It's okay."

They were quiet and the man cried and tried to sniffle the snot that ran down his face along with the tears that dripped off his chin into the dark pool of blood that was all absorbed into the ground as if it were just rain from another day.

"I'll be alone now."

"Are you sure?"

"Yes."

"Okay."

Ernest stood and he pulled his cloak over his head and when they reached the bridge he looked back and the man was still cross-legged and slumped and when they were halfway across the bridge he looked back again and the man was lying motionless and collapsed on the ground. The bridge was sturdy, and constructed of various types of timber, but he kept a nervous hand on the large guard rail as the azure water rushed by underfoot, and on the other side they discovered the supply stash of the guards and they tore into the dried biscuits and bacon and jam and fresh milk and Ernest went to the river shore to vomit once, before returning to eat more.

They finished eating and sat gorged against the bridge posts not unlike the dispatched guards and Ernest said, "Maybe we need to distance ourselves from here before someone comes along."

"Anyone that comes along now owes us nothing but gratitude."

"A lot of people might not see it that way."

"Maybe you're right."

"Do you think we could've tried talking to the three that crossed? Explain to them what happened?"

"Life is full of could'ves, until it's not."

They skirted the east edge of Bontu, keeping out of the village's sight until they intersected with a northbound road not unlike the one that crossed the bridge. They walked the road into the late afternoon without seeing anybody and she kept asking what they were looking for and he would say *we'll know it when we see it*. A short while later, as the sun's light grew thick with its angled descent over the western horizon, they passed a large willow just off the road that had a slanted eyeball the size of person's torso carved into its wide trunk. There were faint, red markings in the lighter underwood that suggested it had been painted once, and he tipped his chin at it and said, "That's what we're looking for."

"What now?"

He oriented himself with the setting sun and pulled his arms around, pointing them north and east, toward the tree line, and said, "This way."

They left the path and crossed a grassy verge before slipping back into the dark forest, like the one of their descent, but they only had to pick their way through the gloomy, dense trees for a few hundred paces before the dim lights of a structure appeared in the woodland. It was a large cabin, well made, and it had a single sentinel guarding the front door and she stood confidently as the strangers approached and then ushered them inside when Ernest gave his name.

The inside of the cabin was beautiful and luxurious. They stepped into a large, open room overseen by a loft that went back, angled beyond their eyesight, and a large, stone fireplace that burned steadily. Across the way was a fire-burning stove and furniture carved from fine, polished wood and a rug in the main room of some large beast that Ernest had never seen before. A single, dark hallway ran back off the main room to a trio of small bedrooms and there was nobody in sight and the two of them stood unspeaking as the sound of movement came from the loft above and they watched as a woman shuffled her way down the steep, open stairway to the room.

She was old, with thin, white hair and a voice that was soft and kind and as she neared the bottom of the stairs she said, "Yas, yas, come in, come in. Are you two still standing in that doorway?" And Ernest and Bird exchanged a confused glance at the obvious nature of the question but as the woman approached them, they could see the milky cataracts floating thickly in both of her eyeballs.

She said, "And your names?"

"I'm Ernest, and this is Bird."

The old woman held up her hands and said, "Do you mind if I see you?"

"Okay."

She moved in close to Ernest and used her fingertips to explore his facial features. Her hands were soft—the kind that had never seen hard labor—and had the leatherlike, taught smoothness that came with age. Her white eyes drifted up over his head and she smiled to herself and said *handsome*, and then she gently pinched his left cheek and said, "There used to be more meat here."

"It was a hard journey."

"Let's get you a real meal."

The old woman made no signal, but a figure came out of the dark hallway, a boyish man that was either in his late teen years or his early twenties and went to work in the kitchen area near the stove. The woman stepped over to Bird next and touched her face and said, "Your name is Bird?"

"Yes."

"It's a beautiful name." And as she touched Bird's face she continued, "For a beautiful woman. A warrior woman, I understand it?"

"Ernest hired me to protect him on his journey."

"Yas. And right that he did. You know, it's unsurprising to me that Lady Kira could send three envoys composed of the finest Olerians she has, and not a soul could make it here, but just two Copperfoot, forced to travel the most dangerous and remote parts of the Dialla, stand before me now—none worse for the wear with the exception of some unintended weight loss. Truly a wonderful people."

"Who are you?" Bird asked.

"My name is Cordilia Vici Merriam, but child, you can just call me Ilia, like everybody else does."

"Ilia, the historian?"

"Yas, child, that's me. But let's get you two out of this doorway before we talk."

They were shown to a room down the hallway on the first floor where they shed their packs and cloaks. Bird looked at Ernest with a quizzical expression and tapped her armor and Ernest nodded and said, "We're safe here," and she began unlatching the armor. She said, "I didn't know you were friends with Oleria's most famous historian."

"Ilia was great friends with Lady Kira's father, Cevrias. She's still close with the family, obviously, but I'm meeting her for the first time today, same as you are."

"Is she the one taking us to the Samsarans? She's blind."

"No, I don't think so. Ilia knows everybody, so she'll get us into the right hands."

They went back into the main room where the fireplace burned, and Ilia sat at a sturdy oak table with one hand in her lap and the other sat on the tabletop with a delicate shake even at rest. There were two bronze plates set out with cuts of bread on them and the young man hovered over a pot on the stove, where a warm scent of stew originated. Ernest and Bird sat and the young man brought them over a cube of fresh butter. Ilia's plagued eyes faced the fire as if the flame was all she could see in her blindness and she spoke in her pleasant tone and said to them, "There's no need for table manners after the journey you've been on. Marcus will be over with the stew as soon as its ready."

They tore into the bread and butter and the young man brought over two bowls of stew, each with a malleable contrail of steam coming out of the top. They ate and the old blind woman spoke and she said, "You know, I've spoken to more Copperfoot people in the last fifteen years than maybe either of you two have in your entire lives. When Ernest here came to work for Lady Kira, I immediately wanted to interview him, but Kira assured me it was as much of a waste of time as all my other interviews with your people. It was obvious, early on, that the Copperfoot held deeply to a faith structure that was not to be shared with outsiders. Of course, even the strongest and most zealous cultures have defectors and disenchanted individuals—but if the Copperfoot has those types of people, I never found them. To a man and to a woman, nobody would share with me your history. I'm old now, and I'll die soon, and it will be the greatest regret of my career, and maybe my life, that I wasn't able to record your story to history."

Bird spoke between a spoonful of stew and said, "It's no regret to us."

"Yas, I know that now," Ilia said. "Know it all too well. And I think it's a shame that generations in the future will never get to learn of your exceptional people."

"We're not all dead yet."

"But if you never speak your story, then you're as good as dead, even as you sit here before me in the flesh."

Bird's tone of voice was sharp, if not rude, as she said, "If we were such a beautiful people then why did your empire kill so many of us? Take our iron? Our horses? Our home?"

Ilia nodded off the tone with a soft, gracious nod of her head and said, "If *I* were the emperor I wouldn't have, but the machinations of an empire are complex, ambitious, and—above all—ruthless. How many people out there, in this moment, dream of the fall of Oleria? How many out there do more than dream, and actively work to make that downfall a reality? Oleria, like all empires, is fragile. Built on a whisper of a better life than the one you knew before or the one you might imagine afterward. And in order to give that to its citizens, the empire must grow—it must continue to dangle in front them commodities and luxuries and progress, or at least the illusion thereof, to keep them content and docile. For the Copperfoot, it was more than that though, because iron, yes, is a commodity, but it is so much more than that. Your peoples' work with it—forging steel—will alter the world. Forever. Every army—every nation and tribe—without access to the steel you created, is inferior to every army with it. It will be what war is waged with, and it will be the reason for the waging of those wars, until it is the backbone of every city and civilization across the planet, with humanity perched atop its shoulders. Someday, somewhere deep in the earth, there might come another metal that will do to steel what steel has done to bronze, but this age will be shaped by the iron of the Copperfoot, and whatever path humanity goes down, will be in part because of the creativity, and ingenuity of your people. It's my feeling that such an achievement should be recorded and preserved for future generations to understand the Copperfoot's con- tribution to the world, but I've long since given up on making that happen."

Bird set her small wooden spoon inside of her empty, bronze bowl and pushed it away from her with the backs of her fingers before using a linen side-cloth to wipe the corners of her mouth. Ernest signaled to the young man at the stove for another bowl and Bird said, "The only history I know is my own, but even in that short amount of time I believe I've seen enough of people and empires to make some unfavorable conclusions."

Bird heard Ernest mumble *oh no*, but she continued anyway. "It seems to me that the Olerian empire is a sickness upon the world. Much like a fever spreading through a household—it'll grow and infect every region and nation that it can until it, or all of its carriers, is dead. You speak so fondly of your idea of who the Copperfoot are, but how many people like mine has your beloved empire ruined on its rise? Dozens? Hundreds? What contributions would they have made had they not been consumed by your already gorged empire just so you could sell your cheap wine and linen to the conquered?"

Ernest bumped Bird with his elbow, but from the head of the table, Ilia responded with a warm laugh. "You're exactly right, of course. I suspect you would have made an excellent historian, child. In fact, with your aura, I think you're one of those who could be exceptional at anything you choose."

Bird's tone was firm, but not rude. She said, "You're exceptional at flattery."

"That's right too, but I have no reason to flatter you. The one thing you have to offer me, I know you'll not give. Your vision of what people *could be* is noble, but naïve. Should a more powerful nation come along, it would do to Oleria what Oleria has done to countless others. Either you're at the top of the food chain, or you're at the mercy of whatever is. What one nation inflicts on another is just a projection of their fear of what would be done to them in the same context. Travel to any corner of the world where one people is at the full mercy of another, and you'll find nothing but cruelty."

"You use their cruelty to justify your own."

"Perhaps, child. But I've been to a lot of corners, and cruelty is a thread that runs through the fabric of every society that I've seen. It's what brought me here to Kardona. It's what brought *you* here to Kardona. And, in all of my years, I've never witnessed a place as cruel as this."

Ernest finished eating and said, "If what we've heard is true, I agree with you on that."

Ilia said, "How much do you know?"

"Just the rumors. If you could paint a clearer picture for us, it might help with the business we're on."

Ilia nodded in no particular direction and said, "That's your right, but I'm old now and I'm tired, so I will try to be quick with it."

Ernest nodded and she started talking, "You must know now that one of the primary principles of the Samsaran faith is one of rebirth—a Samsaran dies, and then is reborn three days later so that they may live and die again. This cycle is repeated for every Samsaran soul until, on this planet, they achieve a high enough status that, upon death, they go into their true afterlife. What exactly needs to be achieved in order to reach the true afterlife is unclear—I've seen the texts—but that point isn't important right now. The Samsarans proselytize heavily, and in the last century their numbers have grown large in Kardona, particularly in the rural regions of the country.

Since Oleria has acquired a taste for herb in recent years, the demand and price for it have surged." Her eyes met Ernest's for a moment, as if she could see him, and he looked away and she continued talking, "With swelling numbers and the majority control of this new asset, a man by the name of Udura Atun saw an opportunity. Discovering who this man was—what he was—is proving to be almost as frustrating as your own people, because everything around him—the stories and the people—became fanatical with his legend, that the truth, I fear, may be lost to history. What is true, beyond any degree of certainty, is that Atun was a visionary and a leader. He traveled around Kardona and sent missionaries outside of it, all carrying with them the idea of a Samsaran nation. He was an exceptional orator. This man convinced simple farmers that it was in their best interest to go to war so that they could secure Kardona and its herb for themselves, and grow out their new, religiously pure nation. Eventually they did just that."

Ernest interrupted to say, "And they lost."

Bird looked at Ernest and they shared a nod of understanding—that everything Ilia said was the same as he had told her back in the Dialla.

"They lost. But a million people and more have lost wars and life in the region has gone on much like before. But not here. Not yet. Atun and his Samsarans waged a dishonorable war, and they made a lot of enemies doing it. Early on, before war had broken out completely, there wasn't a lot of animosity toward the Samsarans around here. When Atun militarized them, he only had the Kardoan army to contend with, which is not formidable. It's largely amateur and relies on volunteers to keep its numbers. But as the atrocities of the Samsarans became more numerous—and it became clear there would be no place for a non-Samsaran in this region if they were to win the war—everybody turned on them."

Bird muttered, "He sounds like an idiot."

"Yes," Ilia said. "There is often a thin line between zealotry and idiocy, but Atun certainly favored the former in most respects. He gambled aggressively, but you can see his logic though, no? His own army was largely amateur, too, and he likely didn't feel confident leading them into an enduring, large-scale conflict. He figured that if he struck hard enough, and fast enough—with iron-hard cruelty—that Kardona would fall before having a chance to put up an organized resistance to his uprising. However, that cruelty has backfired in so many ways. In response to the Samsarans' abhorrent behavior, common civilians—many who would have had no reason to get involved in any war—were running interference on supply lines, and set up their own network of spies to track every move made by the Samsaran army. Many went so far as to destroy their own crops—seasons worth of work—if it looked to fall into Samsaran hands."

"And the war continues?" Ernest asked.

"Ah, yes. Sorry for the confusion—bad habit of a historian to put everything in the past tense. The war is still ongoing, but we're in the final chapter now and it can't end soon enough. The Samsarans are defeated but they can't surrender."

Bird played dumb to ask, "Why not?"

"About one-hundred days ago the war turned at a battle near the village of Bend. A place called Falsom Field. I'm still piecing together the details, but Udura Atun was killed at this battle and, on top of losing their foremost leader and impetus for the whole war, the Samsarans were soundly defeated. For all intents, it should have been the end of the war. However, something happened within the Kardoan army, and they discussed the idea that Atun was dead, but would be reborn again after the battle and it was just a matter of time before he aged enough to start another war."

"But the Kardoans don't believe in that," Ernest said.

"I know, but they understood that the Samsarans did. On this premise they have, since that time," Ilia stuttered and fought a snag in her throat for a moment before continuing, "carried out the wicked act of murdering Samsaran newborns."

Just hearing it said out loud again made Bird catch her breath as Ernest dipped his head into his hands and rubbed the back of his eyelids. Ilia was silent for several more moments and the young man came back to the table and took away their dishes and she continued, "Of course, it's a plan that is as absurd as it is vile. There's no way to tell if any slain child is actually Atun, and if you miss a day, or—forbid it—succeed in killing the right child, then the cycle would go on endlessly anyway. The Kardoans have taken this Samsaran belief—rooted deeply in optimism and eternal rebirth—and twisted it into the opposite. Into mayhem. The stories that I have recorded this last season have been the hardest to write in my life. I can't imagine worse stories. Your business here is between Lady Kira and yourselves, but I hope it plays some part in ending the slaughter."

Ilia stood and apologized and said, "It's long past my bedtime, you two. And such talk before sleeping gives me awful dreams. I'm sorry. We can talk more in the morning."

They were dismissive of her apology, and she made her way back up the stairs and the two of them stood to retreat to their own room. The young man checked on them again and asked, "Does the horse of yours out there need anything?"

Ernest shook his head and said, "She manages to care for herself."

"You guys do it a little different out in the Dialla, I guess."

THEY LEFT EARLY THE NEXT morning, amidst a phenomenon that neither Bird nor Ernest had experienced often in their desert-dwelling lives—fog. It was dense around them, and Bird glanced about nervously as the young man from the night before, Marcus, readied his own horse for their trip and talked quietly with Ernest a dozen paces away. When she heard footsteps behind her in the brush she turned to see Ilia approaching her gingerly, with a cotton shawl draped over her shoulders and her clouded eyes looking like tiny mirrors against the fog.

"Child."

"Yes, Ilia?"

"It was a pleasure getting to meet you last night."

"It was for me as well. I apologize for my attitude."

"Your attitude is justified, young one, and it was no offense to me. Your aura is so strong—like steel. I will write to the Lady Kira about you. I think she would be very interested in meeting you. What are your plans for when you make it home?"

"I haven't had a proper home in thirteen years. Right now, my only thoughts are about helping Ernest and leaving this place alive."

Ilia reached out with an open palm and placed it on the steel armor that encased Bird's torso and said, "Your home is here, child. The state of the Dialla is in flux, but so is the state of the world. In here, you are always yourself."

Bird nodded but the blind woman did not see this and they stood quietly with the old woman's hand on her chest for a moment before Ilia said, "Marcus told me last night of your armor, and your weapon. He said he has never seen anything like it. Do you mind?"

"Of course not."

Bird pulled her cloak aside so that Ilia's hands could explore the crevices in her armor and then she pulled the first weapon from her belt and guided it into the old woman's hands and said *careful it's sharp* while Ilia explored the weapon the same way she explored Bird's face the night before. Ilia said, "I've heard of weapons like this in the far south, but I understood them to be mostly decorative. Yet you use it?"

"I use it."

Ilia handed the weapon back to Bird, "It all seems very remarkable, and I'm sure there is a story behind every piece."

"There is."

"I'd like to tell that story, unless it too infringes on your beliefs."

"We can tell stories about armor."

"Then someday I hope we have the chance to do that. Back in the Dialla if we both live to make it back there."

"You'll live," Bird said.

"I'm old."

Bird said nothing and the two women stood side by side looking toward Marcus and Ernest, who appeared ready to leave.

"I think it's time now," Bird said.

"Yas, yas," Ilia said in her slow dialect. "Marcus there is smart and resourceful. Stick with him. He's armed but he's not much of a warrior. If the three of you get into that kind of trouble, he's not your concern, you hear? He'll get you to the Wolf, if he's still alive, and the Wolf will take you from there."

"That's Kira's contact?"

"Her primary one, and probably the last living one at this point."

"Who is he?"

"A warrior, like yourself. His aura is also very strong, but be careful of him, because it is also guarded, and he hides many things."

"What things?"

"I do not know. It may be nothing but an old lady's superstitions. Just be weary around him. Ernest might know more than me. You can trust Ernest, child—Kira thinks very highly of that one."

THEY LEFT THE THICK WOODED area of the cabin, out to the road that Ernest and Bird came in on, and turned due north in perfect line with Mount Ucari. They walked in silence through the fog for the better part of the morning, until the sun was full up and burnt the moisture off the land and Marcus took them off the trail, still angling toward the mountain. Marcus led from the front, guiding his horse loosely by the reins, with Ernest, Bird, and the mare in quick succession. He stopped after mid-morning at a felled red alder and asked for a minute to catch his breath and wipe the perspiration from his face.

Ernest said, "You know you can ride the horse if you want to. It's no offense to us."

Marcus held up a hand and said, "No, no, it's just something with my boot."

Bird and Ernest each snacked on fresh bread packed for them back at Ilia's cabin, while Marcus took his boot off and shook a pebble out of it. After he got it back on, they continued making their way north and Marcus said, "Sorry about the terrain, but it's best to stay off the main roads in these times."

Ernest spoke up from behind him, "How far are we going?"

"From the cabin it's a shade over fifteen miles. It's going to be a long day. I'm sorry that you two didn't get to rest more but time is an issue, given the situation that the Samsarans are in. We need to make it to the rendezvous by tonight or we might miss the Wolf and then we'd have a whole other set of problems."

"The Wolf?"

"That's your contact. You might know him by another name through Kira, but everybody in Kardona just calls him the Wolf."

"Why?"

"It's a bit of a story."

"I've got fifteen miles worth of listening."

"Fair enough," Marcus said. "If I had to guess I'd say the Wolf is a few years younger than yourself, but the nickname goes back to when he was closer to Bird's age. Kardona has come a long way in that short amount of time. Back then, the Kardoans were the largest tribe in the region, but few people even recognized the greater area as *Kardona*. There were a lot of smaller tribes, and Samsarans were just sprinkled throughout all of them— it was a niche religious choice for individuals, but nothing that divided people, tribe-like. Nothing to fight a war over. Anyway, the Kardoans have a . . .a tradition I guess you could call it, concerning wolves. It didn't happen often, but if the tribe was ever able to catch a wolf in a trap, they'd make a whole event out of it. They'd build a ring—a little arena—and they'd bring in their hunting dogs, or really any dogs, and there'd be gambling and drinking and this big celebration as they'd watch the dogs fight the wolf. It may not sound like much, but wolves in this region are noticeably larger than ones in the Dialla. The fight could go on for hours, where they'd send in two dogs, make their wagers, and let them fight for a bit. Then let the wolf rest and send more, sometimes one, two, three at a time. It's over when the wolf dies."

"I've heard of similar things."

"It's good sport, if you're into that kind of thing. So, the Wolf was born as a Samsaran to parents who were converted by a missionary, and they were members of one of the region's lesser tribes—no longer around. Well, the tribe had a spat with the Kardoans that escalated to violence and the Wolf was captured and taken prisoner, along with some of his tribesmen. This particular outfit of Kardoans decided to do something that, as far as I understand, was *not* a common practice among any of them—they decided to treat the prisoners like wolves. The Kardoans that elected to fight were like the dogs, going in one or two at a time and sometimes to the death, sometimes not, fighting the Wolf's tribesmen. After two nights of the sport only the Wolf was alive. They alternated on and off and held him for days on end, giving anybody that wanted a chance to fight him and kill him. No one could, and eventually, out of respect they set him free. Since then, anybody that knows him knows him as the Wolf."

Ernest glanced behind him at Bird to see if she was listening and she said, "That's some story."

Marcus said, "It really is, and Ilia believes that there is even more to the story than that."

"In what way?" Ernest asked.

"She's still writing this portion of the history, but she has a theory that Kardoans learned from watching the Wolf fight and that they started training to emulate his combat technique and mechanics. From almost that moment in time the Kardoans, always the largest tribe in the area, quickly notched a handful of military victories that gave them providence over the area and has brought us to where we are now. It could be a coincidence, for sure, but it is an interesting thought that the Wolf unintentionally gave his enemies some of the tools that they were missing."

They walked on in silence through midday, skirting unseen around fields of potatoes, green peas, onions, and crops that Ernest had never seen before in his life—all growing fruitfully in this green land of endless rainfall that seemed the irrefutable antithesis of his own home, even as he saw the same beauty in both. Anytime Ernest felt that they might be too exposed on the landscape, Marcus found another hedge of red currant or line of white oak to hide their passing and Ernest concluded that this was all intentional and that this was a route that Marcus must have traveled dozens of times and more. In the afternoon they hit a flat field of flowing grass that stretched, exposed, for several hundred yards, and on the other side of it they saw a tree line that looked to mark the first bit of incline of the base of Mount Ucari.

"I'd like it if we moved fast here," Marcus said.

"Us as well."

They lingered for a moment, letting their breath catch from the day's walking and taking drinks of their water. The mare seemed to understand their plan and she grazed on grass while the others rested and Marcus said, "We'll move fast. If we see anything or anything sees us, show no reaction and get to the tree line."

The two Copperfoot nodded in understanding and Marcus led the way across the field at a brisk jog with the reins of his own horse in tow. Ernest only looked back once to see if the mare was following, and when he saw that she was, he looked forward to the distant tree line and willed himself to it as quickly as he could. It only took them a few minutes all told, but to him it felt much longer, considering what could happen should a party from either side of the war, on horseback, grow curious of their little outfit. They made the tree line and Marcus scanned the plain behind them and, with little beads of sweat on his brow, nodded to the other two.

Within minutes, he had them on a foot trail that kept them heading north and it would weave occasionally to the eastern end of the tree line, and when it did they could see the brown, rutted signature of a large road. They carried on with purpose, and Ernest's legs ached at the slight upslope to the new trail, and the trail would ebb and flow out of sight of the road until late in afternoon when Marcus held up a hand to stop, and when Ernest did he looked out to the road, just a two-hundred paces away, and saw a mass of bodies marching parallel to them.

Marcus cursed and pulled the reins of his horse close to him and looked around the immediate area through the occasional windows in the aspens and cottonwoods with an expression of great paranoia. Ernest asked, "Who is it?"

"It's hard to tell from this distance, but almost certainly its Kardoans. No Samsarans would be marching so openly at this point. They're not great at using scouts but we need to be very cautious right now."

Bird slipped her pack and cloak off and gave them to Marcus, who slung them over the saddle of his horse, and Bird said, "You two keep on the trail. Total silence. I'll be nearby," and then slipped into the trees.

They watched the spot where she vanished into the trees for a moment and Marcus said quietly, "This is very dangerous."

"She scouted in the Dialla when she was fifteen years old."

"I was talking about you and me. How good are you with that sword?"

"Not good at all."

"We better move then."

The two men and the two horses continued up the trail, close to each other and quiet as the sun, which was soon covered by an armada of light, grey clouds that carried with them a soft rain, and an eeriness set itself in Ernest's heart and in the woods too and a shiver ran up his spine at the feeling of being watched. He thought of the army that paralleled their position but he never glanced at them again, and he suppressed his anxiety for the better part of an hour before a woman's voice startled them from behind, "All good here?"

It was Bird. Ernest held a hand up over his heart to show how startled he was, and she approached and patted him kindly on the shoulder and Marcus said, "Did you see any scouts?"

"Four of them."

"Shit all," Marcus said as he took measure of the woods around them with an expression plastered by paranoia.

"They're dead," she said.

"Oh. Right."

Bird slipped her hand under her cloak and brought out a finely crafted dirk and said, "One of them had this."

Ernest looked at it blankly and Marcus shrugged and said, "What's the significance of it?"

"It looks to be steel."

"And?"

"You said yourself these armies are mostly amateur. All the scouts were, without a doubt. So why is one of them carrying a weapon that would be considered precious, even to a professional?"

Marcus nodded, "That's the impact of people like your boss, Kira, getting involved over here. And she's not the only Olerian with financial interests in Kardona. Weapons of iron and steel are coming in everyday from the Dialla, to both sides. It's the primary source of payment for many of these people—weapons come in, herb goes out."

Bird handed the weapon to Ernest and told him to keep it in his belt. They heard a horn sound off at a distance in the direction of the army beyond the forest and all three of them looked quietly into the tree line and then Marcus said, "Stopping for the day, probably."

"Good," Bird said. "Let's put them behind us."

There were still many days before the winter quarter, but darkness enclosed on them quickly under the cover of the tree canopy and Ernest walked on, exhausted, guided only by the soft sound of Marcus's leading footsteps that were soon just another rustle in the forthcoming darkness. Time passed, but he only registered the rhythm of his gait—putting one stride in front of the next—and spitting. A quarter moon made its way through the clouds and lit the world enough to glance the looming Mount Ucari and the well-worn trail of their animal run slowly grew rougher and in a brief time there was no trail at all and they picked their way through the noisy, night woods, with a life separate from the day and, once again, Ernest's desert senses would have been astonished and overwhelmed at the life of this land if it were not the fatigue in his own bones.

A voice ahead of him spoke but he didn't register it and a moment later he walked into Marcus, who had come to a stop, nearly knocking him to the ground. Marcus patted him on the back and pulled his shoulders to direct him to a faint light just ahead in the trees and said, "We're here."

Bird came up behind them and said, "Not very cautious, are they?"

The three of them, along with the two horses and with their cloaks pulled tightly about themselves, approached the light and neared a low burning fire set in a tiny glade. They breached the fire's perimeter without confrontation to find four men sitting listlessly around the fire—their tethered horses grazed at the tree line and reacted to the strangers as dismissively as the men at the fire did. The smallest man among them, with white hair to suggest at his age, acknowledged Marcus with a tip of his chin and Marcus did the same before turning to Bird and Ernest and saying, "Good luck."

"Wait. You're leaving now? It's night," Ernest said.

"I'm needed some place else early tomorrow, and the business you deal with now is between Kira and the Samsarans—it is not my place to be here."

Marcus clasped Ernest's forearm and nodded to him and then did the same to Bird. His back was turned to the men at the fire as he continued talking and he said, "The one second from the right is the Wolf—that's your contact regardless of what any of the others say. He will understand your purpose here, where the others will not. Your packs should have plenty of food. While your business is not my own, I can't help but give the advice that you should see to said business as quickly as possible and then begone from this place and these people. There is nothing but violence here. Try to avoid talking about Atun to them, and if things take a bad turn, go east into the mountains as quickly as possible—there is little activity from either side in the Omoyas and from there you can take whatever path you choose back to the Dialla."

They exchanged nods of appreciation and Marcus mounted his horse and led it into the darkness and back down the trail from whence they had come. A soft breeze made its way through the trees from north to south, and so the four men were in a lopsided position on the north side of the fire, out of the blowing smoke. Nothing of the men's behavior was inviting so Bird dropped her pack near the edge of the clearing and Ernest did the same and they readied themselves for sleep when the one with the white hair spoke, "You don't need to be afraid to join."

"No fear," said Ernest. "It's just been a long day."

"For all of us," said the one with the white hair and Ernest looked at Bird, who shrugged, and they joined the men around the fire, sitting along a husky, fallen tree trunk, leaving a small gap in their circle for the smoke to blow south into the Kardoan night.

All four of the men had beards, and the one with the white hair was not as old as he appeared to be from a distance. He too sat on a fallen log with the one on his left, who was probably the youngest of the group, with dark, smooth skin, and dark eyes to match. He took measure of the newcomers but said nothing. Next to him was the Wolf, perched on a wide, granite rock, whose eyes—the color of iron—had not left the fire since the two arrived, and they did not do so now. He had a forest-colored cloak draped over his shoulders, but Bird could see his large, strong hands where they rested out over the small fire, his elbows on his knees. There were streaks of grey in his beard, the same as Ernest's, but his face held fewer years and his physique, even under the cloak, appeared to be that of a younger man. Next to Ernest was the last of them, a short, heavy man with light, brown hair that looked at them just enough to give a tired nod of acknowledgement before returning his gaze to the fire, much like the Wolf. His eyes were bloodshot, and Bird could see the little bulge of herb he held in his lower lip.

The one with the white hair spoke again, "Might be a good idea to tether your horse, there. The wolves aren't shy around these parts."

"It's fine," said Ernest. "She's not much afraid of wolves, as far as I can tell."

"Did you lose a horse on the journey? Where's the second one at— where's your saddle?"

"Don't have no second horse. Don't have no saddle."

"You two ride bareback this whole way?"

"We didn't ride at all."

"Why not?"

"On account of our beliefs."

"To not ride a horse?"

"That's part of it."

The man's jaw dropped and looked around the fire to the other three, but only the young one with the dark beard raised his eyebrows in an expression of surprise, and then shrugged.

The white-haired man continued, "So what does she do?"

"The horse?"

"Yeah, the horse."

"She just started following us."

"When?"

"Back in the Dialla."

"In the Dialla?"

"Yes."

"To here?"

"Yes."

The young one nodded his head suddenly and said, "In the Dialla? I've heard of your people. The warrior people that walk."

Ernest shrugged and didn't respond while the man with the white hair was staring at the grazing mare and the man said, "You mean to tell me that the two of you walked, on foot, from the Dialla Desert with that pregnant mare right there?"

"Whoa now," Ernest said. "What pregnant mare?"

"Your pregnant mare."

"Who said she was pregnant?"

"I'm saying it right now."

Ernest and Bird exchanged expressions of surprise and confusion and the white-haired man gestured with a finger toward the mare and said, "Look how swollen her abdomen is there. Either that mare is very sick or very pregnant, and she aint sick, seeing how she just walked here from the Dialla fucking Desert." The man shook his head in bewilderment and let out a low whistle.

Out of either caution, indolence, or damp firewood, the fire was mostly embers that exerted the occasional flame, which let off just enough light to see the five other faces and just enough heat to keep any of them from retreating to sleep. All sets of eyes mostly remained buried in the fire, except when Ernest caught the young man staring across the way at Bird. He didn't know if she noticed or not and he pretended he didn't see, but every time he stole a glance at the man, he was still looking at her until the young man finally spoke, "So you're here to talk to Okoa?"

Bird either didn't hear, or pretended not to hear, but the man held the question and his eyes on her long enough to force a response and she spoke for the first time at the fire and she said, "I'm not here to talk to anybody."

"Is Okoa in charge now, with Atun dead?" Ernest asked.

"Yes," the young man said, "But I asked her."

"And I answered," Bird said.

Ernest said, "*I'm* here to talk with Okoa."

"What do you do then?" The man ignored Ernest and was speaking to Bird again.

"I keep him out of trouble."

"Are you his wife?"

Bird rolled her eyes and said, "No."

"What then?"

"His protection."

The young man snickered and then laughed and for the first time the Wolf took his attention from the fire and looked at the two new arrivals with eyes that held a hard grey appearance, even in the poor lighting. Bird kept her attention on the fire, unfazed by the man's implication, but Ernest stared daggers at him across from the fire and said flatly, "What's funny about that?"

The young man threw up his hands in mock defenselessness and did a poor job at stifling his laughter, "It's just that when one of you Olerians shows up here, pretending to be important, they usually have a handful of security, and here you are with just one—and a woman at that."

Ernest spat into the fire and Bird nudged him with her elbow and shook her head but he held his glare on the young talker and said, "I'd take this woman here over any handful of men that I've ever seen. I've lived among the best fighters in the world for nearly forty years of my life. You want to know who the best is that I've ever seen? She's sitting right there."

The young man looked to speak up again, but the white-haired man picked up on Ernest's anger and he cut in before his young comrade could make things worse. "My friend here doesn't mean to offend. In fact, I've seen some women in my time that sure can fight, but—with all ability being equal—a woman will never be as strong as a man. That's just a fact of nature. That's how it is."

Ernest shook his head and was visibly angry. He said, "Look here, friend. I'm not talking about your fat mom or your ugly sister. I'm talking about a woman here who has been singularly blessed by whatever god of war you worship. Strength is just one aspect that a warrior taps into, and with all other aspects tallied—agility, anticipation, focus, experience, instinct—the edge that one fighter gains from being physically stronger than another is so miniscule as to be made irrelevant. Whatever spirit exists that bestows talent and ability into these sorry bodies of ours does so with no regard for the little piece of flesh we carry between our legs."

It was the young Samsaran's turn to appear angry, but the white-haired man kept him in check with a stern glance before the white-haired man directed his attention to Bird and said, "What do *you* say?"

Bird said, "I say that my friend sure has a lot of opinions on the matter."

And the young man said, "For someone who can't fight for shit I'd say your friend sure has a big mouth on him."

Ernest spat again and said, "I spoke nothing but the fucking truth on the matter, and if the truth offends you then try to do me some violence and see if she isn't everything that I've said she is. I can promise that your blood will be gifted to this soil and you'll find yourself weeping your way out of some Samsaran's womb three nights from this one."

The short, heavy man sitting next to the Wolf laughed out loud at the exchange and the young man shot up from his sitting position, only to find that Bird, in reaction to him, was already on her feet and looking him un-flinchingly in the eye.

"Sit down." The Wolf's voice came from across the fire, deep and stern, and the young Samsaran flashed a last, affirming look of anger toward

Ernest before sitting down again. Bird lingered, standing, for a moment longer before she too sat again, except that when she resumed looking into the fire's embers as before, this time she could feel the eyes of the Wolf on her, and she felt them for a long time as he studied her now in the untaught way that his namesake might.

The man with the white hair, in an attempt to make amends, said to Bird, "You know, somebody as gifted as you must be a highly achieved Samsaran. Your past lives must be very impressive."

Bird said, matter of factly, "I'm a Copperfoot, through and through."

"Yes, still. Many Samsaran souls are out there, even if they don't know it yet."

"The only Samsaran that I ever heard of in the Dialla desert was the missionary that murdered my grandfather."

Silence settled over the fire at that and the heavy Samsaran stood and walked to the tree line of their small inlet and returned with a chopped log in each hand. He tossed them both into the pit, bringing forth an exhale of luminant sparks from the embers that popped and hissed as if it were a spell cast by this heavy priest of combustion. He sat again and the quiet among them furthered still until Ernest, recalling Marcus' words, addressed the Wolf, "How far are we from Okoa?"

The Wolf with his grey eyes looked at Ernest with a confused expression for a moment, as if pulled from a thought or surprised that the newcomer had the audacity to address him directly, and said, "The main Samsaran camp is just a few miles from here. Okoa is there."

"Why didn't we just meet there," Ernest glanced around their humble camp, "instead of here?"

"The main camp has been surrounded by Kardoans going on three days now. It's safer if you go through their lines with us than with someone like Marcus."

"The Kardoans are just miles away and we camp openly?"

"The Kardoans don't know this part of the land, and their scouts are shit."

"But they have the main camp surrounded?" Ernest asked, "Is there fighting?"

"There hasn't been any yet—they are waiting for something, but we don't know what."

Bird took her eyes from the fire and turned to Ernest with a look of realization and said, "I know what they're waiting for."

"What?"

"Reinforcements."

Ernest's face took on the same look as Bird's and he said, "Oh shit."

"What?" The Wolf said again.

"On the road here with Marcus," Ernest said, "We passed an army moving this way."

The Wolf's tone was suddenly more alert, and he asked, "How far? How many?"

Ernest looked to Bird and she said, "We passed them half a day back. They were moving slow and I didn't get a great count but I'd guess between four and six-hundred of them."

The Wolf reached out to pat the back of the heavy man next to him and, shifting his eyes to the young Samsaran across the fire, said "Get back to camp. Now. Tell Okoa that an attack will come as early as tomorrow night—the following morning if luck is on our side."

The two Samsarans wordlessly gathered their packs and blankets and within minutes were on their horses and they slipped out west, swallowed by the darkness, into the sound of rustling leaves and chirping night insects. The Wolf said *we leave at dawn* and retreated from the fire to his blanket and pack and the rest did in turn. Ernest and Bird slept opposite of the Samsarans in the inlet and Ernest laid awake for a long time thinking of how he'd been plucked from the Dialla to sleep in this land of water and life among killers of men and just miles from them an army of the same composition slept now too, patiently waiting for more men to swell their ranks that they might get the chance to be killers of children no different than the ones born by their own women and still they found it in their hearts that these children were different and deserving of the kind of wrath impossible for them to understand and if they did and were given the choice would decide to never come howling into this dark world built in the blood of their forefathers and mothers. He shifted on the ground, under his blanket and head resting on his pack, and over the top of the dense canopy to the north he could just glimpse the peak of Mount Ucari and a shiver coursed down his spine for a reason unknown to him but it seemed as if the mountain was living and breathing and it knew of his unsettled form there and it watched him and just as he thought he might not sleep at all before the dawn, his attention focused on the unmistakable heavy breathing of his companion deep in sleep and something about her sleeping while a parade of anxiety marched through his mind made it immediately calmer and he was eventually put to sleep by the idea that if forces had conspired to bring him to this place, at this time, then the same forces had conspired that she be here with him.

HE WOKE TO THE OTHER three already shuffling about and packing up the camp for departure. It was the clearest day that they had seen yet in Kardona. The man with the white hair came over to them and spoke quietly to say that there would be no talking between this place and the Samsaran camp and the two nodded understandingly. Bird was already set to go and stood next to the mare and stroked her muzzle while she waited for Ernest, who rubbed the sleep from his eyes and brought his pack close to Bird so that he could talk to her quietly while he folded his blanket.

"Listen," he said. "I know you well enough now that I know I can't tell you what to do, but what I will say is that I think you should stay here—let me go into the camp, talk to Okoa, meet back with you here and we will go home together."

"Why?"

She watched his eyes and could tell that he wanted to lie to her but he glanced over his shoulder at the two Samsarans just a dozen feet away and softly said, "After the Crimson Shrouds I told you that we weren't the first Olerian emissaries Lady Kira has sent this way. It's true that she nor anybody else knows what happened to them, but it's also true that she suspects that at least two of the parties made it to Okoa and then never made it out."

"She thinks the Samsarans killed them?"

"Yes. She thinks that when they told Okoa something that he didn't want to hear, he had them killed and then played stupid. It's important to know that Kira doesn't trust anybody. It's also important to know that her suspicions have as good a chance as being true as not."

Bird chewed on her lip and eyed the two Samsaran's over Ernest's shoulder and Ernest continued, "You were hired to get me here and you did. And you can get me home still. But there's no job for you to do inside that Samsaran camp. What happens in there is between Kira and Okoa, and if shit goes sideways, even you can't fight their whole army." Ernest's blanket was now safely secured to the top of his bag and he slung it over his cloak, sliding his off arm underneath the strap. "If it is what Kira thinks, then they will kill me and you can still go home and get paid. If it's not, then I'll meet you back here before the day is out. Either way you live."

She kept chewing her lip and she looked about their little camping inlet as if the trees of alder and hazelnut held an answer for her and she looked at Ernest only for a moment before saying, "I come with you."

His shoulders slumped at the answer but he knew better than to argue and so he said, "Be ready to fight then. Every person at every moment."

He shimmied out of his pack and readjusted his sword and dirk so that their hilts showed prominently from under his cloak. Bird understood. She too dropped her pack and undid her cloak long enough to take off the linen tunic that she kept over her armor. She stuffed the tunic in her pack and slid the fist weapon from where it was hiding on the back of her belt so that it was sheathed on her front, left hip, fully visible. She did the same with her sword and the two Samsarans saw this and couldn't help but take second and third glances at the armory this young woman had kept hidden the night before.

When she donned her cloak again, the fist weapon and hilt of her sword were as visible now as Ernest's own, and her armor shown like teeth between the cloak hanging over each shoulder. Ernest looked her up and down and nodded. The Wolf vanished into the tree line headed west and the white-haired Samsaran, pulling both the Wolf's and his own horse behind him said, "Stay with me. Keep your horse close."

As if she understood it all, the mare walked close to Ernest as he set off into the trees and Bird followed the two of them a dozen paces behind, silent and poised like a great cat. There were no trails this time, as there were with Marcus, and Ernest was continually fighting branches off his face and pulling himself clumsily through thick outcrops of thimbleberry that the Samsaran snacked on in passing just as naturally as he navigated through the thick plant life. Ernest never heard Bird behind him and didn't see the Wolf ahead. They moved on through the thick underbrush for over an hour, without a word between them—the only communication being the scowls that the Samsaran continually threw over his shoulder at the clambering Copperfoot man behind him.

After pushing himself over a small incline flush with dogwood Ernest was halted by the Samsaran with a raised hand and he stopped so suddenly that the mare bumped into his back, giving him a kind lick on the neck. He brushed her off and they were still for a few seconds before the Samsaran signaled them on. Fifty more paces along their track and Ernest discovered the reason for the pause—a dead Kardoan with a cleanly sliced throat. So fresh was the Wolf's kill that bright arterial blood still rolled out of the wound and onto the bed of brown, dead leaves underneath. The mare shuffled nervously in the presence of the corpse but the Samsaran had signaled for another stop, leaving Ernest to whisper assurances into the horse's ear rather than ponder the young face of the slain body. They moved on and shortly came across another corpse, this one gored through his torso, judging from the size of the blood stains on his tunic above and his cloak below. Ernest looked for Bird behind him but saw nothing. When he turned back around the Samsaran was waving him forward and though he expected to be introduced to another dead Kardoan, he was instead met by the Wolf and, just behind him, the Samsaran camp.

"Where's the . . ." The Wolf began asking before Bird came up sound-lessly to their position and he stopped. He pulled his head toward the camp and they all followed him in as he gave a whistle and called a greeting to announce their presence to the other Samsarans on guard.

They entered the camp from the southeastern side, weaving their way through rows of staggered, spiked barricades that stuck out of the mud of their felling and came up to Ernest's waist and shoulder in some cases. The barricades ran in a large half circle area ranging from southeast to south-west, guarding the interior of the camp which was set back in a granite nook that cradled nearly four dozen yurts of varying size. At the deepest point of the nook, a small waterfall dropped from the heights above and fed a modest stream that flowed south through the camp before willing itself westward, toward the calling of the Great Water. The many yurts were in good shape—some covered in animal skins and some in felt from the wool of sheep—and Ernest judged the camp to have been here for some time. As they reached the outer ring of yurts, people began to materialize out of corners of the camp that Ernest had yet to see and their faces were dirty and their eyes were tired and there wasn't a soul among them younger than two years in the world. None of them spoke, and some of them exchanged respectful nods of acknowledgement with the Wolf, but mostly all of them were focused on the woman bringing up the rear of the party and Ernest could see in their tired eyes an element of wonder that lit with her passing. He guessed their number to be around six hundred, but as they continued their silent walk to the deepest part of the camp and the largest yurt that waited there, Ernest saw several small cave entrances housed in the granite nook and wondered if there were more of these desperate people hidden in them.

Members of the crowd continued to silently part way for the new ar-rivals and then filled in behind them until they reached the exterior of the camp's largest yurt where the Wolf signaled them to stop and slipped inside through the building's portal. Standing outside the tent was the young dark-skinned Samsaran from the night before, who met Bird's eyes briefly before averting them entirely. Ernest shifted nervously on his feet and Bird spoke quietly to him, "What now?"

"Now I try to convince Okoa to put himself and his people at the mercy of those that look to slaughter them like animals."

The Wolf's head poked from out of the yurt's entrance, and he waved the two Copperfoot inside, and Bird said to the white-haired Samsaran, "Is there someone to look after our horse?" and he said *I'll take her.*

The inside of the yurt was dark and murky with smoke, but they were able to make out the Wolf, who pointed them to a long wooden bench on the curved left side of the interior. There was a modest fire set in the middle that sent a steady trail of smoke up through a single, large hole set in the structure's ceiling. There were four people conversing quietly on the far side of yurt. Two of them sat quietly, admiring the wooden latticework that framed this construction. A minute passed and three of the people wordlessly shuffled outside, leaving the Copperfoot with the Wolf and one of the largest men that either of them had ever seen.

There was seating all around the edge of the yurt, and the big man waved the two of them over to his side, where he sat on a wooden, throne-like chair set before a table made of the same exotic wood. He was bearded like so many of the men here—greasy hair the color of walnut. Atop the table were several maps of the area and a massive double-bladed battle axe that complimented perfectly the size of the man. Bird eyed the weapon as they moved across the room and knew immediately that it was Copperfoot craftmanship. They took a seat on a bench similar to the first one, this time facing the table and the man behind it and when he spoke his voice was unsettlingly high pitched, "Do either of you need food or drink?"

"No, thank you," Ernest said. "Our supplies are strong."

"Good. My name is Okoa, and nothing else."

"My name is Ernest. My companion's name is Bird."

"You are Kira's Copperfoot."

"I am."

Okoa reached one of his huge hands out and tapped the blade of the battle axe on the table before him and said, "One of your kinsmen made this."

"It's a beautiful weapon."

"Yes. And even more deadly than it is beautiful. I could chop down the largest tree in Kardona with this axe and I don't believe it would dull the blade."

Ernest nodded and Okoa continued, "It has been long since we've heard from Lady Kira—I was convinced that we were forsaken by her."

"Not at all. The way here is treacherous. We are the fourth attempt by Kira to send you word."

"We need more than words now."

"Kira's shipments of weapons and armor to you have never ceased. If there were any gaps in their delivery, that is a reflection of the supplier's incompetence, not the lady's support."

"We have no more need of your weapons. We have more weapons now than hands to hold them. We need soldiers—we need Kira's Olerians."

Ernest shook his head. "That can't happen, and it was established with Udura Atun from the start—there would be no Olerian manpower for the side of your Samsarans. I did not come this way to bring word of more support, I came to bring counsel."

"What counsel?"

"Surrender."

Okoa's fist slammed so hard onto the table that even the large steel axe shifted its position. Ernest flinched involuntarily but Bird gave no such reaction. Under the influence of his anger, Okoa's voice came out now even more shrill than before, "The Kardoans murder our children. No, not our children even—our *babies*. They cut their throats. They throw them in rivers. They bludgeon their soft skulls, and you *abandon* us." Okoa sat forward in his chair and placed two open palms on the handle of the axe as he finished speaking, eyeing Ernest angrily. Bird's body was completely still—her posture erect and her weight forward and balanced on the balls of her feet—but her eyes darted back and forth between Okoa and the Wolf, who still stood near the yurt's entrance.

Convinced that he was speaking the last words that he would ever speak, Ernest stood from the bench to face the huge, enraged man, and said, "The cruelty of the Kardoans has been noted and is known widely in Oleria. It will be reaffirmed when I return home to Kira. They will face a reckoning for what they've done to your people. But your war is over. It has been lost. Send them back to their homes so that they can farm the *fucking* herb—as agreed between your predecessor and my boss. You cannot refuse to surrender on the grounds of slaughter when a slaughter is the same thing coming your way if you don't. Your men came to you last night and told you of the hundreds more Kardoans that march this way as we speak. They will probably attack before this day is out, and I just walked through the camp and got a look at what stands between you and the end of your people—what do you have? Six-hundred souls? And how many of them can fight? I saw a lot of faces out there that are too old and too young for the kind of violence that searches them. That fucking axe of yours there may chop down the biggest tree but it won't make you immortal. My own people had finer weapons than that when the Olerians came to the Dialla."

Okoa growled and said, "And your people are gone now, as mine will soon be."

"No." Ernest pointed to Bird and said, "She's there. I'm here. Thousands more of us are back in the Dialla, living quiet lives and waiting for our moment."

"What moment?"

"When Rathalla calls on us to rise again."

"Your deity?"

"Something like that." Ernest looked sideways at Bird but her eyes were transfixed on Okoa now. Ernest continued, "I don't know when that moment will come—maybe never—but I know that there is far greater dignity, and bravery, in enduring such times than there is to throw ourselves like cowards onto the enemy's sword. There can be no martyrs if all who bear witness are dead."

He did well to hide it, but Ernest's knees were trembling and when he finished speaking, he refused to take his eyes from those of Okoa's, though he desperately wanted to. Okoa's expression was still one of anger but his hands came off of the axe and he slumped back into his chair, diminished now in size and looking all the portrait of tired defeat. He looked at the Wolf and nodded to him and the Wolf slipped out of the yurt as if the nod held a dozen words of instruction in it. Okoa righted himself in the chair just slightly and said, "This camp is not the only one—maybe not even the largest."

"How many?"

"At least three to the south, two up north, and another on the coast."

"Get the word out to all of them as quickly as you can that the fighting is to stop immediately. What's the status of the children?"

"We've spent the last two months moving and smuggling new mothers and babies throughout Kardona. Almost all of them now are in trusted situations."

"*Almost* all of them?"

Just as he finished the question the entrance to the yurt was opened again and the Wolf came in followed by a slender figure. It was a young woman with a dark hood pulled tightly over her hair, giving her an appearance even younger than she truly was. She wore the same buckskin shoes and forest green cloak that most of the Samsarans did and appeared unremarkable except for a large lump that was swaddled across her torso with a long, linen wrap.

"What is this?" Ernest asked.

"Another reason we can't surrender," Okoa said. "This is Ayune, and her baby boy, Udura Atul. He was born ninety-two days ago, exactly three days after the death of Udura Atun."

Silence descended over the yurt for many moments, until even the soft crackle of the fire seemed loud.

Okoa said, "It seems that the Kardoans know about this child, and they've shifted most of their resources from the other camps and sent them here."

"Because they think it's Udura Atun reborn?"

"It is."

"How can you know?"

"I *know*. We all know."

Ernest's voice conveyed his frustration, "Then why is she still here? Why hasn't she been hidden like the others?"

"Ayune is here for her people, and her people thirst for the morale that she and this child give us."

Ernest shook his head then addressed the woman, "What do you say?"

She cleared her throat and spoke with a voice that was delicate, but confident, "I cannot leave my people. It's important that they see what they are fighting for."

"Are you prepared to see your son die?"

She reacted to his question physically, taking a step back and reflexively putting a guarded hand to the sleeping baby at her chest. "That won't happen."

"It will. We need to get you out of here now."

"This is my home. These are my people. If we win this fight . . ."

"You won't," Ernest interrupted. "You can't. As long as you stay here, this camp will not surrender, and if they don't surrender they will be all be killed trying to protect you and your son. The only mercy that you'll have to hope for is that they kill you first."

She was clearly shaken by his words, and she said, "What do you think I should do?"

He paused at this question and noticed that sometime after the young woman had entered the yurt that Bird had stood up, now standing next to him with a look on her face that he could only describe as concern. He said to the young mother, "Leave here with us immediately. We will get you out the same way we came in, and then we will find a spot for you with the other mothers."

Okoa shook his head and said, "They'll find her if she stays in Kardona—that the Kardoans know of the child's existence at all is proof that it has already been betrayed by Samsarans in this very camp."

The Wolf then spoke for the first time, "And the way that we came in here has been flooded with hundreds more Kardoans—you saw them with your own eyes."

Ernest pressed the palms of his hands forcefully over both his eyeballs then slid them up to his temples, tracing small circles over each one in a frantic pose of concentration. Everyone in the room watched him in curious silence before he opened his eyes, looked at Okoa, and said, "Rally your camp to battle. If they want to save this child, then this is their chance. You'll lead an attack—with everything you have—into the Kardoan's southern perimeter. As you do this, me and Bird will use the chaos as cover to slip through the perimeter to the east, from where we came. Your attack doesn't have to be suicide—fight as hard as you can just long enough to get a response from the Kardoans, then surrender. Once we clear the area, we will take her, *what's your name?* Ayune to the Dialla with us. Lady Kira will personally see to her and the child's wellbeing while there." Ernest looked at Ayune, "When Kardona is safe again, you can come home."

The room fell to silence again as everyone processed the plan, and Ernest returned to the now empty bench and chewed anxiously at his dirty fingernails. Okoa stood from his chair and paced back and forth with his arms folded behind his back before he stopped and looked at Ayune, "What do you think of the Copperfoot's idea?"

"I would only leave with your blessing, and I would come home the instant you said it was safe."

Okoa nodded and turned to the Wolf, "And you?"

"If the reinforcement numbers are as the Copperfoot say, then winning a battle here is near impossible, but I wouldn't send young Ayune here and the child alone with two strangers—non-Samsarans at that. The Copperfoot is right that a smaller number of people has a better chance of slipping through the Kardoan line, but I believe that I should join them, to act as Ayune and her child's dedicated guardian and see that she makes it to Pridipoa safely."

Okoa nodded and said to him, "You are the greatest warrior I've ever known, and as badly as I want you next to me in this battle, it is right that you see to the child's safety—he is more important than any of us now."

BIRD, ERNEST, AND THE MARE huddled on the ground outside of Okoa's yurt as midday approached, the humans eating the food given to them by Marcus, and the horse blinking sleepily against the commotion in the camp.

"What do you think of our girl here being pregnant?" Ernest asked.

"I think there is too much drama right now concerning babies."

Ernest nodded to that as he tucked a pinch of herb into his cheek larger than any she had seen him take before. He flexed his cheek muscles, settling the herb and then looked up to the sky and said, "This is the first day here that there hasn't been a cloud in sight. If you look up at the sky and nothing else, it almost feels like home."

The camp was alive on Okoa's orders to prepare for imminent battle, as every able-bodied man wrestled into armor and fitted all manner of weapons to his person. Still, in the bustle, many of the Samsarans stole glances at the Copperfoot woman in her armor—some simply observing, some leering.

"Imagine that," said Bird.

"Huh?"

"Going through everything these people have been through—being on the verge of annihilation. And still they won't put a sword in the hands of any of the women."

Ernest nodded, "I understand that it's more common than not. Kira says that the empire sees its people as resources, and to exclude women from any of the empire's many branches is to weaken it by half—as if choosing to fight with one hand instead of both."

"A wise way to put it. I just say it's plain stupid."

He nodded at that and said *let's get ready* and, for only the second time since she started following them, they used their horse as a horse. They tied the straps of their packs to each other and slung them over the mare's shoulders, including their cloaks and water skins—each of them only wearing what they needed to run with, and fight. Bird did a twice-over on her armor and belt, adjusting and readjusting all cinches and then she helped Ernest do the same with his. When they were done he said, "Shit, I'm scared."

"Everyone here is, it's normal."

He put a hand to his stomach and said, "I need to find a latrine."

Bird glanced around the camp and the demarcation was growing clearer by the moment. Women and children separated into the caves and yurts while the men—many of them too old and too young for proper fighting—massed near the spiked barricades that marked the southern entrance to the camp. Bird was doing deep breathing exercises when Ayune approached—no armor, a pack and cloak saddled over her shoulders, and her son awake and alert in her arms. She was beautiful—half a head shorter than Bird but with the same lean figure and her hood was pulled back now to reveal silky, shining dark hair that stretched past her shoulders. Bird offered her a head tilt of acknowledgement as she approached and the young woman said, "Your armor is beautiful, that weapon too. All of you, really."

Bird smiled at her and she continued, "This is my son, Udura."

"He's very handsome."

"Would you like to hold him?"

Bird held up her hands to decline but before she could get a word out the young woman thrust the baby boy into her arms and she had no choice but to bring his tiny figure close to her and snuggle him against her exoskeleton of steel. His hair was dark like his mothers and his eyes were green and perceptive and as he looked up at this newcomer he offered a generous, toothless smile.

Bird smiled back and Ayune said, "He looks just like his father."

"Is his father here?"

"No," The young woman's tone dropped. "He died in battle just as I was beginning to show."

"I'm sorry."

Ayune nodded. "All who were there said he died bravely."

"I'm sure he did—look how brave his son is already."

There were tears in the young woman's eyes and she reached her arms out, "I better feed him before we leave. Hopefully he will sleep."

Bird handed over the tiny figure and Ayune sat on the ground next to the mare and hid her body underneath her cloak, so that she could nurse in some privacy. Ernest showed back up with a bow and quiver of arrows slung over his shoulder and held them up for Bird to see, who nodded approvingly. The five of them stood waiting as the Wolf made his approach from the middle of the camp, expressed in his full battle regalia. His boots reached nearly to his knees and looked to be buckskin, though they had a sheen to them unlike the felty appearance of those like Ayune's. What little of his pants could be seen were wool, but they were covered up almost entirely by iron-coated strips of leather that hung off his main cuirass—eighteen in total—that gave protection to his upper legs. His armor appeared a generation older than Bird's, but it was no less impressive. Iron, black in color, with two large, metallic wolf paws adorned on each pectoral and two shoulder guards, each cast in the shape of a wolf's head. He also had two vambraces, designed in the same style as the cuirass, trimmed with the same metal as the wolf paws. On his left hip was a shortsword almost identical to Bird's and on his other hip a baselard dagger, edged on both sides, and not much smaller than his sword. There was a huge hunting knife sheathed on the outside of his right calf and two strings of leather fastened a plain, steel heater shield to his back.

His movement carried with it something that Ernest could not pinpoint but that he had noted with Bird too—an ethereal, glide-like quality to even their basic movements. Whether it be his movement or his appearance, the Samsarans noticed it too—every man standing half an inch taller as he passed, and the glimmer of fear buried in every one of their eyes dimmed just slightly. He joined their party without a word and then Okoa made his way through the camp with his massive size—and his axe to match—appearing to give the Samsarans another lift in spirits. He nodded to them from a distance and then made his way to the front of the crowd of men, where they could hear his odd voice speaking in melodramatic tones to the mass that offered occasional cheers and rallying cries of their own.

Ernest gripped the new bow in his left hand with sweaty palms and he spat and Bird could see his hand shaking and she said, "Remember what I told you about that?"

"Keep my back straight, and my elbow high."

"I mean don't shoot that thing if I'm within ten feet of your target."

"Oh, right."

Just then a murmur went up through the Samsaran warriors and it spread into the camp to the women and elders. Ernest and Bird exchanged a quizzical look. The chatter grew louder and Ernest saw that they all looked to the north, which was obscured by the nearest yurt. They all stepped back a few paces to see the source of the commotion, and there was Mount Ucari with a huge stream of white gas coming out of its peak like a chimney.

"Is that smoke?" Ernest asked.

"Steam," the Wolf said.

"Steam? The mountain is steaming?"

He looked at the Wolf, whose face was pinched with a mixture of concern and confusion.

Ernest said, "What does that mean?"

The Wolf shook his head and said, "I don't know. It's been generations since there's been an eruption—I don't even remember the mountain's name, far to the south. It is said that it too started with a steaming peak."

The same fear that was painted on many of the Samsaran faces was painted on Ernest's as the significance of the Wolf's words donned on him, but, before he could process anything further, a cry went up from south of the camp as a volley of arrows hit the Samsaran warriors.

The Kardoans were attacking.

Bird's shield was off her back and, crouching, she pulled Ayune and the baby underneath its protective halo, and the Wolf did the same for Ernest. Had Okoa reacted defensively or lost his nerve it might have spelled doom for all of them, but he didn't hesitate to lead his nearly three-hundred warriors charging through the rain of arrows and into the woods at the waiting Kardoans.

"Do we go now?"

"Give them a minute. Let them react to Okoa."

The flat hiss of arrows disappeared as Okoa's charge made the tree line and the Wolf peaked over the edge of the shield before saying, *follow me— don't stop moving.*

Shield up, he led them through the muddy field with the spiked barricades and into the camp's eastern tree line at a brisk jog. They went down the same incline they had come up just that morning, but the Wolf turned sharply to the south and they were swallowed by a huge thicket of thin, but towering evergreen trees. They could hear shouting voices call out from all around them as the Kardoans attempted to react to Okoa's charge. Shadows moved through the trees, as Kardoan soldiers scrambled to get to the southern battlefront, and they weren't more than ten paces into the thicket before a young Kardoan soldier came around a tree at full speed and nearly ran into them. They were all of them surprised and the soldier spat out *who are you?* before his eyes widened with the realization that these weren't his kinsmen. He took two steps backward and gathered his breath to yell, but Ernest had notched one of his arrows and sent it flying true, directly into the young man's chest. He crumpled to the ground and Bird looked at Ernest, in wide-eyed shock at his competence, before another Kardoan from deeper in the thicket, upon seeing the encounter, sent forth a loud, piercing whistle and shouted for help.

Keep moving snarled the Wolf as an arrow went glancing off of his shield with a sharp *tink*, and Ernest could see through the trees at least a dozen figures in the immediate vicinity moving in their direction. "Stay with the girl, Ernest," said Bird as she slipped past him to position herself between the baby and incoming Kardoans. *We can't let them group or we'll be overwhelmed* she said to the Wolf and he agreed and the two of them charged forward, taking the fight to the Kardoans as they streamed in one at a time. Ernest pulled the girl along with the mare following close behind, but even with the circumstance as dire as it was, he couldn't help but be distracted by the Wolf and Bird in action.

They were breathtaking. When he reached his first Kardoan, the Wolf tossed his shield to the ground and pulled out his large dagger and, wielding it hilt down with his sword in the other hand, proceeded to dispatch of the whistler in mere seconds. Bird kept her shield high and active, and dispensed of her first enemy with a quick three move sequence—just in time for the next two to arrive. The Wolf was soon similarly occupied and they danced through the pines, at some points engaged with three Kardoans each, always a step ahead with perfect footwork and never a wasted movement in their upper bodies. Not wanting to get too far away from them, Ernest and Ayune slowed their pace—him with an arrow notched at the ready, as Kardoan casualties continued to mount at the feet of the warriors. He could hear the clamor of the larger battle just west of them, and he looked for the steaming peak of Mount Ucari but the high pines blocked his vision that way.

Rushed by another spear-wielding Kardoan, Bird caught the tip of the weapon on her shield and directed it to the ground, where she trapped it with her left foot and gashed the man's neck with quick jab of her sword. Another attacker was moments away but she found just enough time to turn and check on Ernest before snapping her head back around and dealing with the latest assault. The Wolf was every bit as deadly as she. He continually maneuvered his shortsword, offensively and defensively, until an opening appeared, and, when it did, he struck hard and fast with his offhand dagger. So fast were they all trying to move, and so numerous were the oncoming foes, that there was no time to deliver clean killing blows, and contrasted to the beauty of their skill and movement was the bloody, crying, mangled devastation that they left in their wake. Ernest flanked the mare and he pushed Ayune forward, keeping an eye on Bird and the Wolf and continually repositioning to stay as close to them as safely possible. Arrows continued whistling around them—some thudding into tree trunks while others disappeared into the pine branches with only a minor rustle. With his attention on Bird and the Wolf, Ernest was sent stumbling forward, landing on his hands and knees, feeling as if someone had just kicked him in the shoulder.

Ayune turned and said *oh no* when she saw the arrow protruding from just behind his left armpit, hitting him just at the edge of his armor, and bent to help him up. "Are you okay?"

She pulled him to his feet as a tremendous pain overwhelmed the adrenaline in his veins and sent his head spinning. He stumbled and she asked him again if he was okay, but he only offered a grunt and used his right arm to usher them all forward again.

They were well into the thicket now and the sound of the main battle faded behind them. The evergreen's thinned out and were swapped for smatterings of smaller myrtles and hemlocks and the five-fingered ferns so pervasive to the region came back. The Kardoans thinned out too—already more than two dozen of them left dead or dying back in the thicket. Ernest brought up the rear of the party, focused only on putting one foot in front of the other, while the Wolf and Bird continued to clear pockets of Kardoan fighters along the way. Through it all Ayune was silent and her baby a reflection of his mother—whether sleeping or somehow knowledgeable of what was at stake. They put a mile behind them and then two and still they hurried on against all fatigue until it seemed that they were clear of the Kardoan line and the main cluster of their reserves.

At the crest of a steep incline that ran north to south, Ayune spoke for the first time and, through heavy panting, asked if they could take a break for Ernest.

Neither Bird nor the Wolf was aware of his injury and Bird rhetorically asked *what's wrong with Ernest?* Before she saw the arrow sticking out of his leather cuirass's armhole. *Ernest.* She rushed over to him as he collapsed to his knees and she asked him how long ago he was shot but he waved the question away, breathless.

"We need to get this off."

The Wolf came over to inspect the arrow and the design of Ernest's armor's latch. He realized that they'd have to move the arm in order to take it off.

"This is going to hurt like hell," he said as they unlatched the cuirass and temporarily straightened his arm so that it could be slipped off. He screamed.

Ayune looked on with worried eyes and said, "Can't you just pull it out?"

"If we pull it out now it's really going to bleed."

They got the armor removed and Bird cursed at it as she flung it into the vegetation and she went into her pack to fashion an arm sling form one of her extra tunics.

The Wolf stood over Ernest and slipped his big hunting knife from its sheath on his calf and, gently as he could manage, he sawed a notch into the shaft of the arrow about four inches up from where it disappeared into Ernest's flesh. Ernest groaned in pain at every vibration of the arrow until the Wolf said, "Take a deep breath on my count." The Wolf did a three count and Ernest inhaled as deeply as he could and then the Wolf took the fletching end of the arrow in his strong hands and snapped it off at the notched point. Ernest gasped and fell to the dirt on his good shoulder without a scream—mustering only enough energy to whimper.

The Wolf said, "If it had caught a lung, you'd be spitting blood by now. It's bleeding some but not enough to kill you, yet."

The hill they were on was high enough that they could see over the trees and back toward the camp in the distance. The Samsarans stood idly now—simply breathing—while Bird fitted the makeshift sling on Ernest's arm. She said "It's only right that you had to give up an arm for this errand too. We're even now."

He only nodded pathetically and sat crossed leg on the ground with his head dipped, waiting for the worse parts of the nausea and the pain to pass.

Looking in the direction of the Samsaran camp, the Wolf said, "The Kardoans would burn the camp if the battle had continued and they had won. No smoke is a good sign. Okoa is a wise leader and I hope they allowed him a peaceful surrender."

They breathed in silence, but when Bird went to the mare to retrieve her waterskin she was nearly kicked by the horse, who bucked wildly for a second and then rolled her head back and forth as if she had gone feral. Bird backed off and talked soothing to the mare and Ernest said *what happened?* and Bird held and said, "Nothing."

"What's wrong with her?" Asked the Wolf.

"I don't know. The only other time she's ever done anything like that is when the flash flood . . ."

Bird never finished the sentence.

Beneath her feet a deep, guttural growl reverberated from the foundations of the earth and the world around them began to violently shake. Ernest tipped from his sitting posture to curl on the ground like a fetus, and when Ayune was rocked off her feet she did the same, cradling her baby to her bosom.

The two warriors kept their feet, but even their supreme agility was challenged by the intensity of the earthquake and the two of them looked at each other like wild animals frightened into temporary paralysis, because this enemy was one that could not be fought with sword and shield. Not with iron or steel. What shook beneath them now was the very birthplace of such things and when the time came to reclaim them, reclaim them it would. It lasted for no more than ten seconds and when it was done, Ayune and Ernest got tentatively to their feet—him with one arm—and they scanned the landscape as if they were extraterrestrials set down on this planet's surface for the first time.

Since there was no knowledge or experience in his brain to make him speak these words, it could have only been instinct, or something even deeper if such a thing exists, that made Ernest speak, "The mountain."

They all looked to the steaming peak at just the moment that it evaporated in an explosion so loud and damning that there was no power on this earth or any that could replicate it and a cloud of smoke, such a dark grey as to be black, plumed miles into the sky and the entire southern flank of Mount Ucari—hundreds of square miles of earth and rock—rolled like a liquid outward from the power of the blast. The mare froze and the rest of them flinched and, in their great fear, these acolytes of smoke and fire could not help but bear witness to this—the beginning of the apocalypse if the apocalypse were ever to come, and if any other myth told of the end times differently than this, then it was but heresy. Ernest wanted to run, in any direction, but he couldn't pull his eyes from the cloud that was now ten miles into the sky and rising still and, when it finally hit the upper reaches of the atmosphere, it began to mushroom outward and darken the clear midday sky like an eclipse. Dark and vaporous moon.

There was no precedent for this event in the region, and their group on the hill continued to watch the scene unfold, unsure if they should be dead or soon would be. Moments later a sound came from the overstory of the trees around—a sound like rain—and they realized that debris from the eruption—what used to be the peak of Mount Ucari—was now showering the countryside with fiery rocks that varied from small pebbles to boulders the size of wagons.

"Let's get the hell out of here."

Even in this new world of fire, their plan was unaltered. The Wolf led them on a line as due east as possible and what else could they do but hope that a granite projectile would not find their soft bodies hustling through the countryside? The Wolf, Ayune, Udura, Ernest, Bird, the mare. Ernest labored greatly—the rusty smell of the blood on his shoulder bringing back discouraging images of war in the Dialla, and the hospital tent that he played in. Every breath came with pain and every step came with pain and, so unalert was he, that when the world went dark with ash he thought that night had come, even though it was still early afternoon. The plume blossomed outward and crept toward them like an ominous mold and it brought with it darkness, lightning, and thick, soppy rain. Ernest couldn't keep a shirt or his cloak on without them tugging painfully on the arrow, but the wound's exposure to the warm rain made it difficult to clot, and he continued to lose blood.

Bird called for a break on his behalf but he insisted they keep moving, and Ayune said, "Why don't you get on the horse?"

Ernest just shook his head and the Wolf said, "He can't."

"But he's going to die."

"It's against his beliefs."

Ayune said to Ernest, "Just this one time you can ride it."

"Even if I wanted to, I couldn't stay on. Let's just keep going."

The Omoya mountain range was now just a dark silhouette beneath the ash cloud as it spread into the Dialla, and the Wolf pointed to one of the lumps that had a distinctly round peak and said, "That's Aekren's peak, and just to the south of it is Aekren's pass—that's the easiest way over. Up ahead is Aekren's trail and it will take us all the way up."

Over the next hour the rain began to subside and an uncanny silence settled over Kardona as Mount Ucari continued to billow more and more smoke into the sky. The flash of heat from the eruption had melted the mountain's snow cap, releasing the frozen water onto an already saturated land, and when they came to one of the area's larger bridges, the river was high enough that water pulsed over the wood baseboards. The debris of large trees, caught up in the power of the river, jammed thickly up against the side of the bridge and Bird asked, "Is there any other crossing?"

The Wolf shook his head grimly and without hesitation began making his way across. "Give me your good hand," Bird said to Ernest and she led him out onto the bridge with a very skittish mare right behind them. Two times the water flooded around their ankles strong enough for Ernest to lose his footing, but Bird was there to steady him and they made it across just as another unrooted tree slammed into the side of the bridge, drawing an audible lurch from the structure.

"I miss the Dialla," Ernest said and Bird said, "Me too."

The rain stopped and they found themselves in a relatively developed area, plotted with numerous farms and fields that had clearly been tended to recently, but now stood empty. It was dark, but in a strange, artificial way that, once their eyes adjusted, gave the world a feeling of purgatory—and then the ash began to fall. It came down in huge, dry, slow flakes that in any other context would appear beautiful, and they caught onto what little light there was and turned the whole world grey.

"It's hurting my eyes. My lungs," said Ayune.

The others silently agreed and the Wolf called for a short water break. Bird retrieved her cloak from the back of the mare and pulled it up over her head, giving her eyes some relief from the ash and the Wolf and Ayune did the same.

"Sorry Ernest," said Bird and he replied, "Don't be. The burning in my eyes is distracting me from the pain in my shoulder."

She smirked, hoping his humor was a sign that boded well for his immediate health.

They drank their water in silence for a minute before the Wolf said, "We're going to keep this line, due east. I want you two to take the lead so that I can double back a little and make sure nothings behind us."

"I can do that," said Bird.

But the Wolf said, "I'll do it."

Bird shrugged and capped her water and the Wolf started walking back in the direction they came from.

Ernest spoke quietly to Bird and said, "Do you mind if I set the pace for a bit? Something a little slower."

Bird nodded and Ernest took lead of the party with the mare on his heels—Bird and Ayune next, with the Wolf in the wilderness. The Omoya range gave a clear indication of East and trails were numerous and easily traveled. The ash continued to flake down on them like tainted snow and enough of it had built up on the ground now that it provided a coarse crunching noise with each footstep. They closed the gap on the base of the range, traversing a series of low hills until, presented before them was a final stretch of relatively flat land before the climb into the dull teeth of the Omoyas began.

Ernest continued to lead them with cedars closing tight on both sides, until the trail took a slight turn to the southeast and the trees vanished as the trail, like a river's delta, spilled into a large glade. The glade appeared to be cleared for some defunct agricultural undertaking, given the barely visible and rotted foundations of two wood structures and the decomposing fence posts that occasionally jutted from the ground out of various points around the clearing. Whatever it used to be was now slowly sinking in a rising ocean of ash. They hadn't seen another soul since pushing through the Kardoan ranks, and Bird didn't expect to see any here, as she scanned the glade and the tree line; however, she was surprised to see that the Wolf had joined them again, unannounced, and took his place in line just a couple of paces behind Ayune and Bird.

Moments later, a lesser rumble emanated from the volcano, which caused Bird to stop and look in the direction of the mountain. Ayune stopped too, just paces away from Bird, but she did not turn to face the mountain, and instead looked into Bird's eyes and Bird was drawn to look at her, and an instant later the young woman let out a small gasp, like she had been pinched, and the metallic point of a sword came jutting out of her upper left torso, just missing the sleeping babe clutched to her chest. The young woman's eyes were wide in horror and an indefinable whimper escaped her lips as the sword was withdrawn from her chest, and she collapsed to her knees on the trail. Behind her, clutching the bloodied weapon, was an expressionless Wolf, who looked down at the fallen woman and the now crying baby.

Bird's eyes were wide with horror and her mouth agape. "Fucker," she said.

Ernest turned around when he heard Bird and, upon seeing the downed woman, hustled down the trail to her while the Wolf casually wiped the iron of her blood off the iron of his blade. Ernest panted *what happened?* as he reached the girl and Wolf took a couple steps back away from the body.

Bird said, "He fucking killed her," and Ernest said *she's not dead* while he pulled her to a sitting position up against a waist-high, rotted fencepost just off the path.

"She will be soon," the Wolf said, and Ayune looked at him with unnatural eyes and dark blood filled her mouth and breath started to come to her in short, desperate spats. During their retreat, the baby had been jostled a great deal worse than he had now, ten times over, but he wailed into the empty glade as if his mother's pain was his own. She looked at Ernest and the fear in her eyes made him fearful, but she was able to move her arms enough to gesture that he should take the baby from her. He did—quickly unravelling the wool wrap from her body that had secured the baby—and cradling the upset child in his uninjured arm. She tried to talk but she was only able to spit out a couple of unintelligible, blood-spattered syllables before life left her eyes. Ernest hugged the crying baby to his chest and stood to his feet and said, "What have you done, man?"

"I'm going to need you to hand over the child."

Bird cut in with a tone in her voice as cold as her sword and said, "You're not touching that baby."

"This has nothing to do with either of you," the Wolf said. "If that child is indeed Udura Atun, then the world is better off without it."

"You swore that you'd protect it," Bird said.

"I swore that I would protect *my people*, and that's what I'm doing. That soul has done damage to my kin that will take generations to recover from. We may never. All because of Atun."

Ernest said, "I'm not giving him to you."

The Wolf raised both of his eyebrows at him and said, "Then I'll take it."

"It'll only be reborn again. Isn't that what you believe?"

"Of course. But then let him be born somewhere else, obscure and desolate. Let him be born in the Dialla, away from this land and what's left of his people. The child you carry is already burdened with too much history, and if it's him he will surely find his way back. Already behind us there is an entire camp of Samsarans that knows him." Then the Wolf pointed at Ernest and said, "If it were the fate of your people, it would be your decision to make. Hand it over."

Ernest looked at the slain mother and down at the baby and there were tears in his eyes against the falling ash and the fire in the sky and the unnatural darkness that set in on them and the mare watched them with dispassion from ahead on the trail and then he looked at Bird and she was looking back at him and—against everything in the world—her voice was quiet and calm and she said, "Ernest. You take that child and you take our girl there and you get home." She then turned to the Wolf and said, "Go back to your people and to your home if there's anything left of it. The child will come with us to the Dialla and it will be raised there as somebody else entirely. It will never know its history or the evil that you've done here."

The Wolf spat drily and said, "You know I won't do that."

"I know it."

"It's all your lives then."

"Go, Ernest," Bird said.

Ernest saw the look on her face and didn't argue, and he wanted to match the calmness of her voice with his own but he spoke and his voice trembled and he said, "Be perfect."

He made his way with the baby back to the patient mare through the ashfall. When he reached the horse he stroked her long face and tried to pull her along with him but she kept her gaze on Bird and Ernest too looked back at the warriors, facing off, and part of him wanted to watch the duel to come, but a bigger part knew he couldn't stand to see her lose. The child quieted now and looked up at him with huge, green eyes, but with the world on fire and the sun gone and his friend in the fight of her life, the man didn't have time to weep for the unimaginable tragedy that this child had endured in just a few dozen days of life.

"Come on, big girl. You're the bravest horse I know, but you can't help her now."

The mare whinnied softly and turned to follow him, as usual, as if it understood his words and the situation completely. Ernest's shoulder was completely numb, but the blood ran down his naked back and he could feel it as it was absorbed by, and soon soaked, the back of his trousers. He understood that if Bird lost, the Wolf would come for him, and, though he tried to put it from his mind, it began to set in on him that, even should she win, he would never lay eyes on his homeland again.

THE BIRD AND THE WOLF faced off only paces apart. Eyes bloodshot from the ash. Lungs burning. She unhooded and unlatched her cloak and tossed it sideways, with a heavy puff, into the ash that was now up to their ankles. He did the same and adjusted his belt and said, "I'm glad it has come to this—with your friend's big words about your skill and everyone at the camp looking at you like you're something special."

"I didn't take you for the jealous type, but I didn't take you as some common assassin either."

"The child will someday inspire thousands more to murder if it isn't destroyed. Mine is an act of mercy on the world."

Bird looked at Ayune, stone dead, but still propped up on the fence post with open eyes as if she bore witness to this confrontation from the netherworld, "What mercy is that?"

"To not see the death of her son. To not witness the pain that he would inevitably bring to so many. She is nobody and her death is nothing—just a scared, little girl whose baby was born on the wrong day. And before me stands another."

"This little girl has got a little more fight in her."

"I'm counting on it, honey. You're not in the desert anymore—this is the land of the immortal Samsarans," he drew his shortsword and pounded its crossguard against his iron cuirass, above his heart. "Even if you could kill me here you know what I am. I'll be back in this world three days from now, even stronger than I am today."

She reached over her head and pulled the shield off her back and slid it over her left forearm, fidgeting to get it settled in perfect. She said, "Three days from now you'll come weeping out of some woman's vagina the same as everybody else. I won't be afraid of you then any more than I will twenty years later, should you come for me."

His big, baselard dagger appeared in his left hand and he began stalking around her and she drew her magnificent shortsword from her belt and flipped it deftly in her hand and continued, "I'll kill you then, when I'm fifty, and you can go back to weeping and I'll kill you again at seventy. And if you can find me at ninety you may finally have the advantage but you'll find me with this sword in my hand all the same."

He closed in on her, crouched with his shoulders slumped—a ball of latent energy—and he eyed the fist weapon still at place on her belt and said, "I'm looking forward to taking that off of your dead body. That armor too."

"The days of you squeezing your fat ass into this armor are long past."

The Wolf growled and exploded toward her with a frenzy of motion. Ash went dusting up from the ground in big clouds around both of them as she shuffled backward and used her shield and sword to deflect six, seven, eight attacks in quick succession—the dual-wielding nature of his style allowing him to attack from twice as many angles. After the eighth metallic clink rang off of her shortsword, she was able to swing her shield outward into the Wolf's left shoulder and, though it caused no damage, it allowed her to reset her feet and take her turn on the attack. She used the shield to neutralize most of the action from his shortsword, and then probed his offhand defense with an extensive combo of her own. He handled it with a blend of flawless footwork and perfect angles from the dagger, sending her sword harmlessly in every direction except for where his body was.

They became one entity, witnessed in this glade only by the eyes of the dead mother. They moved relentlessly around the opening, enveloped in a sphere of ash—fallen from above and disturbed from below—as if their conflict was mythological and what was at stake in this contest of titans was to one a child and the other the doom of his people and possibly more.

THE BABY WAS AWAKE NOW. Crying. Hungry. The smell of the linen wrap was still his mother's scent, but this bosom was an imposter's—shoulders that were too wide, a chest that was too muscular. Too hard. Where was the warmth and the softness and the voice that was its world entire?

Ernest hobbled on through ash that now reached up to his shins. The mare followed him closely, every few minutes twisting her head back and forth to shake the ash from her mane. For the first few miles up the sloping mountain base he looked over his good shoulder constantly, imagining the sight of the Wolf in pursuit, but had since surrendered to any thought other than putting one foot in front of the next. With the trail buried under ash, he kept his way by the layout of the trees and the vegetation around him—the five-fingered ferns of the area looking like dust covered spider corpses in a Diallan cellar. For a minute his mind cleared from its foggy, pain fueled coma, and the futility of his errand occurred to him. Like a sick dog, he felt an urge to limp into the forest and find a hole that he could peacefully die in. And should the Wolf win? He looked behind him again for the first time in a while and saw his tracks, dragged through the ash in such a way that the very child strapped to his chest would be able to track him out here.

Soon after the visions of defeat crept through his mind, he came to a turn in the trail that lipped out over a small, rocky cliff before rising further to the east—this time with a far steeper grade than what he had traveled so far. The child quieted again, cried out from its first fit of hunger, and the cliff before him sat just high enough around the surrounding trees that he was given a picturesque, silhouetted view of the distant Mount Ucari and its impressive, horrifying visage. Whether it was the foggy portion of his mind, or the clear one, he decided to stop at this view and, underneath the blanket of the ash, he found a fallen tree and gingerly set himself on top of it. He could feel the child's little strong and steady breaths, and he said to it, "I'm sorry, little friend."

The mare used its snout to prod Ernest in the neck as if to urge him along, but he said *I'm sorry* to her too and he rested his good arm on the back of the child and gazed out, with fearful admiration, through the odd darkness, at the fiery maw of the distant volcano. Its smoke still stacked endlessly out of its gaping wound and its belly of fire would occasionally flare up and across the landscape around the mountain he could see the light of flames and smoke of fires that sprang up from the burning discharge of the mountain. He felt the urge to cry but his eyes, between the ash and his blood loss, couldn't muster any moisture to do so.

"You need to get on, girl. If that murdering bastard wins, he'll probably put you to the sword as well."

The mare moved behind his log and positioned herself so that her chin groove rested on his good shoulder, and he folded his arm upward and traced lines down from her forehead to her nostrils. He reminded her that she had her own newborn to worry about, but she stayed on his shoulder and surveyed the landscape the same as he, and the pockets of fire that attacked the damp vegetation and the volcano that still smoldered and breathed out there in the darkness like a neglected fire pit.

FROM BACK IN THE GLADE came a near uninterrupted clash of steel on iron, iron on steel. Five different elements of her being moved in total harmony, and him too, and all of it with the design to destroy the other. There were no practiced sequences that the other hadn't already encountered and overcame at other points in their lives, and so their fight became one of instinct, improvisation, reaction time, and pure talent, as they were pushed down combination paths that demanded of them to attack and defend in ways neither ever had before. Small victories were won by each—him bleeding from his left thigh and forearm, where his dagger parries were just less than perfect, and her from her shield-side bicep and right calf, where she had gotten a good kick in at the cost of a glancing sword swipe from the Wolf.

The ash was its own enemy. Her lungs burned like they never had before and she suspected to same of him, judging by the bits of blood that dribbled from the corners of his lips. Their footwork suffered too, with the ash piling up high enough that it felt as if they were dancing in ankle deep water. Eyes burned and yearned to be closed. Bird thought that if they went on much longer, then the elements would kill them both. The shield was the foundation of her fighting style, but it was defensive by nature, and she felt the need now to press this matter. She managed to disengage from the Wolf and, like her namesake, took a hop step away from him while slipping the shield off her arm, sending the heavy disk into the ash where it disappeared with a soundless puff. Her left arm slipped into the fist weapon on her belt and the Wolf, attempting to hide his labored breathing, said, "I was beginning to think it was just for show."

She wasted no breath before darting forward and beginning a new attack, this time with both hands. Each time he fought back to neutral footing and thought that there would be a natural break in their battle, she advanced again. The energy she expended was colossal, but the blood at the corner of his lips grew more noticeable and between the metallic strikes she could hear his breathing grow shorter, faster. The fist weapon and its unusual tri-blade makeup was giving the Wolf fits. Strikes and ripostes with his shortsword that would have deflected cleanly off of any two-edge blade got caught up in between the claws of the weapon, causing him to expend more energy disengaging and rebalancing. She lunged forward, low, with her sword thrusting at his exposed legs while catching one of his overhead counters in her claw and, as he backpedaled, the heel of his left foot caught one of the glade's rotted fence posts—not more than six inches out of the ground—and he went stumbling backward.

He tried to roll with the momentum, but his fatigue, combined with the thickness of the ash, slowed him down just enough to give Bird her opening. She followed his tumbling figure, practically stepping on him, and when he was to his feet and still off balance, she swept his sword across his own torso with her claw and came in behind it with her shortsword, puncturing his iron armor and sending her blade deep into his left, middle torso.

She pulled it out and skipped backward again, retreating as if she had scored a hit on a bear and whatever would happen next would be unpredictable, and wild. But he was spent. A feral whimper escaped his lips and he glared at her and he knew he was beaten. He collapsed to his knees, with his arms limp at his side, his hands sinking into the ash and blood coming from him where it spread in the porous cloud of ash like a flame in a warehouse of wool.

When he spoke, his words came out wheezing and hollow, "You lucky bitch."

She sheathed her weapons and crouched down, sitting on her heels, two paces in front of the Wolf, where she looked him in the eyes and said nothing. She breathed.

"They're really going to think you're special now. The little girl that killed the Wolf."

Her throat was parched and when she spoke it was scratchy and tired, "You're no prize to me. I've fought a dozen men better than you, and all of them bitter to the end about being slain by a woman. Go find them in the afterlife and see if they don't all say the same thing as you—*lucky bitch*. You're a story that's been told a thousand times. I won't tell a soul what happened here—you're nobody and your death is nothing."

He tried to spit on her but the blood drizzled off of his lips and down his chin, where it tumbled off and made a tiny crater in the surface of the ash. She stood, with his blood still on her sword, and retrieved her shield. She checked the wounds around her body to be sure they weren't serious and then walked over to Ayune. She closed the girl's eyes and lay her gently to the ground. The Wolf collapsed to his side, the ash so deep that only his shoulder was visible above it, and by the time Bird left the glade, the two Samsarans were completely covered and gifted to this land of their making.

ERNEST WAS SITTING ON THE fallen tree—the child cradled in his good arm and asleep at his chest—when the mare lifted her head from his shoulder and peered through the falling ash toward the trail. A figure approached them—shrouded in ash and just a silhouette of grey—and Ernest struggled to his feet and walked the baby over to the edge of the cliff and looked down at the fatal distance.

"Ernest?"

It was Bird. She flashed a confused look at him before she registered the situation and his intent. Tears came immediately to his eyes, and she guided him back to the fallen tree and told him that it was the right thing. He handed the child off to her and did a controlled slide off the tree so that he took a new position sitting on the ground, leaning up against the wood with a direct view of Mount Ucari still. He wheezed, "I can't breathe."

"Me neither. It's the ash—it gets in the lungs."

She went into her pack and took out one of her linen tunics and, using her foot to pin it to the ground, carved two big chunks out of the shirt's torso with her sword. "Tie this around your face," she said, but he looked pathetically down at his injured arm and the two of them—her with the baby in her arm and him with the arrow in his shoulder—worked together to knot the makeshift masks over their faces.

"What happened with the Wolf?"

"He's dead."

Ernest nodded as if there were some other possibility and Bird said, "I told him he wasn't any good."

"Was he?"

"Yeah."

She handed him his waterskin and he slipped it under the mask to drink and she did the same before the earth began to shake again, this time less than the initial eruption.

They both turned to Mount Ucari and its stack of smoke still billowing up into the sky, but the rumbling ground was accompanied this time by a deep belch from the gut of the mountain that sent forth another plume of smoke. Except that this one didn't travel upward. Down the southern flank of the fractured mountain rushed a fiery avalanche of pulverized rock, ash, and gas that powered down the mountain faster than any living thing could move. It consumed everything in its path and expanded upward, outward, and downward all at once—until the entire mountain and surrounding landscape was shrouded in it. They both watched in awe but the baby in Bird's arms woke again and renewed his crying.

Even from their distance the pyroclastic flow appeared to move fast and Ernest said, "Will it reach us?"

"I don't intend to find out."

His voice was quiet and he said, "I do."

"What?"

"I can't move."

"Ernest."

She looked at his crumpled form and she saw the look in his bloodshot eyes and she knew it to be true.

"I can get you up on the horse," Bird said.

"No. The horse is for you and the child."

She shook her head and she said, "I can't."

"You have to. For the child."

Her head continued shaking and her lower lip welled up and tears formed in her eyes and she said, "I can't."

"He needs to eat and you'll be too slow on foot. Let our girl carry you now."

"Where would I go?"

"Go to the Crimson Shrouds. They're Copperfoot and will help him if you ask."

"I can't do it—I can't ride her."

Ernest wheezed audibly for several seconds and the new cloud out of the volcano blossomed in all directions and looked to consume all the world in its darkness. He said, "Listen to me now. The superstitions of these people have already buried this child in wickedness. Please don't sentence him to death now over another one. Rathalla burns in you. Beauregard himself would lend his hand to get you up on that horse. You are more of a Copperfoot than any person I've ever known, and if at the end of your ride you cease to be one, then such a thing no longer exists."

She was quiet for what felt like minutes—her eyes wandering to the ruined mountain in the distance and the child quieting again and the whole world grey and alien and she said, "Can I move you somewhere more comfortable?"

"I'm as comfortable as I need to be for what I need to do."

"You have a hell of a view."

"I'm looking at it."

She handed the sleeping baby to Ernest again so that she could unlatch her armor and wrap herself in the length of linen that once bound the child to his own mother's bosom. She stood the armor up in the ash next to Ernest—her shield too—and then retrieved his pack from the back of the mare and wrapped him in his own wool blanket and cloak before securing his waterskin into the hand of his healthy arm. "I'll come back for you," she said, and she gave her propped armor a light kick. "And this too."

"I never thought I'd be gifted to any land other than the Dialla."

"You're gonna live."

"I don't feel I will."

"Then you just need a little more herb."

"Shit," he said. "Now you're speaking in deep truths."

She went into his pack and set his pouch of herb in the ash at his side and she placed a gentle hand on his forearm. She looked into his eyes and said, "I'll come back."

"I'll be here," he said, and he gave her a forced, but affectionate smile. They exchanged the sleeping babe again and she secured him in the wrap around her torso. She approached the mare and, though having never ridden her before, the horse dipped her head and offered her mane and, for the first time in her life, Bird grabbed the mane and pulled herself up onto the back of a horse.

Bird was unsure at first—it was higher and more uncomfortable than it looked—but the horse shuffled around and settled this amateur rider into a proper seat. Ernest watched from his position next to the log and, before the mare moved up the trail, Bird looked at him one last time to see a massive smile plastered on his face—this one not forced at all. She grasped the mane with both hands as the mare began her steady and surefooted ascent toward the mountain pass. All sense of time was lost in the grey and the baby would wake and cry itself out until he was asleep again, and then wake and cry more. She took one of the biscuits from her pack and crumbled it with one hand into her waterskin to feed to baby, not knowing if she caused him more harm than good, but knowing she had to try something. Trees closed tightly around their trail and the sky grew naturally dark and the mare quickened her pace, seeming to sense the child's urgency. They made Aekren's pass late in the evening, the sky still unrelentingly muffled and drab. The land flattened, much like the plateau they traversed on their way in, with very few trees and nothing awaiting them in the east except for darkness.

The mare stopped, as if a whisper from the world itself tickled her ears, and she turned to face herself and her rider back to the west. The upper echelons of the sky were still black with the volcanoes' pollution, but out far enough, at the rim of the world, the setting sun lowered itself past the division of smoke and, though it appeared hazier than usual, it was without a doubt the same sun that had risen that morning and the same one that would rise the next. And when it did rise again it would do so on this woman and this mare and the precious cargo that each carried out of one savage domain and into the next.